MITHUN NUMBER TWO

JAYANT KAIKINI

MITHUN NUMBER TWO

AND OTHER MUMBAI STORIES

TRANSLATED BY
TEJASWINI NIRANJANA

eka

eka

First published in Kannada

First published in English in 2024 by Eka, an imprint of Westland Books, a division of Nasadiya Technologies Private Limited

No. 269/2B, First Floor, 'Irai Arul', Vimalraj Street, Nethaji Nagar, Alapakkam Main Road, Maduravoyal, Chennai 600095

ISBN: 9789360458072

10 9 8 7 6 5 4 3 2 1

Typeset by SÜRYA, New Delhi
Printed at Manipal Technologies Limited, Manipal

To the nameless Mumbai commuter
with season pass, comb and tiny lunchbox
sprinting down the platform
jumping into the local train
every single day

Contents

Hello, Mike Testing

As evening approaches, the glass windows of all the buildings at Nariman Point turn a sparkling red, reflecting both the sunset and the Arabian Sea. In his blue jeans and his trademark sleeveless denim jacket, Ghanshyam walks along the seashore for a while before turning right to get to Churchgate Station. More or less around the same time, Charudutt climbs down the rickety wooden stairs of an old building in Maruti Lane near Flora Fountain, stops at Vidyanidhi Book Depot to buy two sketch pens, putting them into his shoulder bag after scribbling on the pad to check their quality, and makes his way towards Churchgate. Although the two men are walking separately, they also walk side by side with thousands of daily commuters like them, heading home to their families. If seen from above, it might look like a dense crowd of sports fans rushing onto the field after a winning goal. But none of these faces look elated. None of them look like each other either. The worshippers of these innumerable faces and postures, Ghanshyam and Charudutt, are about to meet at their usual spot at Churchgate.

The faces of both appear to be just like those to be found

in the stream of commuters, but also somehow different. Charudutt stops at the roadside stalls to pick up a book or a toy. He bends over to look at them closely or holds up the object to fill his eyes with. Ghanshyam is interested in observing the speed and movements of those rushing out of the Churchgate underpass into the station, smiling as he does so. If someone jumps the ticket queue and is pounced upon by other commuters, giving rise to verbal battles, Ghanshyam watches with pleasure and interest. He also observes the street urchins playing hide and seek with loud whoops amidst the passengers. Suddenly, Charudutt climbs up from the underpass, and Ghanshyam says '*Do chai*', asking the Western Railway stallman for two cups of tea. They stand in a corner by the Wheeler bookstall, sipping their tea from paper cups, watching the people rushing headlong into the station like water from the opened floodgates of a dam.

Later, they both catch a Virar local. Without bothering to struggle for a seat, they stand if there is no room. If they get only one seat, Charudutt sits down, because he will alight in Andheri, and when he does so, Ghanshyam will occupy the seat for several more stops until Vasai. In his tiny sketchbook, Charudutt keeps making a variety of sketches. Mostly faces with different expressions. He doesn't look at anyone as he sketches, drawing on what he has seen half an hour ago in the toy shop, in the queue, or in the tea stall. With his sharp memory for faces, they go straight from his mind to the paper. Those sitting next to him peer into the sketchbook to see what he is drawing. Looking at the commuters dangling from the metal manacles above, Ghanshyam feels as though his soul has been distributed amongst them. The smile taking shape in his mind is appearing on the face of another man; drops of sweat emerge on another's forehead, but the person next to him is the one wiping his face. The man who has been standing opposite him for barely five seconds looks like someone he has known for centuries. The faces that continue to appear in front of Ghanshyam, the voices he hears, keep emerging from Charudutt's fingers onto his sketchbook.

If one keeps looking at Charudutt's caricatures, his face begins to resemble one of them. A beard, a long nose, thin face, long hair like a Yakshagana artist – he looks like a mischievous student who has been expelled from Shantiniketan's art school. His caricatures make their way into the *Sunday Observer*, *Debonair* and *Mid-Day*. Mostly they are without words or captions, just wicked lines thrown together. Charudutt can also mime his satires, just like Ghanshyam can sing them. He is fond of the harmonium, and of all kinds of songs: Marathi stage songs, Hindi film songs, Bengali Rabindra Sangeet, Kannada Yakshagana songs. He can imitate all of these. What with their satire, mimicry and miming, these two men are becoming popular as the 'Mimicry Brothers' in a number of small entertainment venues. At the time, stand-up comedy has not yet emerged, or shows like Johny Lever's or *Laughter Challenge*. So at office events, women's associations, housing colony celebrations and other festivities, the Charu–Shyam Mimicry Brothers are always invited to perform.

Children who watch the mimicry in apartment complexes,

government quarters and housing colonies thoroughly enjoy the performance. The Brothers enact jokes, change the lyrics of popular Hindi film songs so they become comical parodies, delight the audience by singing Mukesh and Rafi songs in the voices of those playback singers, and by crooning like the women singers Lata and Asha.

~

Once the organisers of an event had announced that the famous shehnai player Bismillah Khan would grace the occasion. Towards the end of the evening, Khansaheb's name was called out. As the audience began to applaud, Ghanshyam, disguised as an ustad with a beard and a skullcap, walked through the spectators and went up on the stage. He said: 'Please forgive me. There's a situation. I forgot my shehnai in the taxi. But god is great and will not let go of my hand. I will play the shehnai with just my breath.' Ghanshyam proceeded to 'play' the reed instrument through his nose, going pe pe pe pe, pe pe pe pe with the right intonation. Then Charudutt came rushing in from the wings. 'I am the tabla player. When I was about to leave, my wife hid the tabla in her rage. What to do? I have to keep my word. I'll accompany the ustad by playing tabla through my voice.' Boom boom takamaka, he began. The audience was delighted. In these simple ways, the Brothers regaled their audiences.

Vasai is a distant suburb of Mumbai. Those who come to Mumbai for work find new homes along the Central Line, in

Dombivli, Kalyan, Ambernath, or along the Western Line, in Bhayandar, Vasai or Virar. With their greenery, farmland and fisheries, these suburbs still retain the features of the original villages after which they are named. Just as the groundnut is the poor man's almond, these affordable suburbs are the refuge of newcomers to the city.

Ghanshyam was originally from a village in Goa, on the banks of the Mandovi. However exhausted he was at the end of the day's work, when he reached his little abode in Vasai, he was energised by the smell of dried fish and the sight of the fresh vegetables piled up at the stalls. On the weekends, Charudutt would come to Vasai. The friends would chat for hours, thinking up new ideas for their act. Shyam loved to whistle and could 'sing' an entire song through whistling. Something like '*Kisi ki muskurahaton pe ho nisaar*' seemed to have been composed for whistling. When Shyam arrived at the phrase '*Jeena isi ka naam hai*', his listeners' hearts would melt.

One afternoon, Shyam was chopping vegetables and onions, preparing to make khichdi, whistling as he worked. Suddenly, he heard the same tune being whistled from outside. He stopped and whistled again and heard the rejoinder again. He was quiet for a while and then he heard the whistle from the trees outside. An invisible bird was mimicking Shyam's sound. Quietly, Shyam signalled to Charudutt to look out, and then whistled once more, '*Jeena isi ka naam hai*'. Even more sweetly did the echo come. The two were dumbstruck.

There was a small party at the Taj Mahal Hotel after the inauguration of the famous cartoonist Mario Miranda's exhibition. The Mimicry Brothers were invited to perform there. Charudutt was ecstatic because he was a fan of Mario's. That day, for the first time, the Brothers presented a conversation between birds. They mimicked a range of bird sounds, enacting through voice the way the birds spoke to each other, fought with each other. The English-speaking guests were wonderstruck. Charu went up to Mario Miranda and asked for his autograph on his – Charu's – sketchbook. Mario quickly sketched a bird-headed man in a jacket holding a mike and signed it with a flourish.

Of special interest to Charu were the trees that Mario's pictures always had. Along with the street cats and dogs, the post box, the streetlamps, the milk bicycles, Mario drew elaborately every line of every leaf on the tree. If there was more than one tree, each had its own pattern of leaves. Charudutt wondered how a caricaturist, who by nature tended to draw a line and move on quickly, found time to meditatively and meticulously sketch a tree. Although Charu wanted to talk to Mario about this, he couldn't find the right words. Mario looked through Charu's sketches, nodded appreciatively and, looking into his eyes, said, 'Nice.'

Charu was thrilled that this god in civilian clothes had noticed him. Mario went on to say: 'You two imitate the birds beautifully. But you're making them speak like humans. Unfair! Maybe their nature is entirely different. Once you bring in speech, the problem of meaning appears too. And we unnecessarily complicate everything.' He patted Charu's shoulder. 'Your sketches are very good. There's no speech there. The figures are mute, and what they convey is beyond language. You should just get lost in them.' Picking up a glass of champagne from a tray that was being brought around, Mario lifted it towards Charu and said, 'Cheers.'

After this incident, Charu seemed to acquire a different sense of hearing. Any sound he heard, his mind became attuned to it. The sound of a train passing, the sound of the children playing in Nityanand Colony where he lived, close to Andheri Station, the cry of the Versova fish-seller, '*Maashe taaje maashe*,' as she walked with her round basket full of fish, the cry of the kulfi seller, the invisible roar of the peak hour which swelled and receded by turn, all of these had their own unique microtone. One could get quite absorbed in it. Like the harsh sounds of a night bus that turn into a lullaby.

On acquiring a taste for the cries and sounds of his neighbourhood, Charu became more silent. Earlier, when he heard the pressure cooker whistle more than thrice from his neighbour's house, he would feel like shouting: 'Someone turn off the gas!' But nowadays, when the whistling stopped, he felt the new microtone had stopped too.

Ghanshyam did not take long to figure out what was happening. He wondered if Charu was fashioning a new 'mimicry item' from all these sounds, of turning wheels, circling fans, the sugarcane-crushing machine. Charu's inner ear was so transformed that when he went up the wooden stairs of the Maruti Lane building, listening to his own footsteps, he was disappointed when he reached the second floor. He felt the same when he climbed down the steps in the evening. On concrete, different feet shod in sandals, shoes, slippers, each made a different sound in which the wearer's personality manifested itself. Even his own feet, when going sadly down the stairs, or when rushing down in a hurry, or descending in anger, made different kinds of sounds. In this way, the symphony of sound emanating from so many sources brought so many experiences to him, without being verbalised.

Now, when Charu opened his sketchbook, his pictures began to look different too. Like visuals in a film which appeared different when the background melody changed, all of them seemed to be waiting for the magic moment when they would be set free. As though someone had said 'statue', and they could not move until another person came by to say 'over'. But who had said 'statue' and who had said 'over'? Charudutt liked unclarity. He always felt embarrassed about going straight to the point. Ghanshyam wasn't like that. Whatever Charu was trying to grasp, Ghanshyam would speak it out, taking care not to embarrass his friend. Now he said: '*Dost*, your Nityanand Colony's Ganesh festival is approaching. Rao Kaka, the Ganesh Mandali chairman, wants us to do at least four shows. He keeps asking me what new items we can present. It's your home ground, so we need to put up something *dhamaal*. Let's think of a way by which your sketches are set free on the stage. What do you say?'

About five years ago, when Charu was about to get married, he had felt awkward that Ghanshyam, elder to him, was not marrying first. So Ghanshyam said to him: 'In volleyball, one player says "take it" and another has to say "leave it". If both say "leave it", that won't work. There's no time. So just take it.' If one tried to speak about such things, the words came with their own hidden meanings and caused distortions. Because words constantly mocked themselves.

Once Ghanshyam said to Charu, in exasperation at his lack of clarity: 'You speak like a lamp kept on a dividing wall, neither here nor there.' To which Charu retorted that words themselves were lamps on a dividing wall. Ghanshyam remembered this exchange when Mario Miranda commented on their mimicry of the bird calls. To mimic was to break the illusion of meaningfulness, to free something from its binding context.

Like one might say 'a normal delivery', Charu's was a 'normal' wedding. A simple Mumbai middle-class wedding. At the reception, held in the function hall of Nityananda Colony, cassata ice cream was served. The colony's children went around boasting that they had drunk ten bottles of Gold Spot and eaten at least two cassatas each. At the reception, there was an orchestra that performed songs, and mimicry by Ghanshyam. After a few songs, when the accompanists went behind the stage curtain to drink a cup of tea, Ghanshyam entertained the crowd with cricket and hockey commentaries. For the sake of his parents who had come from out of town, Charu had worn a readymade blue blazer with a huge collar, which hung loosely on him. The rosebud in its buttonhole drooped like a traveller asleep on a bus. Charu kept feeling that he must be looking like a hanger draped in a blazer. The bride,

Mandaramala Sakhardande from Nashik, went around speaking to everyone in a lively fashion. Since all the orchestra members were regulars with the Mimicry Brothers, they played songs with gusto, gently joking with the newlyweds whenever they could. Shyam presented a new item: how Amitabh Bachchan and Shah Rukh Khan started fighting in a ration-shop queue while waiting for kerosene. Then the audience had an exciting surprise. The bridegroom himself came on stage in the guise of the Tamil star Rajinikanth to separate the fighting Hindi movie stars. Taking out a cigarette from the pocket of the blue blazer, tossing it in the air and catching it again, 'Rajinikanth' did some dialogues in his gurgling Hindi, to the delight of Ghanshyam, who hugged him and made a congratulatory speech.

'A hearty welcome to Srimathi Mandaramala Sakhardande who is joining Charudutt's family. We welcome her maternal family too. The whole of our Nityananda Colony is a family. The ration shop, the post office, the flour mill, the Irani bakery near the entrance, the money plants hanging in the houses; the flowers in the pots which open their eyes when the alarm clock rings as though they have to catch the 5.30 a.m. local; the invisible, nameless boys who deliver the newspapers, milk, bread, and the packets with a little garland of just four flowers for the household gods, all of them are part of this family. Mandaramala Sakhardande Bhabhiji, I will from now on only call you Bhabhiji because your real name is longer than the title of Rajshri Pictures' *Dulhan Wahi Jo Piya Man Bhaaye*. Perhaps in your schooldays, by the time the class teacher finished calling out your name, the entire period must have ended.' Thus setting off a wave of laughter in the audience, Ghanshyam handed the microphone to Charudutt, saying, 'One song for Bhabhiji please. No Mukesh, no Kishore, no Talat, no Saigal, only Charudutt's voice.'

So now Charudutt had to mimic himself. He was struck dumb for a few seconds. He was like a lamp on the dividing wall between the breeziness of his bachelor days and the seriousness of his new householder status. He waved at the audience, signalled to the keyboardist for a base note, coughed, closed his eyes, and began to sing, trying to see if Mandaramala was looking in his direction: '*Chhoo kar mere mann ko* ..., You touched my heart ...' The crowd cheered. Encouraged, Charu wondered for a moment whether he was sounding like Kishore Kumar, who had originally sung the song. He glanced at Shyam and smiled. Shyam raised his hand, also smiling, as though to wave him on. As Charu embarked on the line '*Kiya tune kya ishaara*, You made such a gesture', his voice seemed to break into something between Mohammed Rafi and Talat Mehmood, veering towards the ordinary Charu voice that would say things like '*Do cup chai dena*'. Like a basketball poised on the edge of the ring, teetering gently until it slipped into the basket, Charu's voice settled into itself. 'How nicely he sings,' thought Ghanshyam gladly.

He signalled to Mala to take the stage. She approached and bent down to touch his feet. Charu did the same. Since the song was still being sung, all this looked like a scene from a film. The crowd turned emotional. Shyam embraced Charu, mumbling '*Arre yaar*'. The audience clapped loudly. After that, the mike was given to Mandaramala by public demand. Her parents looked on, anxious. She began to sing: '*Bole re papihara*', but before the last word her voice choked a little. 'Sorry, I ate three cassatas, my throat won't cooperate,' she said. Shyam reassured her: 'Don't worry, Bhabhi, after you go home you can sing it in Charu's ear.' The crowd clapped wildly. As the couple stepped down from the stage and walked towards the reception sofa covered in China silk, Ghanshyam felt that a decisive turning point in their journey of mimicry had been reached. He adopted an attitude of neutrality, deciding that neither he nor the mimicry programmes would come in the way of Charu's married life.

In a year or two, the number of programmes began to decrease, although when they did take place, they were received with great enthusiasm. Charu invited Ghanshyam for a weekend meal from time to time. If he showed any hesitation at all, Charu would say he had bought some fish, and put down the phone. Shyam would show up without a murmur. If someone were to ask Shyam whether he wanted a fish meal or an interview with Marilyn Monroe, he would choose fish any day. Once a month, Shyam visited the Gomantak Restaurant in Prarthana Samaj and partook of their fish dinner. One day, he bought fresh fish in Vasai and got his Mangalorean neighbour to cook it, since he had invited Charu and his wife to eat with him. Shyam served the delicacy on three plates of different sizes, along with the complimentary curd rice which the Mangalorean family had given. Later, the three of them sat around chatting.

In the stillness of the afternoon, the distant ocean seemed to be closer than it was. Mandaramala stood by the window of Shyam's house, looking at the row of houses across the road. They looked empty, like a camp for labourers which provided a bit of respite before sending them back to the worksite. Had all the people who lived there disappeared into different jobs in different places, or had they gone into Charu's sketchbook? Mala felt there was something in the row of houses that reminded her of Charu's figures, and she stared at them with concentration. Charu watched her watching, as he sat with his feet stretched out, leaning against the wall. Who was this woman, he wondered, who seemed so distant from the world's preoccupations as she stood gazing out of the window? Shyam, who was peeling an orange and laying the segments on a plastic plate, looked at Charu looking at his wife. It's only when they are freed from the past that a sort of glow suffuses the relationships between people. The sound of sparrows pecking the grain outside the kirana shop could be heard. This was the same sound that can be heard at the shop in Nityananda Colony or in Shiroda town in Goa, where they weighed jaggery along with the flies accumulated on it. The three of them never forgot that still and languid afternoon. They came to Vasai many times after that, and Shyam went and stayed with Charu and Mala in Andheri. But that gorgeous afternoon enlivened only by the sparrows' cries never came back.

In these past five or six years, as Charu's sketching commissions increased, Shyam began to learn more and more musical instruments. He came to know a man called Khaleel, who played the accordion in the orchestra of Babla, a musician who was the younger brother of the famous Hindi film composers Kalyanji–Anandji. In Shyam's opinion, the goddess of music dwelled in Khaleel's fingers. Not only that, you could see her making merry there.

Khaleel taught accordion on the terrace of an old building near the Dinanath Mangeshkar auditorium in Vile Parle, close to Andheri. Ghanshyam was a regular there. It was a curious four-storeyed building. If you peeped down from the terrace, you could hear the bustle of the Vile Parle market, but if you sat down leaning against the parapet wall, all the noise and hubbub vanished as though a switch had been turned off. Although there was one local train every minute, the hooting sounded like a distant grumble since the train tracks were not so close by. On the terrace was the blissful silence of the void, as though one had picked up a book and were sitting alone, reading. It was a simple, private space any earnest person could enter. When there was no one on the terrace, only the musical instruments were present. Harmonium, leg harmonium, keyboard, accordion, they all nestled inside their silk-lined boxes. And then there was the piano, swathed in its robes, with all its regal seriousness, almost like the soul of the whole place. No one had the courage to remove the piano cover. It seemed to be in the wrong place, as if a spell had been cast on it. Shyam only knew that the piano was from the time of Khaleel's father.

These instruments were not waiting for anyone to start playing them. It was nonsense to say that the notes were waiting for the instrumentalist to coax them out. Because once the player's hands touch the instrument, what comes out is his melody, his striving, his expression. If Shyam came there before Khaleel did, he would tune himself to the silence of these harmless instruments, watching them soulfully. While other musicians joined their hands in a namaste to greet their instruments, Khaleel would bend, pick them up and cuddle them like a mother would. He would then raise the accordion to his shoulder, and at that point the actor Raj Kapoor became his presiding deity, his muse. The accordion was the metaphor of Shankar–Jaikishan compositions for him. 'That song in *Mera Naam Joker* in the 1970s that enthralled everyone, "*Jaane kahaan gaye woh din*", the entire style of that song, the compositions, the patterns, were present as background score in *Barsaat* twenty years before. So, this amazing tune and arrangement had to wait twenty years to find a story that would suit it. Just imagine, a film director and a music director waiting for twenty years! What an invisible pull there must have been. What promise lay hidden there!' When Khaleel spoke like this, Ghanshyam felt a thrill course through his body. Just as the instruments lay silent without someone to play them, the composition too must have remained inarticulate. Miming breaks meaningfulness just as art breaks time, thought Shyam. Like an accomplished photographer de-focussing to be able to re-focus. Such a tiny, vulnerable movement of the finger, to be able to de-focus and then return to focus.

When the Nityanand Colony Ganesh Festival committee had its meeting on the platform of the cement water tank at the edge of the playing field, Shyam and Charu were there too. This was a preparatory meeting for planning the festival programmes. 'Why should Jayalakshmi Aunty's troupe always perform the *garba*? How is that the most tuneless singers are always near the mike when the aarti is being sung?' These issues began to come up in the meeting. In the post office opposite Nityanand Colony, the postmen were arranging their mail neatly in the carrier bags, slinging them onto the cycle's handlebars, putting some envelopes into their own shoulder bag, and getting ready to head out, carrying those hundreds of missives. Just before getting on the bicycle, if they saw someone, they would stop, sift through the envelopes, and find the one meant for the recipient. How many hundreds of addresses they read each day! It was said that the letters that did not get delivered would be kept in the post office for some time, then sent off to the GPO in the VT station area. Then, after a designated time, they would be destroyed. Just like the figures who were under the 'statue' spell in Charu's sketchbook, these letters would permanently remain mute.

Seeing the Ganesh committee, Postman Desai pushed his bicycle over and began looking through his bags. As usual, Charu had a few magazines and some international aerogrammes. 'My granddaughter Sonali sings really *mast*. Do give her a chance in the children's programme this year?' requested Desai. 'There's no one in our family who sings. Strange she should have this talent,' he said with humble pride. Charu was stirred. All this was beyond his sketches and his mimicry. In these colonies, everyone seemed to achieve an identity only through their children. Even if no one knew their real name, people came to be called 'Pinky ki Mummy', 'Munna ka Pappa', 'Kajal's grandfather'. Mandaramala felt it was typical of Mumbai city. In her small town, all the parents would be known to one another, and every child would be known as the son or daughter of so-and-so. Here it was completely the reverse: the bonds between children who played together made their way into the relationships between those who stepped out of their flats in the evening with their children. Only the boys who woke up early to work in the Irani bakery did not seem to have anyone to look after them. They would pile the fragrant pavs in their square aluminium boxes and take them out to sell. Mala, too, bought her bread from these boys.

After the committee meeting, Shyam went home with Charu. On the TV was playing the song from *Brahmachari* in the Evergreen Songs series, '*Dil ke jharokhe mein*', sung by Mohammed Rafi. When the song ended, Mala switched off the TV and said, 'I love these scenes where the hero sings as he plays the piano. The piano looks so dignified and so beautiful.'

'You said it,' said Shyam in English. 'In my dream house there is always a piano. And even when the breeze blows, it begins to play.'

'And it looks as though it's about to spread its wings and fly,' said Charu. 'And the divine rows of black and white keys waiting for the player's hands, lovely.'

They were all silent, each of them thinking of the piano songs they knew. Charu exclaimed in pleasure as he remembered the song '*Aapke haseen rukh pe*' from the film *Baharen Phir Bhi Aayengi*. The star Dharmendra sitting almost motionless as he played and sang that love song, with Tanuja and Mala Sinha sitting in front and listening like two seagulls, each thinking the song was meant for her. As the song ended, the camera swung gently from side to side. In some films the hero would stylishly end the song by running his fingers over the keys and turn with a flourish to face the audience.

Shyam loved those moments. 'Some foolish heroes don't have a sense of music. Although their faces are enacting the emotions, the fingers are banging mechanically on the keys like the typist outside the courtroom. And others, even when there's only one note to be played, they're swaying like the driver on the ghat section turning the steering wheel,' said Shyam. 'He's a hero, not a mimicry artist,' said Charu, and everyone laughed. 'I want to hear someone play a piano in real life,' said Mala. 'Idea!' said Shyam. 'Khaleel is one of the finest piano players of our time. Let's go visit him. He plays Hindi film songs too, like Brian Silas. It's not easy to play on the piano songs with a Hindustani classical base, and Khaleel is incomparable. Let me call him tomorrow. He'll be happy. He never gets to play what he likes. All he does is rush from recording studio to orchestra practice to hobby classes for rich kids,' said Shyam as he stood up to leave.

Finally, that day too dawned. As the glass windows at Nariman Point turned red in the sunset, Ghanshyam hurried out of his office. Charudutt came down from his building in Maruti Lane and bought a new sketchbook at the Vidyanidhi Book Depot. He wondered if the books spoke to each other when the shop was shut for the night, and said this aloud to Mr Kotian, the bookseller. Kotian was not to be outdone. 'Speak to each other? I wager that they have fights. After all, that's how writers are. The only time they would keep silent is when they are locked up in a cupboard,' he laughed. 'You're in a hurry today? Any programme of bird *awaaz*?'

He continued, 'This building of ours will collapse one of these days. When you walk around on the second floor, the cement dust falls on our books here below. Shouldn't all the owners and tenants get together and make a renovation plan? How come you're not adding your awaaz here?'

Without replying, Charu crossed the street at the traffic signal, and started walking toward Flora Fountain. As he strode through Cross Maidan, he could only hear the cry of 'Ballballballballball' from the boys playing cricket there. It was a cry that came from the depths. None of the other sounds and voices were in focus. Charu had been quite shaken by Kotian's comment that he had not added his voice. It wasn't about his ordinary speaking voice or even his singing voice, but something else from deep down. At Churchgate Station, as soon as Shyam saw Charu approaching, he went towards their usual spot, the Wheeler bookstall, holding his paper cup of tea. Another man threw his empty paper cup into the rubbish bin, but it glanced off the rim and fell. The man pretended not to notice that it had fallen, and started running towards the platform. Shyam went behind him, tapped him on the shoulder, and silently drew his attention to the cup he had discarded. Unable to meet Shyam's direct gaze, the man picked up the crumpled cup and threw it into the rubbish bin, saying 'Thanks'.

Shyam and Charu alighted at Andheri Station and made their way to the east side. As agreed before, Mala was standing near the lottery-ticket seller. She was holding a woven plastic bag.

Her steadfast stance suggested that the entire city was under her control. 'Our Queen of Jhansi ... Look how upright she stands. A ticketless passenger would duck if he saw her,' chuckled Charu. The three of them climbed into an autorickshaw and asked the driver to take them to Dinanath Mangeshkar in Vile Parle. At the Koldongri turn, the open-air fish market displayed all the neatly arranged fish glistening between pieces of ice, looking like school students in uniform.

On his terrace, Khaleeel was going to play the piano specially for Mandaramala. For him Mala had brought homemade batata vada and fresh pav from the Irani bakery. She was about to see a real piano for the first time. At this moment she was utterly grateful to Shyam and his friend Charu. Nothing made her happier than feeding her favourite people with something she had prepared herself. She was also carrying sabudana vada and chutney in a separate box.

As they alighted from the auto, Khaleel met them at the entrance, wearing a serious expression. Stopping them from going further, he said, 'Sorry, Shyambhai, there's some tension. The building owner has been after me for a long time to vacate the terrace. He's not returning my deposit but is forcing me to leave today. He threatened to throw down my accordion, harmonium and keyboard from the terrace. He's going to let loose on me the goonda boys of the neighbourhood. He can do what he likes to me, but why attack these innocent instruments? I'm looking for a new place, somewhere close by, so it won't be far for the students. Please, Bhabhiji, don't be angry. I'll definitely play the piano for you another time, but not today.'

Khaleel spoke breathlessly. He covered his face with his hands. Some of the building's residents were standing around mutely. Shyam patted Khaleel's shoulder, as though to give him courage.

Charu said loudly, 'Who will dare to touch your instruments? We are with you. All the friends of Awaaz ki Duniya are with you. Let's go up to the terrace.' He began to climb the stairs. 'Khaleelbhai, don't worry,' said Mala firmly. 'Darkness always runs from the light. Even lighting an incense stick is enough sometimes. You're a teacher who brings light to children through music. You shouldn't be afraid of anyone. Come, let's go up.'

'The landlord says he will break my piano into a hundred pieces and throw it away,' said Khaleel. 'It's from my father's time. And that leg harmonium is made from German reeds, my father brought it from Miraj. It's the instrument my father used to accompany the legendary Mukesh in all his concerts.' The despair in his voice was disturbing. As they climbed up the stairs, they noticed that the doors on each floor were shut. As soon as they reached the terrace, Shyam switched on the lights, even though it was not yet dusk. He spread out the mats for people to sit on. All the instruments stood peacefully and silently. Shyam took off their covers and moved them to their usual places. Then he got Mandaramala to gently take off the cover of the piano.

Mala stared wide-eyed at the shining wooden instrument with its carved brass floral borders as though she were looking at a newborn infant. It seemed even bigger than she had imagined. Like it had come straight off the pages of an artist's sketchbook. Like a tree on whose branches many birds would have sung.

At every little sound from below, Khaleel was getting nervous. Charudutt went down and spoke to someone. Mala wondered at Charu's demeanour and the voice she had not heard before. Shyam placed a small stool in front of the piano, and bowing, gestured respectfully to Khaleel to take his seat, saying, 'Ustad, please.' Charu, who had returned from below, took a batata vada and fed Khaleel, as though he were putting a piece of cake into the Ustad's mouth. Khaleel had a lump in his throat as he tried to say, 'Oh, no need to do all this.' Mala took out the thermos flask and poured tea into paper cups for all of them. The homemade snack and the fragrance of the tea seemed to give them sanctuary and strength. And Mandaramala's presence seemed to offer them a strange and healthy reassurance that nothing bad could now happen.

Taking a tumbler of water from the earthen jug in the corner of the terrace, Khaleel splashed some of it on his face, wiped it, took a deep breath, and sat down on the stool. He joined his hands to the piano and bent down to kiss it, as though it were his mother, or a child. The other three were sitting on the mat like obedient pupils. The birds of the evening screeched from the trees in the compound. Khaleel, smiling in a teasing way at Charu and Shyam, asked without words, 'Not your cries, right?' They shook their heads and laughed.

As soon as Khaleel's fingers touched the keys, sounds like divine nectar began to take shape. When the first note rose, Khaleel looked towards Mala, as though to say that note was for her. Khaleel played on for some time as though he were enquiring after someone he had not met in a long while. Just when it seemed that his soulful journey was about to begin, he turned to them and asked, 'There's more of that batata vada?'

'Oh, plenty,' said Mala. 'If you want it while it's still warm, I can take it out.'

'Not now, Bhabhi, after I play one or two pieces,' replied Khaleel, diving into the piano like a lone swimmer forging ahead in the vast ocean.

Hello, Mike Testing
2020

Childbirth in the Diamond Circus

Dumpy the trapeze artist, fully pregnant, sat behind the box office on a small metal chair at the Khopoli camp of the Great Diamond Circus, date-stamping the tickets, looking as though she was meditating. If she felt dizzy, she would go and lie down in her tent. The cries of the hungry tigers and leopards, the dust raised by the hooves of the horses and elephants, the circus smell that hung heavily in the air, when Dumpy had enough of these, she carried her heavy belly carefully to the side of the Bombay–Poona highway near the camp and sat there watching the vehicles go by. Nearly forty years old, Dumpy had looked after herself all these months during her pregnancy.

For the last five years, until about seven months ago, Dumpy had shared a tent with Shafi the ringmaster. She could not remember a time when she wasn't part of the circus. She had no memory of her mother, who was supposed to have died after being taken terribly ill. It was Dumpy's aunt, the trapeze queen of Diamond Circus, who looked after the child. She was also the one who trained Dumpy in the art. While other small children in the circus took part in cycling items or in doing stunts with animals, Dumpy persisted in learning the trapeze and became her aunt's protégé. When Dumpy walked along the net, blowing kisses to the spectators with both hands and caught the rope ladder and began to climb, the entire circus shivered in excitement. The spotlight shone on her, unblinking. Her aunt, who was already on the wooden platform above, guided her with claps and finger snaps until Dumpy jumped from the trapeze, looking like a flying fish in her spangled costume. Tiwari, who jumped along with her, was stunned by her speed. In all their shows, the trapeze item was the last one in the first segment, and the first item in the final segment that followed. They did this because it was hard to remove the huge safety net again and again.

If it was Dumpy who reigned over the skies, down below her it was Ringmaster Shafi who reigned over the animals. He had collected a number of coats from secondhand clothing shops and changed his coat for every item. If even one of his hairs turned grey, he would hunt it out and apply hair colour. The entire circus waited on him, calling him 'Master, Master'.

The only item Shafi and Dumpy shared was the one where she put her head into the tiger's mouth and then took it out. Shafi would bring the tiger into the ring and make him stand quietly. Dumpy would come up in a white dress, bow to the spectators, and then position herself in front of the tiger. Shafi would tap the tiger's head with a small stick and get him to open his mouth wide. Dumpy would quickly put her head into the mouth and take it out again before the tiger lost patience. This item had brought a certain amount of fame to Diamond Circus.

If the tiger wasn't in a good mood, they didn't perform the item. If her aunt's mood was off, her beloved niece Dumpy wasn't sent to perform it either. We're trapeze artists, we shouldn't do such things, she would scold the girl.

Things were going well until one day when they were in Jalgaon camp, a huge fight broke out between Dumpy's aunt and the circus owner, Jerry, whose family had always owned Diamond Circus. Aunt was fighting for more pay. Jerry was refusing on the grounds that the takings were not so good these days. After this fight, Aunt's stance changed. Once a week she would take to her bed, saying she was sick. She would ask her trapeze girls not to cooperate with Jerry. But Dumpy continued doing her act. At the Satara camp, Aunt's non-cooperation reached its limit. Jerry came to her tent and took her to task. The verbal exchange escalated. During the second show, Aunt rushed to the box office with a few of her girls, grabbed some cash, got into a rickshaw and disappeared. When this happened, Dumpy was in the middle of her act. When she came down from the trapeze, she looked everywhere for her aunt, in the stables, in the canteen and in the box office. Then she began to cry loudly, beating her chest, 'Why did you leave me?'

Jerry couldn't afford to lose Dumpy too. He told her he would raise her pay. After all, she had grown up in the circus, she was the daughter of Diamond, he cajoled her. Dumpy was so depressed that day that she would have had her head bitten off by the tiger, if it were not for Shafi. Having put her head into the tiger's mouth, she did not take it out even after ten seconds. 'Out!' shrieked Shafi. Dumpy did not move.

Sensing trouble, Shafi inserted his stick between the tiger's teeth, grabbed Dumpy's hair and pulled out her head. Since the tiger had already tightened his grip, a few hairs of Dumpy's and her red plastic flower remained in the tiger's mouth. The spectators exclaimed in horror, thinking it was blood. Dumpy covered her face with her hands and ran inside. Cracking his whip, Shafi nudged the tiger back into his cage. This startling escape seemed to give Dumpy a new lease of life. That night, Dumpy took her iron trunk to Shafi's tent and slept there, hugging him tight.

From then on, Shafi and Dumpy began to live together. Shafi wasn't the kind of selfless man to push away a woman who had willingly come into his arms, and besides, he had Jerry's approval too. Although the circus had a collective kitchen and fed all the artists and staff, such sub-families as Shafi and Dumpy's would keep a kerosene stove in their tent and make bhajiyas, omelettes and tea from time to time. Without this, they would not experience the feeling of domesticity. Washing vigorously the few clothes they had under the tanker's tap, frying bhajiyas secretly, having little quarrels, this is what made them a family. Dumpy was no exception. On the second day after she moved into Shafi's tent, she acquired a wick stove and a kadhai and fried some bhajiyas. Shafi sat with his feet on the trunk and his hands behind his head, looking proudly at her. He wanted very much to grab a few bhajiyas but controlled himself until Dumpy had drained the excess oil on a piece of paper and given him the snacks on a plate. When she did that, Shafi felt his domesticity was complete. And when Shafi dyed his grey hairs or trimmed his moustache to a point, Dumpy sat gazing at him. When she was on the trapeze, Shafi always waited near the net. As a keepsake of their symbolic Gandharva wedding, he had kept the red plastic flower from the tiger's mouth in his trunk. When he had a fancy for it, Cyclist Sushila or Madras Mohini used to come to his tent to be tickled, but now he looked like such a householder that they hesitated even to look at him.

Dumpy scrubbed their two plates and the kadhai outside the tent for a long time so that everyone in the circus could observe the signs of their household. Jerry had told Shafi to keep Dumpy enchanted, but Shafi felt that both his compassion and his love for her were genuinely increasing. Since childhood, she had been called Dumpy because of her thick, rounded limbs. But when Shafi called her by that name, she used to feel happy. Shafi now had a small argument with Jerry and had Dumpy freed from the item involving the tiger. He then trained another woman for it. One day, he brought some mutton in secret and cooked it with garam masala. When the dish was nearly done, he made Dumpy sit in front of the stove and told her to serve it when it was ready. 'How long are you taking?' he said, shouting like a typical city husband, stretching his legs on the trunk. Sometimes, in the changing tent, when Madras Mohini or another female artist shook their bosoms as they changed their glittering bras, Shafi was tempted to pinch their cheeks as if to remind himself of earlier freedoms. Dumpy would then complain to Jerry. Jerry called in Shafi and gave him a peg of whisky. 'If you do such things, she will leave Diamond Circus. And who then will do the trapeze act wearing spangly briefs, you or I?'

Even after some years had passed, the whereabouts of Dumpy's aunt were not known. But when Diamond Circus was camped in the Kolhapur fair, the publicity boy ran into one of Aunt's 'girls'. From him, news crept into the circus that Aunt and her companions were now successfully engaged in a more colourful business than the circus. Dumpy was shocked into silence on hearing this. She cried bitterly, wondering whether this was why her aunt had not taken her along.

Diamond Circus was quite famous in the smaller towns but seemed to lose its lustre in the big cities. But even in those smaller places they did not stay very long, and the losses mounted. During the monsoon, there was no business at all. The Diamond remained closed for many days. Some of the artists went away to their hometowns. People like Dumpy for whom the Diamond was their only home, spent those days in boredom. Shafi went off to his town, Lucknow, and also to other places in northern India. Sitting in the dripping tent, Dumpy wondered if things might be different if she had a child and could play with it. When she brought up the matter with Shafi, he said, shaking his head and sticking his tongue between his teeth as if to indicate it was a sin, 'How can a trapeze artist have children? You'll lose your job'. So her monsoons passed in mending torn costumes and looking after the circus animals. Those animals that were sick tended to get worse and die during the rains. Each time Shafi visited his hometown, he would come back with a new animal.

During the monsoons, Dumpy would spend most of her time with the tiger from whose jaws she had escaped. She felt a strange connection with this creature, perhaps because it was linked to her relationship with Shafi. The tiger had developed a skin disease. Clumps of its hair had fallen out, the patches looking like furrowed earth. The ulcers on its gums did not seem to heal.

This time, when Shafi returned, he did not bring an animal. Instead, with him were two identical-looking teenage girls. Having met these Ranchi girls in a Kanpur circus, Shafi had lured them to the Diamond with promises of greater pay. He introduced them to the artists at the Diamond as Rekha and Surekha. The beautiful, slender girls had small eyes and tiny navels. The arrival of the Ranchi sisters brought a new spirit to Diamond Circus. At the Mahad camp, in the empty tent the girls showed off their stunts to the others. When they demonstrated the twist jump, or jumping from the trapeze with scissored legs, Jerry's jaw dropped. Walking on the wire, Rekha balanced cups and saucers on a pole, throwing up each one until twelve cups and twelve saucers were piled one on top of another on her head. Surekha jumped from the back of a galloping horse, slid under its belly and came up on the other side in one swift movement to jump back onto the horse. Even their costumes looked different from what they were used to in Diamond Circus. Shafi swaggered around as if to take sole credit for bringing in these new artists. The world Dumpy had glimpsed when she had taken her head out of the tiger's mouth seemed suddenly to shrink.

Dumpy looked at herself in the large mirror in the green room. She felt the flesh above her ribs was sagging below her blouse. She stopped eating dinner. She scrubbed her face with turmeric powder. At night, when the rehearsal was taking place, Shafi told Dumpy to watch the Ranchi sisters' item. 'Show her your twist jump,' he said to the girls. Dumpy felt as though her body was on fire. When the girls called her 'Madam, madam' she felt a bit better. 'If you look like a hunk of meat from the mutton shop, how can you ever do the twist jump,' commented Shafi, looking at the girls and laughing. Unable to stand the humiliation, Dumpy retreated into her tent. After a long while, Shafi came in and shouted furiously, 'Call yourself the trapeze madam? And you can't bear to see the new item from these girls?' 'You bring these threepenny girls from nowhere, and in front of them you trample into the mud all the esteem I've earned over all these years. Do you have any idea you're destroying my livelihood by doing that?' shrieked Dumpy. 'It was my foolishness to let you stay with me. The times are changing. You're now past your prime. Learn to eat what you have.' With these words, Shafi marched out of the tent.

Dumpy felt as though she could not breathe. She waited for him to return. After the searchlight and the coloured lights went off and the circus was covered in darkness, Dumpy began to feel afraid. Had Shafi gone off to the tent of the Ranchi sisters? First she went to the stables. She could hear the horses munching hay, the anklets of the elephants, the yawning of the tigers and leopards. Because the smell of the animals was strong, no one slept in the stables. But Shafi was there, lying on a folded tarpaulin by the side of the leaves piled up to feed the elephants. Perhaps he didn't quite have the courage to go to the sisters.

Dumpy sat by his side for a long time, while her eyes adjusted to the weak light inside the stables. In the cages, the animals that couldn't sleep were making various noises. Her tiger was rubbing his back against the iron bars in pain. Shafi used to call it King Kong, this tattered creature with wounds all over his body. Whenever his cries became loud, the Diamond's animal doctor Venkatrao would inject him with a tranquiliser, but that was not enough to make him sleep. If they dragged him from the cage, the tiger came unwillingly, resisting, his loose-hanging skin swung from side to side. They had stopped bringing the tiger to the ring so as not to disgust the spectators. Since they couldn't sell the creature to anyone else, they cancelled the item permanently from the show and started giving him less food. But when the circus publicity van went out in the town, the tiger's cage was sometimes hooked to the van on a trolley. Children who saw the tiger always demanded that their parents take them to the circus. Dumpy felt her heart wrench when she thought the tiger might one day lie dead in that same cage.

As though possessed, she leaped on Shafi. 'Forgive me, forgive me. I'll do whatever you say,' she said. As she beat her head on his feet, Shafi woke up in alarm and fell into the elephant feed. Dumpy pressed herself close to him, licking him in the way that he liked, almost stubborn in the way she approached him. She wasn't taking her pills by then. If she became pregnant in her fortieth year, what little work she had might also disappear. The child might become a noose round her neck. Would she spend the rest of her life in this circus? Even as these thoughts came to Dumpy, in the dim light, amidst the ruminating horses and the collar bells and the animal cries and the stench, she drew Shafi into herself. As if clutching on to something she was on the verge of losing, she erupted in joy. And then closed her eyes.

At dawn, the next day, the motorcycle artist was practising in the well of death, his engine producing distorted sounds. Dumpy woke in fright, as though someone had shaken her. She looked at Shafi sleeping by her side and felt he would surely not leave her now. He might push her away saying that she had grown old and fat. But how could he push his child away? Would the Diamond community let him do that? Elated at the thought that a new life was going to take shape in her, she left Shafi sleeping in the stables and, walking very carefully, went to the tanker to fetch water for her bath. For the next two or three days she moved around with great care. When she stood on the trapeze plank and waited for the one on the opposite side to swing to her, she shivered slightly. As the plank swung closer, she could barely see it. When Tiwari clapped, she caught his cue late, and leaped forward at the last minute to grip the plank with fingers that slipped a little. But with an agility that even the Ranchi sisters applauded, Dumpy somersaulted and jumped onto another trapeze. With a rush of feeling, she lost herself in thinking that no one amongst the spectators, or the Ranchi girls, or even Shafi, knew the secret that was fluttering inside her. She began to feel quite light. Fearing that she might lose the unborn child, after four jumps she waved to the audience, blew them kisses and came down from the trapeze.

Her bitterness about the Ranchi sisters melted away. She

began to touch and pat them, talk to them nicely. Invited them to her tent. Learned from them how to tie her hair differently. She told Jerry that all the Diamond artists should wear costumes like those of the sisters. She got the accordion player, Gadkari Master, to go to Mumbai to buy a ream of China silk and one of zari work. With Rekha and Surekha's help, Dumpy fashioned new silk tops and shorts for all the Diamond women. Excited by the newfound enthusiasm of Dumpy madam, the Ranchi sisters shaped her eyebrows for her.

The one who felt confused was Shafi. Having ended the relationship with Dumpy and wasted many days wondering which of the sisters to draw close to himself first, Shafi was in a predicament because of their newfound closeness to Dumpy. He had thought her attack on the sisters would allow him to escape from her, but now that door was shut. He made some false accusations about each to the other, leading to both sides ignoring him. And as if to manifest his private agony in public, one day Dumpy sat on the trapeze plank under the spotlight and began to throw up.

Given the precarious financial situation of the company, there had been no room for pregnancies in the Diamond, and this sound of Dumpy throwing up was harsh in Jerry's ears. He sent for Shafi. Before Shafi arrived, Jerry had counted the months on his fingers. 'You bastard! You've made Dumpy pregnant just when our peak period is starting. By the time we get to Khopoli, Panvel and Mumbai camps, she'll be ready to give birth.' Shafi said helplessly that the bitch didn't tell him anything. Jerry said, 'You didn't know either? Shameless fellow. Then go and tell her to get rid of it. Our main trapeze artist gets pregnant, that too at the age of forty, and without her companion's knowledge? How can that happen?' He sent Shafi off with curses and imprecations.

Shafi could not figure out what to do. Dumpy wasn't his wife. He had taken care of her because her aunt had gone away. He had felt sorry for her and rescued her from the tiger's mouth. He slept with her because she didn't have anyone else. He stayed with her because she provided company. And now, without a word, she had put his child into her. Oh oh oh, he clenched his teeth and hit his head. Unable to articulate his humiliation, he plunged into her tent, grabbed her by the hair and shouted, 'Don't you know the company rules? Already your brand is losing value. Although you look like a gunny bag, they still keep you on the trapeze. You ungrateful woman. And you didn't say a word to me either.' Shafi began to kick her trunk and her pots and pans. Seeing his fury, Dumpy thought her plan had borne fruit. In a calm voice, she said to him, 'You can leave me if you want. This is my child and I'll look after it.' Shafi said, 'You fool! Already you look like a pig. After you have the child, you'll look like a hippo. Then, even the street players won't look at you. What will you do then? Will you hang yourself with the child under your arm?' Hearing the commotion, the Ranchi sisters had come in. 'Don't you dare come this way again. I'll get you thrown out of Diamond Circus,' Shafi screamed. He pushed the girls out of the tent and followed them, kicking the ground as he went.

All at once, things seemed to go silent for Dumpy. Did

Shafi not care that she was bearing his child? Had she wrongly calculated that he would eventually melt? Would he simply take the chance and kick her away? Why should she have this child then? Unable to sit, she walked out of the tent. The coloured bulbs and the searchlight had been switched off. All the tents were silent. The King Kong tiger, failing to reach his wounds with his tongue, was rubbing his back against the bars of his cage and whimpering. The elephants stood like boulders. Dumpy wondered if Shafi was in the Ranchi sisters' tent. She thought of what he had said: how would she look once the child was born? Would she take her child onto the trapeze? For how many more months would she able to pull the gold zari-work panties over her swollen belly and climb the rope ladder? All said and done, she was an older woman having a baby. What guarantee that she would not lose it before term? If the child did not survive, her nine-month-long meditation would have been in vain; she would have lost the physique for her job and lost Shafi in the bargain. Was tying down Shafi the only purpose of this pregnancy? Dumpy was at a loss. If it would induce Shafi to stay, perhaps she should get rid of the pregnancy? With heavy steps, she returned to her tent.

She stayed dull for a week or more, and constantly dizzy. She threw up frequently because of the smell of the animals around her. She would try to find a spot outside where there was a breeze and sit there until she felt better. Meanwhile, Shafi was busy putting the final touches to the twist jump trapeze act of the Ranchi sisters. New posters had been prepared, and they were attracting a number of potential spectators.

Shafi did not come anywhere near Dumpy. Just when she was deciding to get an abortion, the day of the new twist jump item dawned. It was a custom for all the artists to be near the ring to encourage the performer whenever something new was introduced. This time, too, it was the same. Looking like multi-coloured parrots, the Ranchi sisters came and stood by the net. They touched Jerry's feet in respect and did the same to Shafi. They joined their palms in respect to the lightboard. They began to look around for Dumpy, saying 'madam, madam'. Dumpy was hidden behind the curtain, watching them. 'It's not just her body but her mind too that's out of order,' said Shafi, lifting the girls and throwing them into the net. Swaying as they walked on the net, the sisters blew kisses to the audience. Over the loudspeakers one could hear the extolling of their achievements. As the specially composed music track began to play, the sisters grasped the rope ladder and started climbing.

Gadkari the accordion master, who never played anything but '*Jeena yahaan marna yahaan*' from *Mera Naam Joker*, now started to play '*Nazar ke saamne jigar ke paas*' from a much newer film, *Aashiqui*. All the lights of Diamond Circus shone on the Ranchi sisters. Dumpy felt numb: the sisters hadn't bothered to wait for her blessings, and no one went looking for her when the girls started calling out to 'madam'; even those who saw her behind the curtain did not bother to draw attention to her. It seemed she had no connection to what was happening around her and that the only connection she had was with the child in her womb. She placed her hand on her belly. The stench of the animals wafted towards her. Gagging, she ran to the tent, a hand to her mouth. Jeep jumper Jasmine, who was preparing for her act, came running to her side. Stroking Dumpy's back as she kneeled, puking, Jasmine held her head and stroked her back, saying, 'Did you need all this at your age?'

As though grasping at her new life, Dumpy returned slowly to her tent. In the middle of the night, Shafi turned up, seemingly drunk. 'It's nearly a month since you climbed on the trapeze. If you sit around vomiting, Jerry will cut three-fourths of your pay. And I won't give you a paisa. I'm telling you nicely, get rid of it,' he said. Dumpy sat up, asking, 'What did you say?' 'I haven't married you,' said Shafi. 'I'll say the child isn't mine at all.' He had an ugly expression on his face, and his eyes glowered. Dumpy stood up, shouting: 'Hey you, just because you leaped on my body like a donkey and spat into me doesn't give you the rights over the life of this child. Get out of here!' As though possessed, she picked up Shafi's trunk, his boots, his clothes and his mirror, and threw them out of the tent. All the half-asleep animals began to make a noise. The watchman came running, flashing his torch. Seeing Shafi, he caught hold of him and took him away in the dark. As though she had won a fight, Dumpy went over to the tanker, turned the tap, and sat with her head under the water.

In the morning, Shafi took away all his belongings. Dumpy began to throw up with renewed enthusiasm. She made the animal doctor Venkatrao write out a prescription for tablets and a tonic and got Jerry to buy them for her. She went to the nearby village in the publicity van and bought herself a jar of pickles. But Gadkari Master told her sternly that pregnant women shouldn't eat pickles or they would get swollen feet, and took away the jar to keep for himself. Dumpy roamed around regally in the Diamond. On one side was Shafi, who had moved permanently into the Ranchi Sisters' tent, and on the other side was Dumpy, who was strengthening her womb at the cost of the company, both causing worry to Jerry. He couldn't let go of either of them. Not in the state the circus was in. Then Jerry made a farsighted plan. When he realised that Dumpy's child could become part of the circus, he felt a weight lift off his chest. Not many young people joined the circus these days. Even those born in the circus would run away when they grew up. Only the girls were not bold enough to leave. The circus entered their bodies when they were barely able to crawl. If Dumpy could bring a wonderful trapeze artist to the circus, why worry? Jerry prayed in secret that god should grant only a daughter to Dumpy.

As the months passed and the camps changed, Dumpy's world grew along with her belly. She looked after herself with great vigilance. She would ask the women of the nearby town what was good for a pregnant woman and what was not. She cooked greens and ate them. At midnight, when she felt like making bhajiyas, she gave some to the watchman because she did not want to eat alone. Someone told her she should gaze at the coolness of the moon. She sat up all night with drooping eyes, looking at the sky. She went to the town doctor and got injections, keeping the pregnancy record card under her pillow. When she saw other pregnant women knitting in the doctor's clinic, she begged someone to teach her, and began to knit a tiny pair of socks. Now it was a common sight to see Dumpy knitting away with her large belly and her puffy face on which she had applied a light layer of powder to highlight her kajal-lined eyes. She sat near the animal cages, at the box office, or by Jerry's side as she knitted. As though none of this concerned him, Shafi kept changing his coats and shoes and cracking his whip. When someone told Dumpy that Shafi was sleeping with Rekha and Surekha, she laughed. 'I wonder if he sleeps between them, with one hand on each. I wonder who he takes first. I wonder if the other one watches them at it,' she gurgled as she knitted a sock.

Sometimes, she drowsed on her stool. Between sleep and waking, the empty planks of the trapeze swung in front of her inner eye. In her ears she heard the cues ringing, and the applause. Sometimes she seemed to see herself as a little girl swinging on the trapeze. When the children jumped and couldn't catch the trapeze flying towards them, Dumpy woke with a start. In one of her dreams, she was standing at the ring with her little daughter dressed all in white. The girl was taking colourful doves from her pocket and letting them fly away. These dreams were very brightly lit. They left her feeling sometimes tearful, sometimes elated. They made her feel a strange love for all the animals and humans in the circus. She would prepare snacks and call whoever was passing by to come and eat them. 'Let us know if you need any help, Dumpy,' everyone would say as they vanished into their tents. Dumpy lay down alone amidst her stove and her boxes, looking for the cool moon in the sky.

When the circus came to its Khopoli camp, Dumpy looked

fully pregnant. Now all she did was sit in the box office and stamp the tickets, count the takings, and hand out the tickets if there was no rush. She would also help out a little in the costume room and in the canteen. The little town of Khopoli was just below the Khandala ghat on the Mumbai road. Close to the Pune–Mumbai highway was the Diamond camp. From Khopoli to Mumbai was barely two hours, a fact causing some excitement among the Diamond artists. Dumpy was glad they were near a big city and big hospitals. Venkatrao said again and again, teasingly, 'Dumpy, I hope you've calculated right? Your stomach is looking really big. I'm sure you're going to have twins. Maybe there's two artists in Diamond's future.' Anxious, Dumpy went with the publicity boy to the doctor in Khopoli town. 'There might be two in there,' said the doctor, a possibility giving rise to great happiness in Jerry. He was glad that nine months of free salary wouldn't go in vain. Dumpy felt there was just a month to go, but the thought of twins made her feel scared. To get over that feeling, one day she made bhajiyas and invited the Ranchi sisters, Gadkari Master and Shafi to eat with her. Except for Shafi, the others came. As she fed them the bhajiyas, she said, 'If you hadn't joined Diamond, I would never have had this good fortune.' The sisters blinked, not knowing what she meant. Gadkari Master, on the other hand, stroked Dumpy's head, and said in a choked voice, 'Don't be afraid, Dumpy, we're all here.'

After they left, Dumpy lay down with difficulty, wheezing. It was hard for her to turn on her side, so she sat looking at the sky through the gap in the tent top. Like always, the empty trapezes began to swing slowly into her eyes. From a great distance, she heard a woman wailing. The sound began to draw her into it. As though hypnotised, Dumpy got up with difficulty and began to follow the sound. It was dark all around. The wailing was coming from the side of the highway beyond the camp, where the adivasis lived. A few people were standing around dejectedly at a little distance from the thatched huts, looking at the wailing woman, who could be glimpsed in the faint light of the night sky. On her lap was what seemed to be a newborn baby. A woman came out of her hut and stopped Dumpy from going further. 'This woman just killed her male child by drowning him under the tap. Her husband was thrown into the lockup just a few days ago. Last year, too, she killed another baby of hers in the same way.' She added, 'Don't go there', and led Dumpy all the way back to the circus camp. Dumpy could not figure out how she reached her tent. Her mouth was dry. She could still hear the woman wailing. Dumpy's heart was beating fast. In the stables, all the animals lay as though dead. Sweating profusely, Dumpy wondered whose tent she could go to, but hesitated. Instead, she woke up a deer by prodding it, and began to sob loudly.

Next day when she sat down to stamp the tickets, she did not have the courage to look towards the highway. The wail still rang in her head. For the first time, Dumpy began to worry about her unborn child rather than herself. This child with whom she had sought to ensnare Shafi would make her a new woman. Because of the pregnancy she had experienced the pleasure of independent motherhood. Asserted her rights too.

But once the child came into the world, what would happen to it? Who was it going to be? Dumpy's throat dried up. Near the box office a woman began to say to Dumpy, 'Definitely a girl child. The belly's very big.' Venkatrao, who was close by, said laughing, 'Not one but two.' The Ranchi sisters began to shriek: 'Yes, give us girls. We want only girls for the trapeze. Madam, give us only girls.' Inside the Well of Death a motorcyclist was testing his accelerator. King Kong the tiger was yawning, its wounds gaping. The red jeep standing in the sun looked as if was on fire.

Dumpy rushed into Jerry's office. She sat on the stool next to him with her enormous stomach, breathing rapidly. Jerry asked kindly, 'What happened? Did you want anything?' In a trembling voice, Dumpy said, 'My children are not for the circus.' Locking his drawer, Jerry stood up to leave, and laughed, 'What does that mean?' Raising her voice, Dumpy said, 'They are not for the circus. Only over my dead body.' Jerry glanced at her with a chuckle, as though she were a madwoman, and went away twirling his key. Dumpy sat there for a long while, breathing heavily. Outside, the animals were being decorated for the parade. The publicity van boys, dressed as jokers, were dancing around. One of them came running to Dumpy and asked if she wanted water. He brought her a glass and then asked how he looked, this boy who was wearing the joker costume for the first time. Dumpy made a sign that he looked good. Holding herself carefully, she got up. The first show was beginning noisily. She walked slowly towards her tent. She just couldn't sleep. Her throat was hurting too, as though it was being pressed from within.

Seeing that Dumpy had not appeared for dinner even after the second show was over, Ekka, the canteen boy, took a tray to her tent. Dumpy was still breathing heavily. Ekka helped her to sit up. 'I'm feeling very sick,' said Dumpy, so Ekka ran off to find Venkatrao. Since the second show had just finished, there was a lot of commotion and Venkatrao was nowhere to be found. Ekka finally caught hold of Jerry near the music platform and told him about Dumpy. Jerry sent several people to look for Venkatrao. If Dumpy had gone into labour, he would get Venkatrao to do the delivery and not waste money on a hospital. Also, he might have a greater hold on the child if it was born inside the circus. Ekka passed on his errand to one of the jokers, who was actually the publicity boy. By now, everyone had taken off their costumes, but the joker boy still wore his. When he couldn't find Venkatrao, he went to Dumpy's tent, only to find a large number of people there, making suggestions about where to find the pregnant woman. 'Take the jeep to the town hospital. Maybe you'll find her there,' shouted Jerry. A few people ran towards the highway, where the headlights of the passing vehicles lit up Gadkari Master, who was racing up and down calling Dumpy's name.

After watching everyone for some time, the joker, as if something had suddenly occurred to him, ran in the opposite direction, towards the back of the camp, where there was an irrigated field. When he had left behind the lights of the Diamond, he saw a pale white shape in the middle of the field. The mountains seemed to have placed Dumpy there and moved away to either side. Under the starlit sky, she grabbed the joker's hand and held it tightly as she tried to lie down at an angle. Here, one couldn't hear the vehicles on the highway or the circus generator, and the coloured lights of the camp had vanished. It was as though the field was covered with a mosquito net made of moonlight. Without letting go of the joker's hand, Dumpy began to call out for her aunt as her labour pains increased. The clouds had come to a standstill. She could not hear anything. She could not see anything. The breeze was polishing the dull glow. The headlights of the cars and trucks descending the distant Khandala ghats seemed like stars coming down to earth. As the faint light of dawn suffused the skies, Dumpy gave birth, holding on resolutely to the joker's hand. In the trembling dawn, the joker held up the newborn infant. Where there should have been two arms, there were four. The gleaming infant moved fitfully. 'Tap the baby on the head,' muttered Dumpy, as though in her sleep.

By now, groups of people were arriving at the field. Truck drivers who had heard the news at the petrol station abandoned their vehicles and rushed to the field to see the wonder. But the entire community of Diamond Circus had surrounded the field and was guarding it so that no one else could come near. Jerry tried to push his way in, saying, 'Keep the infant as it is. It will be the new attraction of Diamond Circus. Like a god with four arms. It will be the new item.' The circus members ignored him as they tried to make a plan. Venkatrao was shouting, 'The baby should be taken to Mumbai instantly. They can operate on him there. Where's the jeep? The jump jeep....' The red jump jeep was reversing bumpily into the field. The crowd made way for it but watched from a distance. In the arms of the mother, who slept peacefully, the infant was crying. The joker was touching all his four rosy arms gently, making crooning noises.

Diamond Circusnalli ondu herige
1992

Milk Moustache

Punda had wiped dry all the utensils he had washed and was now wiping down the Cuddapah stone kitchen counter in the first-floor flat where the entire family had gone to sleep. The flat was in Supriya Apartments on Rajaji Road in the Mumbai suburb of Dombivali. The eleven-year-old had been doing housework here for the last two years. Although his given name was Pundalik, the second half had long fallen off, making him Punda – the mischievous one – although he was hardly that. He did not remember exactly how old he was. But everyone knew the age of Pinky, the child of this house. Today had been her birthday. Whenever there was a party with cake and balloons, when large heaps of dishes piled up in the sink, the woman of the house quickly picked out the chips left by the guests on their plates and put them into a small tin, saying, 'Pundu, these are not touched at all. They are for you. Have them whenever you like.' Whenever she tried in this way to make him happy, Punda did wonder on which day his own birthday fell.

When *Chhayageet* or *Chitramala* played on the TV, Sir

always told his wife to call Punda, who would be filled with delight. In order to save them the trouble, he would rush to finish his chores by the time the advertisements came on, and stand by the living-room curtain. 'Why did you come before you were called?' he was sometimes scolded. When a Kannada song was played on *Chitramala*, Sir would teasingly ask: 'Which film is this from, Punda? Who's this hero? Why does he have a potbelly?' Responding to this banter, Punda would say, 'This is Srinath. This is Ambarish. This film was shown at the Honnavar rath yatra. My older brother took me doubles on his cycle all the way from Bhatkal to watch it'. When he started blabbering like this, his chest puffed up, and they shut him up with a 'shhh'. His job was to wash the clothes, scrub the floors, wash the dishes, help Ammavru with the cooking, and in his spare time play with Pinky.

The afternoons, when Ammavru took a nap, was when the empire of Pinky and Punda flourished. Three-year-old Pinky hung on to every word he uttered. In the beginning, when he was asked to tell Pinky a story, Punda used to fall into a predicament. Slowly he began to spin the stories into a fine thread, becoming quite an expert at telling tales to the little girl. He would narrate her to sleep and earn the parents' praise. Sometimes, even when Pinky had fallen asleep, Punda kept on telling the story to himself, being unable to stop the pace of his narration. His Sir was like that too. On the pretext of putting Pinky to sleep, he would sing a few film songs, and continue singing even after she had gone to bed, until Pinky's mother told him to stop. Each day Punda added new elements to his story.

Once, Bhima from the Mahabharatha and the paanwala in his little shop across the road came together in one character. Not knowing how to resolve the narrative, Punda made his Bhima pummel the paan shop into a hundred pieces with his mace, grab a fistful of paans, shove them into his mouth, and stride away towards the railway station, chewing. In this way, Punda added a dimension of astonishment to his stories, keeping Pinky entertained through her dinner, teatime, milk drinking and bedtime.

From a relative's house where there were boys of Punda's age, Ammavru got him a couple of sets of used clothes. If they had to go out somewhere or if they had visitors, Punda had to wear trousers and a shirt. The pants were a bit long, and so Ammavru shortened them for him. There was a T-shirt the collar of which had become loose but Punda liked the picture of the boat on the front. Pinky loved to see Punda in his 'good' clothes. She kept running around after him, calling out, Pundoo Pundoo. When he stood up on a stool like a street acrobat to put up the washing on the wire above, Pinky handed him the wrung-out clothes from below. When the waterdrops fell from the clothes onto Pinky's eyes and chin, both she and Punda were overjoyed.

When he rolled out chapatis, she sat with him. He would give her a small ball of dough and she would roll out a tiny chapati. Then she would cling to his neck and swing gleefully, while he continued making chapatis. When Punda pulled out his simple bedding which was put away during the day, and quietly spread it out at night, Pinky looked at him with pride.

She would bend down to help him roll out the dhurrie. Then she would fall asleep, sitting with him and listening to his stories, even when her mother scolded her for doing so. And even though Sir didn't like it either, there was no other way of getting Pinky to sleep. So he would pretend to grumble at Punda, while he picked up the child and took her to the bedroom. Punda would then get back to his chores. During Diwali, all the loud and flashy fireworks purchased for Pinky were actually lit by Punda, because Pinky was a cowardy cat who could not even hold a sparkler. When she finally managed to light one that was tied to a stick, a jubilant Punda came running home excitedly to relay the news.

Each month, without fail, Punda received a postcard from his hometown, Shirur, near Bhatkal, which his mother got someone to write for her. Ammavru always wrote back saying that he was doing well. You've passed second grade and can't write your own letters? Ammavru would say. Look at Pinky, how clever she is. Praising Pinky was a way of getting her to do her homework. Pinky would scribble circular objects on a piece of paper and laugh, calling it Pundu's Kannada. In the beginning, when the card arrived from home, Punda would become quite listless. Pinky would keep calling him to come and play, and complain that he wasn't coming. 'He's got his mother's letter. He's thinking of home,' Ammavru would say compassionately.

Slowly he got used to the letters. He used them to teach Pinky the game of blowing-down-the-card-train. Each postcard was folded neatly in the middle and lined up one behind the other. Then, when Punda blew on the last card, it would fall on the card in front, and one by one they would all tumble down, causing great merriment to Pinky, who would clap her hands in glee. Punda would then make a stack of the cards, put a rubber band around them, and keep them in Pinky's toy chest. When asked where this train was bound, he would say, 'Bhatkal'. 'Here we are all fine. Your elder brother is working in Shanbhag's truck service. Your little sister Tulasi is refusing to go to school. She doesn't even do the daily flower plucking. Don't worry about us.' These words, give or take a few, would appear on all the bogies of the train. When a new postcard arrived, Sir would say, here is one more bogey for your train, as he handed it to Punda. Sometimes the boy would say: 'My sister Tulasi is very smart. Much more than me. I used to play with her just like this.'

Punda's family worked for a Nayaka's house as the gardeners, with the family consisting of Punda, his mother, his brother and his sister. They had made a small thatched hut for themselves in the Nayaka's backyard. Their work was to water the plants and trees in the garden, pluck the coconuts, pluck the hundreds of different kinds of flowers blooming there, and take them to the Nayaka for the daily puja of the household gods. It was the mother's task to pluck the flowers. While doing this she seemed to be talking to each plant and caressing it. After his father died and his brother began roaming in search of work, it fell to little Punda to collect the flowers. Punda used to do this with great delight, immersed in the dawn light, holding a cane basket in his left hand and a rod with a hook in his right. The backyard was full of plants and creepers and trees dripping with flowers. So many kinds of flowers. Clock flowers, conch flowers, hibiscus, needle jasmine, pearl jasmine, sugandhi, kanakambara, red champak, yellow karaveera, sone hoovu. Punda would gently hook the giraffe-like hibiscus plant and delicately pluck its flowers. In the monsoon, the petals were covered with raindrops. The yellow karaveera tree's branches next to the compound wall were like swings hanging from the skies. Climbing its smooth, worn trunk, Punda would sit in those branched chairs, swinging like a king as he plucked the karaveera flowers and sucked the nectar from their leafstalks. As he sat holding a flower between his fingers like a cigarette, sipping the nectar, his sister Tulasi would whine from below: 'Anna, give me some too.' Then, in godly fashion he would throw down a few flowers. The brother and sister would make their way to the Nayaka's house, sucking on the sweet flower cigarettes.

Sitting on his big porch, the Nayaka would take the flowers out of the basket and make three large heaps and one small one. The three heaps were for him and his two brothers. Even here, the big flowers went into the Nayaka's heap. The ordinary-looking hibiscuses, karaveera and a few other daily flowers went into Punda's heap, for his stone god. Punda called it the stone god, because he had seen the Nayaka's shining gods of copper, brass, silver and gold. His own family's god was a meek idol in the alcove outside their thatched hut. For him, the hibiscus and the everyday flowers were enough. Once in a while, the children would find a blue dahlia near the guava tree, or some white sugandhi, and hide those away in the yard. Until they faded, they would look at them from time to time and inhale their fragrance. On such days, when the Nayaka portioned out his heaps, a mischievous smile would appear on Punda's lips.

In the light of the dawn, it was easy for his mother to know in which direction Punda had gone, since she could see the discarded yellow karaveera flowers, sipped dry, that he left in his wake.

After coming to Mumbai, Punda hardly ever went out of the house, but whenever he went with the family to a wedding or took Pinky to the park, he would struggle to find flowering plants. There were, however, flower shops aplenty. Apart from the parijata tree with an oddly twisted trunk he saw outside a Tamilian temple, he could not see any plants that bore flowers. He envied Tulasi, who now plucked the flowers in their village. Taking the seeds from the tiny garland of flowers that the household got from the flower vendor, Punda planted them in a vanaspati tin, in spite of Ammavru's protestations. On the balcony, in the midst of old newspapers, footwear and Pinky's small bicycles, the bulbs pushed their way out of the tin. Pinky called the flowers 'Pundoo flowers'. Once, Punda was so preoccupied with this 'flowerpot' that he forgot to iron Pinky's uniform, and her mother yelled that she would upturn the tin and its flowers on top of Punda's head. For some reason, this made both Pinky and Punda laugh.

Taking Pinky to and from her nursery in the city was a task done with great zeal by Punda. Both times, before he stepped out, he combed his hair. He looked at everything on the side of the road and pointed out several things to Pinky. Her nursery was sandwiched between a garage and a flour mill with a small factory on top. When school was done, the little slatted wooden gate was opened to let the children out. As though they were being auctioned, each child was held up for viewing. If their minder did not come forward, the child was put back inside and another one hauled out. Even if one reached there a second late, the child would be pushed inside and had to wait for half an hour before her turn came again. As soon as Pinky spotted Punda, she would call out to him – 'Pundoo' – and wave. When they left the school, Punda checked her schoolbag to make sure all her books were there, and her pencil and rubber. If she hadn't drunk enough water, Punda would threaten not to tell her a story and make her drink some right away.

On the way home, Punda would ask Pinky who she wanted in her story that day. Pinky would point to people and objects on the road. See that green car, Punda would say. It came first in yesterday's story. Pinky would go closer to look at the car.

They both were deeply interested in the mobile paanwala. If they saw him on the road, they would stand near him to watch how his hands moved. He walked with a small box tied to a strap around his neck, with his ingredients in tiny bronze jars. Anyone walking along might stop him and order a paan. Compared to the paan in his hometown which was pre-prepared, Punda felt the paan that took shape in front of him was pure magic. The paanwala took things out of his shiny jars and smeared them on the betel leaf, filled it with colourful masalas, folded it and handed it to his customer. Even before the customer had put the paan in his mouth, the paanwala had taken his money and moved on. When he walked, not even a sliver of arecanut moved in his tray.

One day, when he was coming back from dropping off Pinky, Punda gathered his courage and spent fifty paise to buy a paan. Wrapped in a muttuga leaf, the paan nestled in his shorts pocket, waiting for night to fall. When everyone had gone to sleep, Punda folded all the clothes drying on the balcony, watered his plants, and only then took out the paan from his pocket. Carefully he opened the packet, spread out like a flower the paan mixture which lay huddled in a dark heap, looked again at the masala, folded the paan again, and as the lights started going out one by one in the nearby buildings, he slowly put the paan into his mouth. Without swallowing a single drop, without spitting anything out, he held the paan in his mouth with eyes closed. He felt he was floating. Suddenly he heard Sir speaking to him: 'Pundoo, heat some salt water for me. My throat is itching.' Abruptly he swallowed as much of the paan as he could, rushed to the kitchen and lit the gas stove, all the time making sure Sir was behind him and could not see his face. Like an angry daughter-in-law with a scowling face, Punda just grunted assent to whatever Sir said. He handed the glass of salt water to him and fled to the bathroom. As he scrubbed his lips clean, he was glad to see in the mirror that they had turned red with the paan. Next day, on the way to school, he did not forget to show Pinky his red tongue. 'How did it become red?' she asked, and he said that it was because he had eaten a lot of red ice candy in his dreams.

The night before her next birthday, Pinky's mother applied mehendi on her hands. Pinky insisted that she apply it for Punda too, so she drew some pretty flowers and vines on his palms. 'Don't go and wash the dishes now. Do it tomorrow. The mehendi colour won't rise if you get water on your hands,' she said. Like prisoners, both Pinky and Punda sat with their arms raised. Punda felt a little foolish sitting like this, so he washed his hands and went off to do the dishes. Next day, Pinky's mother must have kissed her little girl's hands and said 'Arre waah' when she saw the pale colour of the mehendi. Pinky came running to Punda, who was washing clothes in the bathing room, pulled at his hands, wiped off the soap and saw the faint colour there, and kissed it, saying 'Arre waah'. 'Sheee, soap!' she said, and ran off. That day in their stories all the king's subjects were wearing mehendi. Some children got together and applied mehendi on an elephant. For the elephant's birthday, there was a cake as big as a palm tree.

One day, a new visitor came to the house. He was wearing glasses, and sat with Amma and Sir, chatting for a long time. When Punda took them water, tea and fruits, the visitor called him by his name and said, 'How are you, Pundalik?' Punda ran off shyly. Who was this man who seemed to know him? Punda turned off the light and stood in the dark by the door, looking at the man. From his speech he seemed to be from Punda's home region. But his was not a familiar face. Pinky sat there for some time, expecting to be given chocolate. When nothing came her way, she ran out, calling for 'Pundoo'. She sat in the kitchen with her toys spread out. Even as he helped Pinky build a tower, Punda was shelling peas and throwing them into a pot of water. From time to time, he would give her a few raw peas to eat. You eat too, said Pinky, stuffing them into his mouth, but Punda refused to part his lips, as though his life depended on it.

Just then, Ammavru came in saying, 'Pinky, Uncle is leaving.' The bespectacled Uncle came behind her: 'This Sunday you must come to our house for a meal, Pinky. Bring Pundalik too.' As soon as he left, Ammavru said, 'Punda, we have to go to his house in Andheri the day after tomorrow. It's far away, so we have to leave early in the morning. Tomorrow night don't make preparations for idli batter. We'll just eat some bread and leave early.' Then she said, a little haltingly, 'Pundu, some good news for you. This man Rao who had come. They have a six-month-old baby. Your sister Tulasi is looking after the child. It seems she's been demanding that she see you. Such nice people. See how they came all this way to talk to us. So let's go visit them. You'll get to see your sister, and she too may feel better when she sees you.'

Punda could not believe it. Tulasi? Here? As though she had appeared in one of his stories. He couldn't figure out whether to believe it or not. She was so small when he left home. Her hand couldn't reach even the hibiscus buds on the small plants near the well. A stubborn girl. She must have given their mother a lot of trouble.

Punda started doing his tasks with greater vigour. When Pinky made her usual fuss about drinking her milk, Sir asked Punda to help. Punda sat her down in the balcony and started telling her about his sister. 'Tulasi can walk on the sandy beach even in the midday sun. Others run because their feet burn. But not Tulasi. She can eat raw banana without flinching. She can chew on a bitter, unripe guava and eat it up. But when she sees this brother of hers, she trembles'. Pinky listened with eyes wide open, guzzling down her milk. Then she ran to the mirror. 'Chheh, today the moustache isn't right,' she grumbled. The bigger the milk moustache, the greater her joy. 'Tomorrow we'll make an even bigger moustache,' said Punda as he went to spread his bedding. Pinky began to roll about on the sheets. 'Go brush your teeth. Otherwise no story for you,' he shooed her away. After Pinky had fallen asleep, Ammavru said to Punda, 'You've washed your pants and shirt? You should do it tomorrow if you haven't.'

The next day, after dropping Pinky to school, Punda washed his clothes and hung them on the balcony wire. Ammavru saw Pinky's panties on the sofa and said, 'Arre, she's gone without wearing them. Go, go and take them to her school.' Punda ran out without even wearing his chappals. At the door of the nursery, he asked a teacher for Pinky. When she came out, he drew her to one side and and quickly put the panties on her, calling her Nangoobai. 'Shall we go home?' asked Pinky. 'No, there's still time,' Punda said, sending her back inside and running back home. He saw the mobile paanwala on the way and regretted not having fifty paise with him. It would be nice to take a paan for Tulasi.

When he returned to the school to fetch Pinky, the electricity department was cutting down branches on the roadside that interfered with its wires. The truck had a ladder like a fire engine and uniformed men were climbing up and down. They were using ropes to make sure the cut branches did not fall on the wires. Praying that the work would continue until he fetched Pinky, Punda made his way to the school. Picking up her schoolbag and making her drink some water, he said, 'I'm going to show you something fun, a truck that's cutting trees.' Although they rushed to the spot, the work was finished and the men were piling the cut branches on one side. The ladder too was now sleeping on the side of the truck. Punda was sorry that Pinky hadn't got to see the action.

Doesn't matter, I'll tell you all about it, he said, talking about it on the way home. 'Why did they cut the branches?' asked Pinky. 'So that they won't grow on the wires,' said Punda. 'Why shouldn't they?' she asked. 'Because it'll give the trees a shock.' 'What will happen if a tree gets a shock?' 'The tree will start talking. It will start walking. It may come into your house and sit down. Or it might stretch out all its hands and start grabbing food from all these shops.' 'Baap re,' said Pinky in awe, as they reached home.

Ammavru said to Punda, 'It's nice for you that your sister's here, isn't it? You can go and see her whenever you want to. But she doesn't seem to be liking it here. She really makes a ruckus. And it's a house with a small baby. You should speak to her since she listens to you. Tell her to do as she's told.' Again and again, Ammavru repeated these words.

Tulasi's little face came before Punda's eyes, but it seemed to resemble that of Pinky. 'Sure, sure,' he said, as he ironed Pinky's clothes for the visit. Ammavru switched off the iron and said, 'It's still hot. Why don't you press your own clothes too? You should look good tomorrow.' Punda rushed off and got his shirt and pants. As he finished running the iron over his shirt, it became cold. But he ran it over the pants all the same and thought he would place them under his pillow. When Ammavru was napping, he heard the paanwala's cry and went down quickly to buy a paan which he slipped into the pocket of his pants.

Next morning they were all at Dombivali station by eight a.m. Because it was Sunday, there was a long queue for the tickets. Punda, who was holding Pinky's hand, was dumbstruck by the sea of people. It was as though Pinky was the one giving him courage. Sir came with the tickets. Amma held Pinky's hand, Sir held Punda's. A train approached the platform, but seeing the crowd, Sir said they would take the next one. Passengers alighted onto the platform like ants coming out of a nest on fire. Those who were outside were now inside. In a second, the train had left. 'Do you see how quickly we have to climb in, Pundoo?' said Sir. In a few minutes, another train approached. They all pushed themselves into a compartment. Punda's face was pressed against Sir's stomach. They were being jostled by the crowd. Now Sir was carrying Pinky. Ammavru couldn't be seen. At some point, Pinky shouted, 'The sea, the sea.' 'That's only a stream, Pinky. Now wait till the bridge comes,' Sir said. Punda could not see a thing. All around him were stomachs, pockets and bags. When it went over the bridge, the sound of the train seemed different. Punda remembered that when he had first come to Mumbai, Sir had taken them somewhere near the sea. There was a hill and a park on top of that hill. With an enormous cement boot house. Sir had pointed to a blob in the sea and said, 'Punda, look, that's your Bhatkal. See how close it is. If you take a launch, it's only two minutes away,' he had laughed. Even though he knew that was not true, as long as they were in the park, Punda sat looking at the blob in the distance.

When they changed trains at Dadar, they were able to find seats. Sir said in Punda's ear, 'Tell your sister that if she looks after the baby well, without making any fuss, we will give her a present.' Pinky kept looking at Punda. Drawing his chin towards her, she said, 'I'm tired of this train, Pundoo. Our Bhatkal train-of-cards is so much nicer. We can always stop it when we get bored.' Sir spoke into Punda's ear again. 'Talk to Tulasi nicely. If you like, we can arrange for you two to meet once a month. Tell her to behave properly and not break anything. The other day, she threw a cup in anger and broke it. They kept quiet because she's just an eight-year-old child.' Punda began to feel a bit afraid. When they alighted in Andheri and got into a rickshaw, he forgot to hold Pinky's hand, causing Amma to fly into a rage.

After they rang the bell of Rao's home, he took a few seconds to open the door. In that short time, Ammavru said quickly to Punda, 'If they put snacks before us, don't put out your hand. They will give you a separate plate. And don't try to sit on the sofa.' Having glimpsed them through the peephole, Rao opened the door, saying, 'Oho, come come.' He asked them all to sit down. Pinching Pinky's cheek, he said, addressing his wife, 'See who all are here.' 'Pundalik, you're looking good.

Sit down, sit down.' Worried that he would sit on the sofa, Ammavru said quickly, 'That's all right. Pundoo, sit on the carpet over there,' pointing to a spot near the teapoy. As he was about to sit down, Rao pointed to a dining table chair a little distance away and asked him to sit there. Amma signed to him with her eyes not to sit. Mrs Rao came in, wiping her hands. 'Namaskara, I was putting the baby to sleep. My mother was here and has just returned to our hometown.' Turning to Punda, she said, 'You must be Tulasi's brother. How smart the boy is! Tulasi, come here!'

Punda's eyes turned towards the inner part of the house. His heart was pounding. Moving the curtain aside with thin hands, little Tulasi came and stood before them. Her eyes looked at her brother with longing. Seeing her brother grown fair and plump, she smiled shyly. Then she saw the others and took a step back. Punda too smiled at her. Then Rao said, 'See how nicely he's grown in two years. If you stay here, you will also look like that. Come here, come and talk to him.' Tulasi did not move. In the peculiar dress she was wearing, her hands and legs looked like sticks. Pinky ran to her and stood examining her as though she were a toy. Her mother scolded her, 'Pinky, come over here. Let brother and sister talk to each other.' Then Pinky went and stood near Punda. 'Wah, she's really attached to him, isn't she?' said Mrs Rao. She continued: 'They must be feeling shy to talk in front of us. Let them sit comfortably in the bedroom. Please go there, both of you. The baby's asleep. Talk softly.' Punda too stood up and followed Tulasi. Stopping Pinky from going after him, Rao told her she could follow them later. When both Punda and Tulasi had gone into the bedroom, he partly closed the door, leaving it a little ajar.

A kind of deafness began to envelop Punda. Almost Pinky's size, this baby sister of his. What to say to her? What to do with her? He had no clue. On the big double bed in the middle of colourful bedsheets, the baby was sleeping like a tender flower amidst soft pillows. There was a small mosquito net placed over the child, just like those nets that cover the jamuns in a sweet shop. By the window stood Tulasi, as scared as he was. No words came to Punda's lips. Tulasi was looking unblinkingly at him. Who plucks the flowers there now? Why did you come here? Why do you make a fuss? Why did you break the cup? None of these questions came to him. He couldn't even sob. The silence was palpable, like a noisy kerosene stove had been turned off. The infant twitched, having wet itself. Tulasi came swiftly forward, lifted the child's legs, removed the diaper and tied a new one after wiping down the infant. She tapped the child gently on the chest. The child fell asleep again. She fixed the mosquito net.

After some minutes, Ammavru opened the door. 'Pundoo, Pinky has started her fussing again. Please make sure she drinks her milk.' She dragged Pinky into the room holding her glass. Pinky got absorbed in looking at the sleeping baby. She lifted the net, touched the baby's fingers, and stepped back. Tulasi came forward to adjust the net. When Pinky was bent over the baby, Punda made her drink up the milk quickly. An unbelievably large moustache loomed on Pinky's face. He signed to her to go and look in the mirror. Jumping in joy at the sight, Pinky went outside to show the others.

In a little while, preparations for lunch began. 'So is your conference over?' They asked the brother and sister to come out. In the serving of food and cleaning up, Punda played a major role. 'See how well trained your brother is', everyone kept saying to Tulasi. Punda ate sitting beside Tulasi. 'See how neatly he's eaten', they showed Tulasi. When Mrs Rao made the afternoon tea, Punda was at hand to carry the tray of cups out. She whispered to him, 'You told her everything, right? I hope you scolded her a little.'

At four, they got ready to leave. 'Now you should come and visit us. Pinky, do you want a baby to play with?' As these farewell words were being uttered, Mrs Rao said to Tulasi, 'If you don't do your work properly, your brother won't come to see you again. Isn't that so, Pundalik?' Tulasi was sitting cross-legged on the carpet. On her little thighs the baby was sleeping, clad in a blanket. 'Hold the baby with both hands. Your legs are too short. The baby might fall off,' said Ammavru on the way out. Everyone stepped outside for the goodbyes.

Punda, who was holding Pinky's bag, turned around to look at his sister. The little girl holding the baby with both hands and gazing unblinkingly at him looked like their mother. As though he had forgotten something, Punda went back inside, took the paan out of his pocket, and placed it near Tulasi. Then he rushed shyly out to join the others.

Haalina Meese
1992

Kekoo and Pyarelal

Between the Xerox shop with its deep yellow signboard at the corner of Lal Bahadur Shastri Road outside the suburban station and Pyarelal's immutable 'temporary' stall – basically a plywood box piled high with fruit next to a shiny metal balance – there didn't seem to be any connection. People heading to catch a train to their office, school or college dashed into the Xerox shop to photocopy something or the other. Early in the morning there was always the whiff of soap, attar or perfumed oil about the place. In the evenings, the same people would stop in front of Pyarelal's stall to touch and smell the fruit before they agreed on a price. On Sundays, since offices were closed, the Xerox shop also remained shut. Pyarelal, on the other hand, did not have any holidays. Only if he fell sick did the spot remain vacant. On such days the plywood box clung to the Xerox shop as though seeking protection.

Kekoo Shukla of the Xerox shop was always busy counting the hot sheets that came out of the machine, counting them and collecting the money that was due, then moving on to the next task. If by chance he looked towards the street, a sheet was sure to get jammed in the machine. It was a second-hand machine.

Kekoo was the middle one in a family of three brothers who lived together in Mahajanwadi, an old set of buildings in Mulund. The elder brother, who was considerably older than his siblings and the younger one, who constantly twirled his moustache, did 'business' in Danabazar and Tarapur respectively. Knowing that Kekoo did not have their business sense, they had bought this machine and installed him in the Xerox shop. If they hadn't done that, Kekoo may have continued to while away his time in his baggy pants and pygmy boots, spraying himself with imported perfume and talking about film stars and singers as he leaned against someone's car or scooter. For ten years after leaving school he had done exactly that.

His younger brother had suddenly fallen in love with a Marathi girl and married her against the family's wishes. The two daughters-in-law had conspired to get the Xerox shop for Kekoo, annoyed that all he did was eat and sleep and grow fat. But no one had the time to think about a wife for him. And his parents were long dead. Now that he was nearing forty, Kekoo found it difficult to figure out which generation he belonged to. When he looked at his youngest brother he felt older than him, but when he saw his brother's children, the cradle in a corner, and his bhabhis folding the brothers' underwear, he felt he was actually the younger one. When he escorted the children to school, he felt he was the older brother. When he took the family's clothes to be ironed, and touched the bhabhis' blouses, their salwars, their saris, he felt a strange ethical dilemma. So, once in a while, he would shout at the children for no reason at all as he brought them back home after school. And don't you dare tell anyone I shouted at you, he would tell them.

Until he crossed thirty-five, he kept hoping he too would have an affair, get married. But before he could blink, the years had rolled by. The world, the town, the families of the brothers, all grew older. Along with grey hairs a bald patch began to appear on Kekoo's head, making him feel dispirited. But what tied him to his Xerox shop were the attractive young women with long fingers and painted nails and crackerjack chatter who came to the shop. Their splendid locks flowing in the breeze were enough to keep him trapped there.

In the beginning he used to be impatient with the old people who came to get copies of their ration card or a property deed, but now he managed even those with great care. If the original document was torn, he would mend it with some Scotch tape. Watching him at work, Pyarelal once said: 'Waah, Kekoobhai, how neatly you dress. So well-ironed your clothes are when you arrive in the morning, and they look the same at the end of the day. Quite tiptop. And you take such pleasure in your work.' From that moment a link was forged between the shop and the stall. 'I'll just go and get a cup of tea. Please mind the stall,' Pyarelal would say. If customers came when Kekoo was away Pyarelal would tell them he would be back soon. From this sort of aloof friendliness, they progressed to having tea together or giving change on behalf of each other when one of them had none. But Kekoo stood warm and neat and well-ironed in his shop, while Pyarelal continued to stand outside, buffeted by the wind, exposed like one of his fruits.

Pyarelal was from the northern state of Uttar Pradesh. Bitten by wanderlust from a young age, he had washed up on

Mumbai's shores like so many others. His dwelling place was under the wooden staircase in a dilapidated building. He would buy his fruits in Crawford Market and sell them in this suburb. Pyarelal was probably between forty-five and fifty years of age It wasn't something he thought about much, though. When his work was done for the day, he would eat dinner in a small hotel that he patronised. Throughout the day, what fuelled his body and his labours was strong milk tea with a little sugar. He needed to have that at least eight or ten times a day. And each time he would offer half a glass to Kekoobhai or to the paper boy next to him. Kekoo was a lassi lover. However, each time he ordered a glass of lassi to be delivered to the Xerox shop, he wondered if he should share it with Pyarelal. And being money-minded, he didn't fancy that. So, once in a while, he would come out of the shop, say 'Pyare, I'm going to the toilet', take the narrow path through the vegetable market to the dairy parlour and drink his lassi. He did worry that Pyarelal might see him. But not wanting to spoil his own pleasure for which he had paid good money besides, he would say to himself, 'I have the good fortune of being able to afford this', as he downed the glass boldly. Afterwards, when he had come back to the Xerox shop a little sheepishly, he avoided looking at Pyarelal for some time. If the lassi caused him to burp, he did feel bad about Pyarelal. Kekoo's behaviour was thus sometimes secretive and his manner not always expressive. The fruit seller, on the other hand, always laughed loudly and openly when someone said something, however insignificant.

One day, Pyarelal was cutting the slightly damaged fruit from the bottom shelf of his box and handing a few pieces to

Kekoo. 'Kekoobhai,' he said, 'you've got plenty of room in your shop. You could have a built-in cupboard. These days there's huge demand for audio cassettes. All kinds of people are selling cassettes on the street as though they are vegetables. Why don't you think of selling them? When someone comes for a Xerox, they stand around for a few minutes, don't they? Play them a song and they may end up buying the cassette.'

Kekoo took his decision that very night. In a couple of weeks, two speakers began blaring from the Xerox shop. The walls filled up with cassettes. In a flash an astonishing cassette business had begun. Pyarelal's hunch was right. The five-rupee Xerox customer began to buy a thirty-rupee cassette. Kekoo began to get cassettes for customers on demand. When Pyarelal went to Victoria Terminus on his way to Crawford Market where he purchased his fruit, he would pick up new cassettes for Kekoo without taking a paisa for himself. Cassettes of Mehdi Hasan ghazals smuggled from Pakistan and brought to the Bhendi Bazar shops, Talat Mehmood's radio songs, the trending '*Choli ke peechay*' – all of these could be found in Kekoo's little shop. Outside, as though he had nothing to do with this music wafting from the shop, Pyarelal stood polishing his fruits like Kapil Dev polishing the cricket ball before bowling, listening happily to the songs. It was as though Pyarelal did not know there was a link between his suggestion and Kekoo's growing prosperity. It was as if he didn't seek to benefit from it at all. Once in a while he would make a request: 'That song you just played. Play it again, na.' Seen from inside Kekoo's shop, Pyarelal's contentment appeared even more exuberant.

Inside the shop was the hot, sooty smell of the machine, the sheets and sheets of paper, the plastic-wrapped singers who sat in the cupboards. The same opening phrases, the same concluding lines, the same melody – no matter when the cassettes were played. Whether fast forwarded or rewinded. But each of Pyarelal's fruits looked different, and the ones that got sold and the ones that remained were equally fresh.

Along with this phase of good fortune was growing a powerful anxiety in Kekoo. How would he repay this debt to Pyarelal? He knew only one kind of expression of gratitude – either to make free copies for someone or to give them free cassettes, a free service or object from his shop. Neither of these would mean anything to Pyarelal. It wasn't possible to gift Pyarelal a cassette player either. That would mean mocking the tiny transistor radio that the fruit seller had held close to his heart for many years. This faded transistor nestled amidst the fruit, with melodious songs coming out of it at all times. From the early morning devotional songs to the soldiers' special to the *Bela ke Phool* at midnight, the transistor that played them was Pyarelal's faithful companion. When he laughed aloud at some dialogue in a radio play, he may have looked foolish but he did not seem to care.

Kekoo asked him once in a light voice, 'How about if you had a cassette player?' 'No, I don't want one. It's very predictable, isn't it? Reports to us obediently. The listener thinks he's the one who holds all the pleasure in his hand – isn't that stupid? The radio isn't like that. There's always some suspense even in a known programme, and that makes me happier. Isn't it grand that it comes from the skies, without any wires, and reaches everyone without discriminating? My only job is to tune into the right station. For a vagabond like me, what could be greater than this?'

Kekoo fell silent. The lassi that he had been drinking behind Pyarelal's back seemed like a shameful thing. Even if he were to start sharing the lassi, the weight on his chest would remain. When the municipal trucks came to clear away the unauthorised stalls, Kekoo would step forward like a warrior and hide away all of Pyarelal's fruits in the Xerox shop. When the goods of all the other stalls were being carried away by the municipality, Pyarelal's fruits looked like little children hidden between Kekoo's cassettes. 'How *bechara* they look, na?' commented Pyarelal, handing Kekoo a half glass of tea. Kekoo could think of his assistance as help offered to his friend, but was it really?

Finally, he tried one more time. Letters to Pyarelal from his hometown used to come c/o Kekoo Shukla. One day, handing over such a letter to the fruit seller, Kekoo said, 'How long will you have a "care of" address, Pyarebhai? Why don't you get a small kholi of your own? You can keep your fruits safely there. You can sleep safely there, you can cook for yourself. It won't be very expensive.' In a firm voice, Pyarelal said, 'Absolutely not!' Then he added, 'This "care of" address gives me such satisfaction and such happiness. Even if the illusion that someone cares for you lasts for a second, isn't that good enough, Kekoo? Who cares for anyone in this town?'

Then, wondering whether his words had insulted Kekoo's concern for him, Pyarelal said quickly, 'I'm a wanderer who thinks the whole world is his, not just a few square feet. I'm renting the world, so why bother to tie myself up trying to own a piece of this earth? In rented homes there's a feeling of being very light, like with this transistor. So many songs come flying out of the air, settle on borrowed branches and then fly away.'

In this way, although there was a difference in perspective between Pyarelal and Kekoo, they came closer in another way. This was demonstrated one day when the Shiv Sena called a bandh without any prior notice. It was a city-wide 'Mumbai bandh'. Before the day had advanced, the entire city came to a standstill. When the Xerox shop opened that morning, there had been no sign of the bandh. Kekoo had lit the usual agarbatthi and done his aarti for the Xerox machine and the rows of cassettes. Having had his half glass of tea, Pyarelal was arranging apples and pomegranates on his plywood box. Kekoo had just started playing a cassette when a group of men shrieking 'Band karo' came running, with stones in their hands. The market shut down. Those who had set out for their offices went back home, glad for the unexpected holiday. With no buses or autorickshaws plying, the road began to look like a path cleared for a funeral procession. As the day wore on, the market emptied out completely. There was no tea stall open either.

'This is what happens in these bandhs,' raged Pyarelal. 'Those who call for a bandh check to see whether everything is shut, then they go home to eat a huge meal and settle down for a nap. Those who live on daily wages, those who eat from street carts or in hotels, no one bothers about what happens to them. The success of this bandh depends on how many children go to bed hungry today.'

Kekoo sat on Pyarelal's box for some time. In the silence of the marketplace, the music from Pyarelal's transistor could be heard even from a distance, spreading all around. The waiters in the nearby restaurants came out to play cricket with stumps and a bat. The auto drivers sat down with the policemen on a mat and began to play rummy. The Telugu women who sold strings of flowers ran to the temple which wasn't shut, and seeing that there were no people there either, they let the flowers go dry in their baskets and sat picking lice from each other's hair. 'Let's go,' said Pyarelal to Kekoo. 'We'll never get a chance like this. Let's walk around the place.'

The market was quiet except for wealthy young men in coloured shorts wandering around looking for soda for their drinks. Since there were no people on either side of the road, the bazaar looked different, as though sitting with its face covered. Kekoo said, 'The trains haven't stopped. Shall we go to VT and see the Gateway and the ocean?' After a moment of silence, Pyarelal said, 'Let me show you a gateway right here.' Taking a side street, they came to where dozens of empty carts that belonged to the bhelpuri and pav-bhaji sellers were parked. On a normal day, the area would be filled with people who had come there to eat the snacks. Now there were no customers and no sellers. Some of the vendors were sleeping on the carts. On the side of the street was a huge wall like that of a fortress. On top of the wall were pieces of glass embedded in the concrete, and the door had rusted bars. 'Have you ever seen this?' asked Pyarelal. Kekoo was noticing it for the first time. Behind the wall seemed to be a rusting structure completely covered by a metal mesh. 'Do you know what this is?' asked Pyarelal. 'It's where they put away criminals. To preserve the world from their murdering and thieving ways.' Pyarelal's demeanour was sombre. Kekoo felt a strange fear.

'Don't be afraid,' said Pyarelal. 'The place is well guarded. No one can come out.' He walked quickly to the municipal garbage bin next to the prison and climbed on to its edge. He gestured to Kekoo as if to say, one can see better from here. Kekoo climbed up with some difficulty. He could see iron bars across the galleries. Behind the bars he could see some creatures in ill-fitting uniforms, like hundreds of owls sitting in silence. The creatures seemed to be moving their limbs about in the darkness. It suddenly occurred to Kekoo that these were human children. He held his breath as he watched. Children ranging from the age of three to twelve were waving their arms, as though calling out to them. In the same compound could be seen a large worn-out metal slide and a pair of broken wooden swings. Were these children waiting for someone to look in their direction so they could wave to them?

Jumping off the edge of the garbage bin, Pyarelal said, 'Let's go.' As they walked, he continued, 'They bring child convicts and orphans to this remand home. You should listen to the evening prayer. It sounds exactly like the wailing of a family when a corpse is borne away from the house. Amidst the noise of the marketplace, the pani-puri carts and the balloon sellers, you can't hear the wailing so clearly. Last year, on Children's Day, seventy children broke a gate near the toilet, jumped over the ditch at the back, and escaped. Only a dozen frightened little sparrows remained. So the security has been doubled now.' Kekoo was digesting all this very slowly. He had walked along this road thousands of times all these years. Why hadn't he seen it before? Why couldn't he still see it?

As though infusing life into the empty streets, a tea boy ran up and down hitting a coin against his aluminum kettle. The two friends drank some tea. Worried that they might not get any more tea, Pyarelal drank two glasses just to be safe. He spoke to the tea boy: 'Where do you live, child? If you fall sick and have trouble finding food, come and see me. I sell fruit near the station.'

It was tending towards afternoon. 'Arre, Kekoo, it's your lunchtime,' said Pyarelal. 'Go home and eat. Anyway, I only eat one meal at night. This tea saved my life.' Kekoo's home was close by. 'Pyarebhai, it's rare that you're free at this time. Come and eat with us today.' Holding his hands to his ears and sticking out his tongue a little, Pyarelal said, 'Don't spoil me, Kekoo. Go and eat, and rest a bit also. I'll be near the shop.' His words were too emphatic to be undone through persuasion. Defeated, Kekoo walked to his house.

Because of the bandh Kekoo's brothers were at home and it felt like a festive lunch. They were all watching a new film on cable TV as they ate. The TV-watching children were being fed by hand by their TV-watching mothers, with morsels sometimes getting into the children's ears, noses and eyebrows. In this house of washed clothes hanging out to dry, heaps of already dried clothes, tin trunks, rows of kitchen utensils, wedding albums, embroidery frames, spice jars, jars of pickles, and betel nut, how would he have brought Pyarelal for a meal, Kekoo pondered.

After lunch, he tried to lie down but could not. He looked at them. His elder brother, who was playing with his little daughter on his stomach, burping as he played. His younger brother, who still showed everyone his honeymoon album from the trip to Ooty. The children, who believed there were only strangers in this world, because their mothers had taught them never to accept food from strangers and never to go anywhere with such people. Hundreds of hands from the remand home that stood like a dark, silent tomb kept appearing in front of Kekoo's eyes.

Once Pyarelal had asked him if he was married. And he had replied: 'If the world is ready to give me the friendship that won't be spoiled by either money or bodily needs, why should I bother to collect bundles of small troubles?' Pyarelal never dwelt on the details of his personal life and thought them irrelevant. Neither did he ever ask about Kekoo's private life. When his mother passed away in the village, he did not close down his fruit stall. Kekoo tried haltingly to comfort him. 'When someone has become part of you and your strength, to make a fuss about the end of their bodily existence is to push them away even more,' said Pyarelal. 'If I stop working for a day, would that have made her happy?' he added.

Once Pyarelal had taken a hundred rupees from Kekoo to make change for a customer. He hastened to return it as soon as he possibly could. 'What's the hurry, Pyarelal? Am I running away somewhere?' said Kekoo. 'You won't run and I won't run.

But this money will. Then you won't treat me the way you do. In this day and age people keep track of the money they've spent even on their kids.'

If it wasn't for the bandh today, Pyarelal would never have taken him down that road. He would never have seen the gateway of that dark sea. In some distress, Kekoo stood up to leave the house. Seeing him put on his shirt again, his older brother said, 'There's a bandh today. Why are you going back?'

'I think I may have forgotten to switch off the Xerox machine,' said Kekoo as he stepped out.

In the afternoon sun on that bandh day, the streets were still empty. Kekoo strode quickly towards his shop. On the little porch of the shop, Pyarelal was sleeping with his head on his left arm. By his head, as though standing guard, his little transistor radio was humming. The toes of one foot trembled slightly. His hair looked greyer than before. Kekoo felt like wiping the sweat off his friend's forehead. Just then, Pyarelal woke up, as though sensing that someone was standing near him.

'Our fate. Not even a cup of tea ...' he said, wiping his face and head with his handkerchief. 'Where shall we go, Kekoo? To VT perhaps?' As he was about to step into the street, they heard a cry: 'Save her, please. Save my daughter!'

An old woman came running from the direction of the vegetable market, crying loudly. As the few people who were in the street, including Kekoo and Pyarelal, started moving towards her, she sat down in the middle of the road, her jaw clenched, shivering. Her teenage daughter, eight months pregnant, had suddenly started labour pains. Hoping to catch a rickshaw, the mother and daughter had walked for nearly ten or fifteen minutes. As they reached the vegetable market, the labour pains had increased and she sank to the ground. The helpless mother had come running towards the Xerox shop.

Pyarelal looked around for a rickshaw and found none. He grabbed Kekoo's hand and ran towards the vegetable market. A number of curious people had crowded around the pregnant girl, who was weeping. A woman was giving her some water. When Pyarelal came running up, the others stood aside, as though making way for someone from the girl's family who would take responsibility for her. Pyarelal picked her up gently, as though she were a small child, and holding her with care he began to run towards the municipal hospital. All along he kept reassuring her, 'Don't be afraid, child. Everything will be fine. We're here with you.' He said to Kekoo, 'You have money if we need it, right? I only have a couple of hundreds.'

A few hours after reaching the hospital, the pain subsided. But because the girl was already eight months gone, the doctors said it might start again. They made her lie down on a white cot with her feet raised. Outside on a wooden bench sat her mother, Pyarelal and Kekoo. As though she had just found her voice, the mother told these strangers all her woes. About how Rickshaw Chandu had said he would marry the girl and persuaded her to enter into a sham marriage, and sent her back to her mother within three months. As usual, such things did not affect Pyarelal. The only thing that bothered him was the fear on the face of the young girl. He was well aware of transactions that did not involve love. But the thought of a new birth that did not involve any affection pulled him to pieces. He put his hand on the shoulder of the mother. 'Sister, forget him. He's just an excuse. His work is over. Do you seriously think there's no space on this earth for a baby's little feet?'

Kekoo was looking at the other patients. Rows and rows of cots. On each cot a human being. Each cot surrounded by relatives. Biscuits, fruits and a flask. Each patient gained courage only through a fellow patient. Each pregnant woman given courage by another pregnant woman. Because it was a bandh day, nobody had been discharged and the hospital was full. Ward boys were taking away bedpans. Outside, it was growing dark. When the visiting hour ended, the hospital became a little quieter.

The girl, who had been taken away for a while, was now brought back on a wheeled stretcher and lifted onto a bed. The three of them went close to the cot. The girl, who looked even smaller than the child growing inside her, was sleeping peacefully. A saline drip was affixed to her arm. Pyarelal bent down and stroked her hair. She opened her eyes a little and then went back to sleep. 'You're alone here, sister,' said Pyarelal to her mother. 'You may need help at night. We'll stay here. You can go home for a bit if you like.' To Kekoo he said, 'I'll go get some fruit.'

The mother did not move but continued to sit on the floor at her daughter's feet. Kekoo went to the nearby window. He did not have the courage to look at the dark structures that could be seen from the first floor of the hospital. The dark sea waves beat in silence against his chest. *The children who escaped on such a night, where are they now? What are they doing? Are the children behind the gateway asleep?'*

Down in the unpeopled marketplace and the narrow lanes, the streetlights shone wastefully. Kekoo turned to look at the ward. A very old patient was being fed like a child by another man nearly as old as him. Wiping the specks of food from his chin, he kept saying, 'One tiny bit more.' By the pillow of the old patient was the same kind of transistor Pyarelal had. It was singing softly, as though it could be heard only when listened to intently. In the ward, the song seemed to convey a collective sense of release. The sleeping girl twitched as she tried to turn over and then slept on. Kekoo walked towards her, praying that the same secure feeling the little pregnant woman gave him might reach the children in the remand home.

Santheya Dina
1993

Spotless

Through the window of a hospital, the sun usually looks like a flower. But this hospital on the third floor in a lane near Charni Road Station didn't seem to have windows at all. Just rows of cots in a narrow room with wooden partitions. Above, a huge fan like the wing of an old airplane. It was dark even during the day. The dull tubelight burned through the day and the night. If you thought there was a window and went near it, all you would see was the wall of the neighbouring building. In such a room, KK lay on a cot like a figure cut out from a sheet of paper.

This man who spent all his life on the streets of Mumbai had been involved in leftist movements since his youth. The textile mill satyagraha, the dockyard and railway workers' strike, he had taken part in all of these. After working in film studios as a set artist on daily wages, he went to study art in Rabindranath Tagore's Santiniketan. On his return, having gained a new awareness, he gave up all his impassioned speeches and started teaching drawing to the children roaming in the streets. He wandered around with a cloth bag, coloured chalk in his pockets and holding a rolled-up black clothboard wound around a plank. His hands and body were constantly smeared with chalk dust.

In the strange belief that unfortunate people living in squalor would have the doors of fortune open to them if they learnt about beauty and cleanliness and neatness, the artist would gather these dirty, snivelling children around him, stroke their backs, and make them draw a colourful parrot, a peacock, a sunrise, a brinjal, a rainbow, a bus. His friends scolded him: 'What's the use of art? Why don't you teach them how to write instead?' 'Chheh ...', he would reply. 'This isn't vocational training. Just an effort to give them the strength they need for their life.'

'If you learn some art, you can draw posters, make decorations for the Ganesh Festival and for Navaratri, become a set designer in a film studio, create banners,' he enthused the children. The mothers would dress them in a relatively clean set of clothes and send them to the artist. Whenever he saw an unkempt child by the roadside, he would immediately ask him whether he wanted to learn how to draw. Which child would turn away from colours and sketching? Pulling out the chalks and some blank sheets from his cloth bag, KK would conduct the class right there on the street. Later, he would distribute lemon peppermints to the children and hand out blank paper, a notebook, a sketchbook and some colour pencils, saying that they should fill the pages with drawings by the time he came by next. It was natural that the children should call this man who carried coloured chalk 'Khadoo Kaka', Chalkpiece Uncle. Some would tease him as 'Khadoos Kaka', Short-tempered Uncle.

Without ever getting provoked, Khadoo Kaka would go around collecting the old pencil boxes and the blank pages remaining in the notebooks, putting them all into his bag. Slowly Khadoo Kaka became KK.

Let alone a wife, KK did not even seem to have a distant relative. People did wonder how he earned his living. All his old activist friends had already retired and lived in their children's flats, dandling grandkids on their knees. Dealing with scowling sons-in-law or daughters-in-law, they had melted into the suburbs. Without being concerned about any such obligatory relatives, KK led his wandering art-filled life.

The children of the women from the mujra halls near Kennedy Bridge were also brought into KK's orbit. The sickly women who lay around all day put on their make-up at lamp-lighting time, shrugged into their padded blouses, and as the sarangi struck up a tune, they would make seductive gestures to the passersby. All night there would be a darbar of notes and coins and spitting of betel juice. The children, who had seen all the fake expressions of love and the cinema songs and the posturing from their hideouts behind the curtains, seemed fearful and warped. KK sat them down in a separate room and got them to draw. But however much they drew, the strange fear in their eyes did not go away, and this made KK sad. The orchestra members who got up to drink some water or to eat a paan in between two dance numbers would peer into KK's art room and ask, guffawing: 'Don't you teach any *naach gaana* in your kindergarten?'

KK soon realised that the slum children from Dharavi,

Koliwada and Kherwadi had a sparkle in their eyes that the Kennedy Bridge mujra kids did not have. Thinking of all the eyebrow-plucking and seductive laughter, and of how simple emotions like shyness or excitement were acted out, KK felt that the only way to enlarge the children's minds was to take them out on trips. Walking by the sea at Chowpatty or along Marine Drive, these children revelled in their freedom. The energy gained by the Dharavi kids through drawing and sketching was obtained here by going past the double-grill doors and looking at the far horizon. KK would feel acute pain when delivering the children back to the mujra hall. They would hold KK around his waist as though they were hugging their mother, weeping all the time. 'Tomorrow let's go again to see the sea.' This one sentence was enough to help the children get through the night.

On the Mumbai streets, it was becoming common to draw giant portraits of Shirdi Saibaba. Long after the original artist had disappeared, the saint's picture helped quite a few street children to earn a living. Although the wind and the rain had made the portraits indistinct, it was still possible to add new colour to the original lines and collect coins from passersby. Once KK was caught in a thunderstorm near Charni Road Station. As he stood by the side of the road, he saw a large portrait of Saibaba on the other side, with a little girl with two pigtails standing guard over the coin collection. As the force of the rain increased, the saint's features began to disappear. Putting the coins into her skirt pocket, the little girl covered the Saibaba face with a piece of plastic and kept on sitting there. She didn't budge even though she was as wet as a drenched crow. Aghast, KK dragged her under a nearby awning.

She began to scream, 'Don't you understand? The rest of the picture can be drawn again, but not the face! If even a slight change, business will go phut. No more coins!' She shook off KK's hand, ran back through the rain to the portrait, and sat on the plastic sheet covering the face. KK stood watching in silence. Like a statue welded together by art, hunger, money and rain, the girl sparkled in the street. Until the rain stopped and the sun came back to dry out the road, KK waited with the girl. He took her to get a bun pao in the Irani restaurant close by. 'Don't worry. I'll repair the whole picture for you,' he consoled her. Crouching with her on the street, KK took out his coloured chalks and created a brand-new Saibaba. When he used his fingers to shade the colours on the saint's face, the little girl sat on her knees with her face in her hands, totally captivated. At the touch of KK's fingers, the lines began to come alive. The peaceful face was as clearly drawn as on a calendar. Unable to contain her joy, the little girl – perhaps seven years old – took out a two-rupee note from her pocket and put it into KK's. Her movements as she transferred the money to him were practised and serene. The gesture seemed to distil the essence of the streets. KK did not pay attention to it, as though it didn't concern him.

Before he went to bed that night, KK put his hand into his pocket and found the two-rupee note. He thought for some time about whether it was merely a piece of paper, a value or a cost. He had surprised himself when he noticed the girl putting the note in his pocket and did not mind the act. If he had reacted, the gravity of the moment would have been destroyed.

Feeling there was a lesson in that moment, he put away the priceless note inside the cover of his old diary.

As though beauty itself was beckoning in a formless and abstract way, KK began a new practice from the following day. He gave each of his children a plain white paper the size of a postcard. 'Keep this carefully along with your drawings, chalks and notebooks. Keep it as it is. Keep it clean,' he told them. Into each ear he whispered, 'Do not write anything on this paper. No scribbling. Don't make it dirty. Guard its emptiness. Then it will guard you too.' In the trembling little hands, each piece of paper looked like a swan's feather, a mysterious secret paper. Wherever he went, in the midst of his chats and lessons KK distributed these papers as though he had taken a vow to do it. Everyone hid their piece of paper in a safe place. Each of them felt an emotion beyond anxiety, carrying the responsibility of the paper. 'KK might return, KK will ask for the paper.' The papers had no blemish. They all thought that touching the papers would make them dirty, that they would fade if they kept looking at them. In thousands of holes in the city, KK's pieces of paper sat quietly like freshly made kites. Just like the black dot a mother places on her child to avert the evil eye, the paper pieces too seemed guileless.

One day KK was sitting with the children of the dockyard coolies in a nearby field and talking to them about line, movement, cleanness and beauty. The seamen from the ships which had been put into harbour because of the monsoon were also standing around, listening to the lesson. The children were making their own drawings based on the figures on KK's blackboard. Just as the lesson was drawing to a close, the piece of blank magic paper appeared in every child's hands. They all looked at the paper as though looking into a mirror. KK then distributed the paper pieces to the coolies standing there, and to the seamen. Even those who hesitated at first began to accept the pieces, sensing something extraordinary and invisible. Those who laughed dismissively also came up and took the paper. Along the harbour, the wet breeze from the sea was blowing. In the dim light from the sky, the paper in everyone's hands was gleaming. 'No marks for this. You don't need to show it to anyone. Don't write anything on the paper. Look after it and make sure that it stays spotless.' KK's humble voice reached everyone. As they sank into solitude, thinking of the strange spaces opened up by the piece of paper, a boy called out, 'Khadoo Kaka, there's a spot on my paper. I didn't do anything to it.' Saying this, he began to tremble in fear. Stroking his back, KK took out another piece of paper from his bag and gave it to him. He took the dirtied paper and threw it so that the breeze carried it away. Shining in the air, the paper floated crookedly like a paralysed bird and disappeared behind the nearby huts. For some unknown reason, everyone raised a shout. 'Ho!'

KK's piece of paper became such a private matter that no one spoke about it. They thought if they did so, its power would diminish; they also believed that their efforts gained strength and support from this paper. Like a nameless secret. Like a good deed done in all innocence, it began to grow within them. Those who lost their paper would sidle up to KK near the public tap, or outside the Irani restaurant, and express their anguish mutely.

KK would tell them: 'You must have put it away somewhere. It's your paper. It will never leave you. Don't worry, you'll find it.' 'Please give us another paper,' they would plead. 'Chheh, only one piece for each person,' KK would say. 'It will not be lost. Don't keep looking for it. Go about your business.' The little girl near Charni Road Station with the Saibaba portrait had learnt freehand drawing from KK and made a border for the portrait herself. She felt that this Saibaba inside a border was safer and more tranquil. She complained to KK that he hadn't given her a paper.

Having given out the pieces of paper, KK did not return to visit everyone with the same interest and enthusiasm as before. By this time, he was nearly eighty years old. If he sat down tiredly in front of a hut in the slum and the children surrounded him, he would take out some peppermints from his pocket and hand them out. If the slum women asked him whether he would like some tea, he didn't refuse vehemently like before. Instead, he would say, 'Give me half a cup', and sit quietly without speaking until he was handed the tea. He would then drink it in silence and go away. People still wondered where this weak old man lived and how he earned enough to feed himself. Although liberties were often taken in this open and informal public place, it also had its own boundaries. And so the questions remained unasked. One day, KK fell down near Indira Gate and someone from the Artists' Centre brought him to the hospital.

Since the past week, KK has remained in a half-conscious state, and quite weak. Everyone seems to feel a strange and irresolvable burden. Someone comes to the hospital and sits by KK's bedside.

If he is awake, they mumble a few words. Someone has brought rice gruel in a bottle and it remains by the bedside, now gone stale, because the bringer probably didn't return. Office, home, children: many responsibilities, many reasons. Somehow they are taking turns to come and visit KK. Whenever KK opens his eyes, they go close and speak loudly into his ear, 'Don't you have any relatives? Any blood relatives?' KK simply blinks. 'If you need anything at night, do call the nurse,' they say. KK looks at the window. It looks to him like an odd blackboard. Why is there no light there? Or is it that he can't see it? The words don't come to his mouth. He is too weak to raise his arm. Another patient next to him asks, 'Was that your son?' 'The one who came yesterday, is that your brother?' 'What's your illness?' 'What's your caste?' The questions come at him from time to time.

When the nurses tell him that dozens of little boys come to see him every day and stand outside the hospital gates, and that they are not allowed in because they look dirty, KK is anguished. He remembers the faces of his students and is thrown into turmoil. He begins to imagine that at nightfall all the children he had ever taught come to the hospital gate and stand there like a row of marks against the evil eye.

Whenever anyone came near his bed, KK would ask: 'Are there any children outside?' He would add humbly: 'If you see any children hesitating outside, please don't shout at them. Do bring them to me.' The nurses would smile at his words, tell him to go to sleep, and disappear. In front of KK's eyes would appear the little Saibaba girl's face, and all those tiny bangle-less hands that were trying to draw. When the wardboy came to change his saline bottle and cajole him to eat proper food rather than take the drip, KK wondered whether he too was his student. He wanted to call him back and ask him but fell silent at the absurdity of his train of thought. He had kept wandering all these years without accumulating or recording anything. He began to fear that his journey of dissolving his inner and outer worlds had come to a halt.

People stopped coming to see him. KK gained the strength to walk a dozen steps, and the doctor patted him on his shoulder and said, 'Let's send you home tomorrow.' Before KK's gaze, nothing called 'home' materialised. He thought of the ruined mills of Parel.

The huge, rusted iron gate of one such mill is opening slowly. There's a metal ladder nearby. Underneath it an old iron trunk. The lid of the trunk is opening. Inside it are two pale blue kurtas, a pair of cotton pants, a much-mended cloth bag, brushes, colouring books, a Solapur bedsheet, a tin of Amrutanjan balm, a torch with two battery cells. There is no blank paper there at all. None at all. However, the two-rupee note given by the Saibaba girl is there.

Outside the hospital, the rain is pouring down. The little children, drenched in the rain, stand close together in silence, clustered like honeybees. Hundreds of chalk portraits of Saibaba are getting washed away. The wind from the harbour is lifting the tin roofs of Dharavi's huts. The cycle tyres that were meant to weigh down the roofs are falling down and rolling away on the wet and empty streets. They roll into one another on the slope and go down with a rivva rivva sound.

'Amma,' cries a little child, startling KK. As the slumber

clears from his eyes, he sees a poor mother on a bed on the far side of the ward. She looks sick and hungry and weak. But she has managed to sit up on her bed and is plaiting the hair of her four-year-old daughter who has come to visit her. The child cries out because of the tugging of the comb. Her mother bends down to soothe her and continues to make two pretty braids. Seeing the magical appearance of beauty amidst this dirt and disease, KK is dumbstruck. He sits smiling.

Dittibottu
1998

A Door in the Well

Rocket Tejbali, who was walking along the long beach at Alibag, shone red in the light of the setting sun. At a casual glance, you couldn't tell whether he was walking towards you or away. He was certainly quite far from the crowded area that had the bhelpuri and ice cream stalls. For Alibag's inhabitants, this ocean and the sunset were not special, and they did not venture out much at this time. But groups of picnickers from Mumbai, hoping for a respite from the commotion of the city, would come a hundred kilometres to splash around in the red waters here. Those who were familiar with the terribly crowded beaches of Mumbai were frightened by the long stretch of deserted beach. Far from the picnickers Tejbali had stopped, but perhaps he was still walking. He glowed like a burning coal in the strong sea breeze.

He couldn't remember when he – chief motorcyclist of 'Milan Well of Death' which had set up camp near the Alibag beach – started being called Rocket Tejbali. Perhaps he had become Rocket Tejbali when he left the Diamond Circus fifteen or twenty years ago. There he had been the fastest motorbike warrior in the 'death globe'. After leaving the circus, he had worked in a number of Death Wells until he came to Milan, where he had been for five or six years and where he performed hair-raising bike stunts for the audience. Tejbali, now nearing fifty, had greying sideburns. When he sat on his motorcycle with the deep red petrol tank and no mudguard at the top of the Death Well and kicked the accelerator to produce a sound to split the skies, he looked like the hero in an old Hollywood Western. He would sit by himself, motionless, with great concentration, like a rocket that was about to take off.

Today was the last day of the Alibag camp. The ten p.m. show was the final one. For the last fifteen days, without fail, Tejbali had been coming to the seashore at sunset. Even if it was for a few seconds, he would climb onto the old Yezdi that looked like a black scorpion and come quickly, fatafat, to the beach. If it was low tide, he rode the bike along the sand for a stretch and then went back to Milan. If little children ran after him, whooping, he would rev the bike and disappear behind the miserable scrub bushes in the descending darkness. For a long time, the phut phut sound of the scorpion bike without a silencer continued to linger in the breeze.

Perhaps the thought that from tomorrow this sunset and this beach would not be there for him has affected him. He leaves the black scorpion by the tender-coconut vendor and walks along the beach. It is low tide. On the wet sand Tejbali's footsteps appear light, lit by the setting sun. In the hollows made by the footsteps, seawater is seeping in. The old fort emerging from the sea in the distance is being covered with shadows as the night sets in. He has seen it every day this fortnight, but hasn't felt like going to the fort itself. When the tide is really low, he has heard that people walk along the sand to the fort.

Even when the tide is higher, people go swaying in small boats and launches to reach the fort that stands like an island. The fort is like an old dream that crumbled a long time ago. Darkness is gathering in its dimly seen windows. Black birds appear to be sitting on the tree in the courtyard. The fort's broken tower looks like a torn map. Tejbali calls out: 'I'll be back!'

He has lived in thousands of places, he thinks. But none has drawn him like this one. When he opens the door at the bottom of the well of death and enters, he sees hundreds of eyes looking down on him, against the backdrop of the deep sky. The applause floats down into the well. When he kicks the starter of the red bike the audience stands to attention. Like a rocket Tejbali comes rising up rivva rivva rivva. That's all. The entire wooden structure of the well of death shakes and the audience is scared. After the item is completed, Tejbali rides the bike down in a zigzag fashion, leans it against the lamppost, pushes open the tiny door at the bottom of the well and goes out. There, too, the same crowds. In the town too. Crowds unseen in any dream. Crowds that vanish at ten p.m. as though someone has magicked them away. Jostling through the crowds, Tejbali comes to the seashore, stands at the edge and watches the fort. The sea surrounding the fort wets his feet and recedes forcefully to make the sands shift. He calls out: 'I'll be back!'

It was Milan's owner Rampyare who had magnanimously allowed him to come to the seashore today. Without fussing about Tejbali not being around for all the shows on the last day of Milan's camp, Rampyare said, giving him the key to the black scorpion, 'You go and roam around at your leisure. Let Chhagan and Pattoo do the item today. Anyway, they have to learn to do it by themselves. Go, have fun. We leave town tomorrow. Don't forget.' Rampyare looked like he was in a bit of a dilemma. His eyes always seemed to be secretly worshipping Tejbali. He used to behave as though, if Tejbali had wanted to, and luck had smiled on him, he would have been somewhere else, somewhere better. His calibre was what Rampyare had a deep respect for. So, even though Milan's takings were reducing by the day, Rampyare never failed to pay Tejbali's full salary, and to ensure that his bike servicing took place regularly.

Whenever Rampyare had a major decision to take, he would have the habit of speaking to Tejbali about it. 'You're a great artist. And as great a man. Your luck has turned against you. That's why you're in a two-paisa stunt company like ours. We have benefitted from you. But we're not in a position to give you the position and honour that you deserve. Let's manage with what we have?' Rampyare's conduct seemed to suggest all this. Since last year, when they were at the Ichalkaranji camp, the laundry service for Tejbali's attractive costumes had been discontinued. That was when Milan Death Well was doing really badly and not drawing spectators at all. The generator, the bribe to the electricity department, the rental for the wooden gallery, the deposit for the camp site – spending on all of these had emptied out Rampyare's pockets. Considering that, Tejbali did not think it right to hassle the man about his laundry. He began to look after his costumes himself.

One night, in a drunken state, Rampyare fell at Tejbali's feet and began to weep. 'We're unable to look after you like you deserve,' he wailed. 'No, Seth, no master,' said Tejbali, and Rampyare screamed, 'Don't call me Seth,' and slapped himself. Looking at the owner in his patched jeans wiping his eyes on his sleeve, Tejbali felt something well up in him. He patted the man's greying head, saying, 'You'll come into a phase of good fortune. Don't worry.' As though wanting to believe this, Rampyare widened his eyes, saying, 'Really? Is that true? Let my luck turn, Tejbali, I will look after you like a god. I'll give you a full-time assistant.' He walked off enthusiastically. After this moment when it seemed that they were both giving false reassurances to each other, Tejbali began to feel that he had become a burden to Milan. Just like children who played house-house, who pretended to cook a meal and served each other with tiny spoons, he felt that he and Rampyare were feeding each other dreams about the future and about life.

A few days after this incident, there was a small problem while they were in the Arnala camp. A little girl accidentally touched a naked bit of wire, part of the string of light bulbs fixed around the well of death, and fainted from the electric shock she received. Although she recovered, the Milan Death Well became the target of the audience's fury. People broke the wooden seats, smeared tar on the posters, went in search of Rampyare, who had gone into hiding in the nearby Arnala hills, and beat him up. For ten days or more, the loudspeakers of Milan were silent. The Shiv Sena youth leaders who came aggressively to collect compensation for the little girl looked at Tejbali, who was giving his bike a shine with some Brasso, and said, 'Ha, hero! Don't you have any work? Come and work for our election campaign; we'll give you food. Chicken curry.' Tejbali experienced this as a naked moment of realisation. And he also felt that it was in this naked moment that change was possible.

This might be the best time to lessen Rampyare's burden, he thought. He went up to him and said gently, 'Pyareji, you have your own problems. And I'm not of any help to you. I shouldn't become an unnecessary burden now. I don't want last month's salary. Let me go look for another job. If nothing, I'll get a job as a driver in Panvel or Kalyan. In the last two years, many factories have closed down in Mumbai and the workers are taking this thing called voluntary retirement. With their handshake package they're going around saying business business, and buying maxi cabs and SUVs like Tata Sumo or Qualis to set up car rentals. Because of this there's a huge demand for good drivers. Let me go. I certainly won't go hungry, Pyareji. Believe me. Let your situation improve, and then I'll come back and join you.' He held Pyare's hand as he spoke, almost as if in someone else's voice.

For a second, there was a flash of freedom in Rampyare's eyes. To hide the fact that Tejbali may have noticed it, he took the bike rider's hands in his and pressed them to his face. 'Chhheh, did this day also dawn for me?' he sighed. 'You are a tiger, Tejbali. A tiger. The tiger may stay hungry but won't eat grass. You shouldn't eat grass – you're a brave warrior. An artist. Society should worship you. Useless people. And me? How can I not care for you?' Even as he said this, he stopped abruptly, frightened that the moment of freedom had been lost. His eyes looked like the empty well of Milan.

In those defeated eyes Tejabali too glimpsed his path to freedom. If he said anything else, he thought he might confuse things more, so he went to his tent instead. That night, when everyone was eating dinner under the single naked bulb, Rampyare began to shout, like a motorbike roaring, 'Let them go. Let all the big people go. We can't tie them up for our benefit, can we? Who am I to say you should go hungry with us? Whoever wants to leave, leave. But I don't have the capacity to pay anyone's dues now. I'll sell the generator and then pay you all. I need at least a month. Please go, but do keep faith in me.' After a point, both Tejbali and Rampyare realised that the shouting was once again like the playing of children. When it came to words, it all sounded very dramatic. And the more dramatic it got, the greater the illusion of transcending their grim reality. The more untruthful it seemed, the lighter the situation became. Suddenly both of them laughed. As though to scare the trees that stood silently in the dark, they laughed so hard it was as though they were sobbing.

In the publicity for the next camp, Rampyare began to screech: 'Our Amitabh Bachchan, our Sachin Tendulkar, our Rocket Tejbali.' But along with this passion, he kept feeling that due to his own weakness he had let slip that moment when things could have taken a different turn. Younger audiences were not attracted by a figure like Rocket Tejbali. However much he dyed his sideburns and however tight his jeans, the slack skin at his neck and the visible veins on his arms told a different story. Although Chhagan and Pattoo did not have Tejbali's experience, the enthusiasm with which they performed their stunts and the glow of their youth drew attention. It promised mysterious futures, and people could forget themselves in the show. Beside the boys, Tejbali appeared like an ancient ruin. If the sweat on the youths' faces appeared like dewdrops, Tejbali's looked like a stream of exhaustion. This wasn't a fact unknown to Rampyare. But he lived the fantasy of his youth through Tejbali, who was approximately his own age. When the bike rider tore around the well of death and snatched the handkerchief thrown at him by someone in the audience, Rampyare would think, 'Not bad, there's still something here, something's remaining.' But after the show was over, and the bike riders were all standing outside lined up like warriors, the departing audience – especially the youngsters – wanted to shake hands with Chhagan and Pattoo and didn't usually come near Tejbali. The spectators of Tejabali's age would already have slipped away, back to their daily routine. So, finally, Tejbali remained a Rocket only in Pyare's imagination. Although he knew this, that world of imagination was for him his true world, and he held onto it to the best of his ability. Whenever he ordered mutton from a Military Hotel, he picked out the best pieces and sent them to Tejbali.

Somehow the belief that he was not contributing anything to Rampyare's business had been strengthening in him the last ten days as he paced the Alibag beach. The fort in front, the vast empty beach, the casuarina trees clustered together like birds that had forgotten to fly. All of it suggested a relinquishing.

Walking through the reddish light that was turning dark, Tejbali rehearsed in his mind: 'Rampyare, I know you'll be sad. I know you're afraid. We both know we need each other. But enough now. I'm leaving behind the Milan Well of Death. We've both done what we could for each other, Pyareji, and that will stay with us forever. Let me go. You're old now. Those boys should look after you. Don't drink too much and ruin your liver. Just give me this black scorpion. It might take me somewhere else. Let me carry that debt with me. And that debt will tie you to me always. Look Pyare, leave me on this shore. On this soft sand, where there are only steps and no paths, let me walk in peace.'

Until well after midnight, Tejbali sat on the sand with his legs stretched out. The spot seemed to have appeared there for this moment of his nakedness. The sound of the waves, their beauty, had begun to take on new meanings and shapes. The fort pierced through the tender clouds, dispersing them. With its flickering lights, it looked like a ship about to leave the shore.

The last show ended. Every stick of Milan Well of Death was packed away in two large trucks. 'Seth, Rocket Sir hasn't returned. He's not here yet,' said the workers and the young bike riders. 'He'll come,' said Rampyare. 'I know. You look to your work. We should leave now. We must reach the highway before the dawn traffic begins. Come, let's go,' he barked.

'Seth, does he know where our next camp is?' asked Pattoo. 'Let me go and fetch him. He'll be at the beach.' 'Chup,' said Rampyare. 'No need for anyone to fetch him. He knows everything. He knows everything,' he shouted in a high voice. It's as though Rampyare knew. In his depths trembled the thought that he should not lose once more this chance of mutual freedom.

By dawn, the trucks had turned towards Lonavala and everyone was asleep. Except Rampyare, who stayed awake, as though the truck was his body. He sat immobile, staring at the road ahead.

On the seashore, Tejbali had fallen peacefully asleep. Some children surrounded him, bending over and whispering, 'Rocket Tejbali, Rocket Tejbali.' They gazed at his curls stirring in the breeze. As though at a large idol that had been washed ashore after an immersion ceremony.

Like the secret link between two different worlds, the black scorpion at the tender-coconut stand sparkled in the rays of the sunrise, waiting to start at the first kick.

Baaviyallondu Baagilu
2000

The Recluse

Digoo Mama must be about sixty now. I used to see him every year during Shivaratri in my childhood in Gokarna. He would come for the Shivaratri fair. Waking up at dawn before everyone else, bathing in cold water without waiting for it to be heated, washing his own clothes and wearing them again as soon as they dried, taking me to see the temple chariot procession and buying me sweets, this is what Digoo Mama did. He would then climb onto a bus and vanish before all the other guests had left.

Year after year, he looked the same. As for me, from year to year I kept changing the clever opinions I had formed of him. That he had remained a bachelor seemed unique to my child's eye. His bachelorhood made him an object of curiosity amongst our relatives. The fact that he reserved his affection for children, the fact that he never came into our kitchen, the fact that he never got involved in family discussions showed him to be a *bairagi*, someone disinterested in the everyday world. But the sparkle in his eyes couldn't be matched by anyone else in the family, including my own parents.

I didn't bother to think that Digoo Mama had secrets in his past, or that there was any story there. He used to read the Penguin paperbacks that were popular then, with their reddish edges. He never entered conversations about politics, or familial concerns with expressing sadness at someone's death, asking about the exam success of growing children and whether they were going to be engineers or doctors, or discussing the taste of special snacks. Once he heard me humming a tune and bought me an eight-rupee flute so that my musical aptitude could grow. 'Sadoo, if you learn to play this flute well by next Shivaratri, I'll buy you a much better one for twenty-five rupees,' he said.

I couldn't figure out whether Digoo Mama came to the Shivaratri procession because he was devout or simply because he liked the crowds at the fair. My mother, Aayi, had a special fondness for Digoo Mama. During her wedding ceremony, she had not wanted to wear the conventional nine-yard sari and Digoo had convinced her bridegroom, my Baba, that it was fine not to stick to the convention. He was also related in a distant way on my mother's side. During the Shivaratri commotion, Aayi always found time to ask after Digoo – had he come, had he eaten. At one point, Aayi and Baba, swelling with affection for Digoo Mama, had even tried to get him married. At that point he must have been forty or forty-five. The alliance was with a schoolteacher from Kodkani. My parents arranged to have the party come to our home and made sure Digoo would be there as well. Digoo found out about the plan as soon as he arrived but didn't seem to be surprised. Didn't show anger. He went up to my mother swiftly, said 'I'll take your leave', came straight to my school and called me out with the master's permission, stroked my head and caressed me, put five rupees in my pocket, went down the school steps and disappeared. I was disappointed that he wasn't staying.

In the evening when I came home, there was dead silence. 'We should have alerted him beforehand,' my mother was saying. 'He's insane,' my father said. But Digoo Mama showed up for the next Shivaratri like always. Aayi and Baba were relieved. There was some discussion about my college education in which Digoo Mama participated enthusiastically. 'Don't wear tight pants. Bad for your circulation,' he told me.

Once I left for Sirsi to attend college, I did not come home for Shivaratri. So I didn't meet Digoo Mama either. Later, when I was at university in Dharwad, I remained out of touch with him. Then I got a letter from home, saying, 'He's in the KMC Hospital getting some tests done. Do go and see him.' I went through all the wards of the hospital but couldn't find him.

When I obtained a rank, I received from him a letter in a crooked scrawl, 'You didn't defeat our expectations. Now keep your own aspirations in focus.' When I got this letter, his image took on a new shape for me. Joyfully I preserved it amidst my report cards and diploma certificates.

Now I was working in Mumbai and leading an unthinking life which seemed to be galloping away in all directions, mired in questions of hierarchy and efficiency. As Aayi, Baba and the Kannada school in Gokarna became indistinct to me, Digoo Mama too receded into a corner of my mind. The least thing could irritate me now, whether it was Anuradha's behaviour, or the Mumbai heat, or the train that was running five minutes late. At twenty-eight I was caught up in a strange kind of distress. The curious business with Anuradha irritated me and I wanted to end it. 'What then?' 'What will I do when I go home?' While I was struggling with these empty questions, I received a letter from Aayi about Digoo Mama. 'Digoo is in Mumbai. Staying with a distant relative in Mahim, and at death's door. Go and see him before it's too late,' she wrote. The address was mentioned too.

Although it was difficult to prepare for this new chapter, I must have felt it was the break I was looking for. Applying for two days Casual Leave, I set out early one morning for Mahim. Alighting at Dadar to change trains and sweating profusely as I stood in the crowded compartment, I wondered how it would be if I brought Digoo Mama to stay in my bachelor kholi. Would I be able to look after him? I got down at Mahim and searched for the address. It was to the east of the station, and in the municipal quarters. Because it was vacation time there were children everywhere, playing and whooping loudly. A middle-aged woman opened the door. 'I'm Sadanand,' I said. 'Is Digoo Mama staying here?'

'Yes, come in,' she said. Offering me a chair, she went inside. It was a congested house. As though it were a Ganesha idol, the TV set was displayed on a stand. Perhaps Digoo Mama was asleep. I wanted to ask the woman not to wake him up, but she came back just then with a glass of water. 'It's good that you came. Ever since he arrived here Digambar has been saying that he wants to see you. We're too busy to go looking for your address. You're in Thane, quite far away. And my husband usually works the night shift. We lied to Digambar that we had phoned your office. But he's been asking time and again,' she said. 'Where is he now?' I asked. 'He's so stubborn. He can barely walk but he wants to go by himself to the hospital. That KEM Hospital is like an ocean. You can't find anyone there,' she said. I was alarmed. It was painful to think of Digoo Mama winding his way through the Mumbai crowds all by himself.

Without waiting for tea, I stood up and said, 'I'll go to the hospital. If I don't see him there, I'll come back here.' I climbed the overbridge and jumped into a taxi, saying, 'KEM.' When I reached the hospital, I was aghast at the commotion. In the OPD were heaps of injured people from a bus accident. In the midst of policemen and nurses and attenders the injured lay groaning on the grey stone floor. In front of the payment counter, there was an enormously long line of patients. I couldn't remember what Digoo Mama looked like. Had he come here for his daily check-up? Or had he gone to some quack by the side of the road? I had forgotten to ask the Mahim woman what the nature of his ailment was. I wondered briefly about the source of Digoo Mama's finances. In the midst of all this confusion, my office cabin and my everyday life seemed to belong to someone else.

Braving the smell of phenyl, I went up and down the corridors looking for him. Somewhere I got lost and went into the anatomy department where there were dozens of tables on which dissected bodies were lying. I dashed out, willing myself not to throw up. Leaving the hospital, I went towards Mahim. I didn't feel like taking a taxi. I got into a bus in which there was standing room only. I felt a woman's breast, soft and pointed, protruding into my back and in that embarrassment the tumult in my mind diminished. But I saw that it was merely the purse under her arm that was poking into me. I started thinking about my office politics. The conductor flew into a rage because I did not have enough change. My back began to itch badly in a place my hand couldn't reach.

I alighted at Mahim. The sun was beating down mercilessly. A burst pipe in the street had erupted in a fountain in which little sunburnt children were splashing around. I felt exhausted. How much self-interest was there in my quest for Digoo Mama? As I climbed the bridge and walked towards the municipal quarters in the throbbing sun, I told myself that Digoo Mama should rest now after returning from the hospital and turned back to the station. It was two p.m. by the time I reached Thane. Outside the station I ate an omelette from a streetside cart and went home for a nap. The sleep that had been chasing me now caught me in its grasp. A dreamless sleep. Five p.m. when I woke up. As I washed my face I thought of my behaviour earlier today and it startled me. Two possibilities: Was I so distressed about my useless life that just the pretext of looking for Digoo Mama overwhelmed me? Or was I trying to recall the innocence of my childhood days and the memory of a time when the mystery of life was still intact?

All through the peculiar affair with Anuradha, with its sorrows and joys, Digoo Mama had not once come into the picture. This magician from my boyhood had now come closer to me during his last days, prompting me somehow to think of Anuradha. I seemed to have loved only the love she had for me. After pretending to be passionate, I had become tired of it and said, 'Anu, enough of this journey. I'm getting off here.' I had rung the bell and alighted. Bewildered, Anu had continued onwards, loving herself now in the guise of a pining and sad woman. And I? I couldn't establish the reasons for loving myself, and like someone who has just found a white hair on his head, I was perhaps awakening to the possibilities of Digoo Mama. Feeling quite at odds, I made myself a cup of tea and drank it. Then felt sad. Was this how it felt, to be afflicted with the disease called Mumbai? Why was it making me fearful, this solitude of Digoo Mama who had not shared his life with anyone?

'You say you don't want to get married. When are you going to settle down then? When will you stabilise?' wrote Aayi and Baba. People said, 'You must take your life seriously.' Those who used to laugh at my jokes began to invest in the share market. Those who shared my room bought land in their faraway villages. Confusing emotional thirst with sexual desire and the other way around, I got into complicated relationships with women and gained a reputation for being unreliable. I found my work boring. I looked at the fresh MBAs who were being hired and felt jealous. I developed a 'so what' mentality which I threw even at the rays of sunshine that came through the window. Once a female colleague wished me good morning and I said 'So?' and then felt embarrassed.

I felt I was meant for something else. This job and its routine may only last a few days. Perhaps I had competences that I wasn't yet aware of. And so I minimised the importance of the days that had gone by. Getting used to this habit of worrying day and night, not having the strength to make new friends but still trying to avoid the tedious old friends, moving from light beer to strong beer, writing my name in a new diary every year, distributing the old blank diaries to the neighbourhood kids, noticing wryly that girls did not look at me that much anymore, being aroused by married middle-aged women, paying a ten-rupee deposit for borrowing porn from the supplier on Dadar bridge, I began to proclaim loudly to myself that I was loving life.

Irritated even with Aayi and Baba, I took to saying cleverly that it was a tragedy that working and earning a livelihood were one and the same thing. In the half sleep of early dawn I heard the faint clapping from the debating halls of my college days. The smell of the earth after the rain, after my tenth standard exams, came to my nostrils. A healthy Aayi and a strong Baba appeared before me. When I woke, a new morning was ringing the doorbell. Along with the milk packet, the newspaper and the bills.

How did Digoo Mama survive without being close to others? What were his relationships like? Did he act or did he react? I should have stayed in touch with him. The fact that I couldn't meet him that morning felt like a terrible injustice.

I set out for Mahim again. I took some extra money with me. On the way I bought some fruit. When I reached the place it was getting dark. The TV was blaring from every house. The woman opened the door. There was such a crowd of children and adults watching television that one could barely step into the house. I wondered if Digoo Mama was among them. I couldn't see anyone's face in the darkened hall. 'Digoo Mama is sleeping inside,' someone said. Without waiting for anyone's permission, I dived into the room. There was no one there. I wondered if he had gone to the toilet but there was no one there either. It looked as though someone was asleep in the narrow kitchen. Digoo Mama. My heart sank. He was sleeping on a sheet spread over a mat. His beard was gone. He seemed to have lost a lot of weight. When he embraced me during my childhood there used to be the smell of sweat which, in the spice-laden kitchen air, was hard to discern. Outside was the commotion of the TV. Here the hissing of the pressure cooker. All of it seemed strange. Strange that my childhood's Digoo Mama was in this tiny Mumbai kitchen.

If he had married, he would now be staying with his children. Looking at his weak body, I wondered how I could possibly take him to my place. I gently stroked his arm. He turned over and woke up. On seeing me he clutched my arm and sat up suddenly. I was seeing him for the first time without his beard. 'No beard,' he laughed. He did not seem so weak now. He spoke in quite a lively voice: 'Where do you stay? Where do you eat your food? Do you write letters home?' The questions tumbled out one after the other. 'Glad that I've seen you,' he said. 'Do I look very old? I heard you'd come in the morning. Why didn't you wait for me? No, no, no doctor-poctor. I had just gone for a walk.'

He stood up and took me to the balcony. 'Arre, you've

become taller than me.' He continued, 'Come early tomorrow evening. Do me a favour – I need to go to someone's house. A Marathi man called Shirodkar. His house was in Borivali. It must still be there. If it were closer, I would have gone myself, but Borivali is very far. Please take me there.' 'Of course, I can come tomorrow morning also.' 'No, no, don't waste a day's leave. Go to your office and come in the evening. We'll go as soon as you come.' He sat down on a stool and began to drowse. I wondered where all he had wandered that day. I woke him up and took him inside. He did not go into the kitchen but entered the room where the family slept at night and went to sleep on a chair. He looked like a child. Even now he must be washing his own clothes. So as not to trouble his hosts, he must be avoiding mealtimes. Even if he was hungry, he must be going to sleep without telling them. He was not the kind of person who would become dependent on others. Or maybe my understanding was incorrect. I had pieced together my knowledge of him through random observations.

Beneath the cotton vest his shrunken chest rose and fell. The woman came in saying, 'We ask him to sleep on the cot and he doesn't. We ask him to drink milk and he refuses. He's stubborn.' I stepped out, saying I would come the next day. I searched for my footwear in the pile of children's chappals. Thinking of Digoo Mama's lively words, I felt happy. As I braced against the wind on my way home, my mind felt unburdened. Deciding I'd take him wherever he wanted to go tomorrow, I set the alarm and went to sleep.

As usual, the office work ended at five. I rushed to catch

the train to Mahim. Digoo Mama was standing in the balcony looking out for me. He seemed to be observing very closely the way I was walking. As soon as I came to the door, he said, 'Shall we go?' The woman said, 'Tea?' 'No, no, we'll get late. We'll get something outside,' said Digoo Mama, holding my hand as he stepped out. As usual, he was wearing pyjamas and a cotton shirt. 'Come back quickly,' the woman said. When we climbed down the stairs, Digoo Mama occasionally missed a step and leaned heavily against me. On the second floor, the door of a flat was open and a fierce fight was raging inside between women. 'Must be the daughter-in-law and mother-in-law,' said Digoo Mama. 'It's been going on since yesterday.' We started walking on the left side of the road. He spoke without gasping too much. As we climbed onto the overbridge, he said, let's stop for a bit, and took out from his pocket a dozen pieces of paper through which he sifted, looking for the address. Then he said, 'I know it by heart.'

Under the bridge the Harbour and Western Line trains were rushing past. On either side of the railway lines were dense clumps of huts. Perhaps it was not a new sight for Digoo Mama. Women with tired faces were returning from work holding bags of tired vegetables. 'Wherever they are, in hut or flat, these women can't escape pregnancy,' he laughed sadly, hehhehheh. Then he said, 'Listen, here is the address. I was last there in 1960. An old type of house. Called Rajat Mansion. Just get me to Borivali. I can find the house by myself.'

'There's a huge difference between the Borivali of 1960 and that of today,' I said. 'There are so many large apartment buildings now. It would be difficult to find the old houses.'

'Let's see,' he said. 'The name was Shirodkar.' Again he was lost in his thoughts

'Stay here,' I said, and went to the ticket counter. When I returned Digoo Mama was not to be seen. He wasn't on any of the nearby benches. I looked near the newspaper stall. Not there either. I started heading towards the toilet but then I saw him. He was standing within the station fence and looking out at the street that lay beyond. When I looked in that direction I saw a group of women, migrant labourers clad in scraps of cloth, who were bathing on the footpath. Thinking he might be embarrassed if I called out to him, I waited for him to return. I darted glances to either side to see if anyone had noticed us. But there were many people, old and young, watching the water games as though they were at a circus. The women were laughing as they scrubbed each other's backs. I forgot Digoo Mama for a second. When I looked for him again he was back at the old spot, standing impassively. Because of the rush, we let two trains go past and got into the third one.

'Digoo Mama, you never asked me whether I was married.'

'Are you?' he asked.

'No, I'm afraid to think of spending my entire life with another person. I don't know if I have the ability or the frame of mind to do that. I don't know what satisfaction is,' said I. Although I had the appearance of an adult, I felt like the boy 'Sadoo' waiting to be comforted by Digoo Mama. 'I need your blessings,' I said in a thin voice.

It was as though he hadn't heard me. 'Whatever it is, amidst all this chaos you mustn't forget to live your life for yourself,' he said.

It was eight in the evening when we reached Borivali. Digoo Mama seemed to quail at the thought of looking for the house in this unrecognisable mass of buildings. 'How did so many people get born without our knowledge,' he mused. We caught a rickshaw and went looking for Rajat Mansion – through this alley and that, there near the mill, here (after having asked at a hotel) near the theatre, behind the park ... No luck. Everywhere, as though mocking us, were unfamiliar, grinning faces. For an hour and a half we searched for Rajat Mansion. Digoo Mama said in a strange voice, 'Isn't there a zoo somewhere here? I wonder if they feed the animals properly.'

We went into an Udupi restaurant to eat. Digoo Mama liked the vegetable curry we ordered and asked for a second helping. When I said I would pay, he became angry. Insisted on paying himself. As we came out he said, 'I don't have much longer to live.' I burped and he said, 'It's the truth, Sadoo. At the most another three months.' I didn't ask him why or what or how. I didn't feel like hearing about his illness. But I felt sorry for him, wearily engaged in this futile search for Shirodkar's house.

'I don't know, Sadoo. An incompleteness I've never felt before is haunting me now.' Suddenly he asked, 'Are you married, Sadoo?'

'No,' I said again. He didn't ask why.

'This Mother Nature is strange, isn't she? Tries so hard to emotionally blackmail us to continue the family line.'

'Yes,' I said. We both urinated at a public toilet standing in adjacent stalls. This peeing is something one can't avoid,' he laughed, and yawned. Because he was so weak, he kept standing there even after he had finished urinating. A man waiting behind him screeched, 'Arre bhai!' I held Digoo Mama's hand and brought him outside. Why was I making this poor man suffer in Mumbai's crowds? I decided to hail a taxi.

Once we were in the taxi, I began to speak. 'Digoo Mama, do you know why I'm hesitating to get married? For me, a woman is magical, a mystery, a treasure house of beauty and exhilaration and freshness. In the company of a woman, I can't imagine anything dirty. A woman smelling like jasmine, when I wake up beside her in the morning will she be the same fragrant being? I can't digest that thought. It may be an exaggeration, but I can't think of a woman as having to poop or pee or do anything dirty. Maybe it's a version of a sexual fantasy. But I feel this for sure.' It didn't trouble me that Digoo Mama might or might not be listening. He was a living witness to my truth and my grief. As though telling him a deep secret, I said, 'I've escaped from Anuradha. Because I grew afraid of my tendency to assert my rights over her. Maybe she wanted that. She loves me fiercely. She keeps my nail clippings. She takes my half-smoked cigarettes and smokes them in secret so as to remember me. I made myself feel meaningful by taking in her scent, by kissing her. I began to feel ridiculous when I stood apart from her. In sexual pleasure, there were obstacles to my being the centre of the universe. In the midst of our ferocious love, what if I commit suicide or she does? Or I make her pregnant and we have a wedding with jewellery and silk saris and then have a baby boy in our one-room house and I buy fifteen rupees' worth of mangoes – three for fifteen – and the darling boy samples them and throws them away, and I don't fly into a rage but instead go into a paroxysm of delight? What meaning would that have?'

Digoo Mama was holding me tightly. At the traffic signal the van that had stopped next to us contained a wedding party. In their *zari* and silk and jewellery and jasmine, the women were sweating and wilting. The men were pretending to protect their wives by turning their arms into courtroom railings. We got off before the Mahim bridge. Digoo Mama, unable to walk by himself, was holding onto me. I had begun to feel the strange pleasurable sorrow that used to cloud my thoughts after Shivaratri ended in those days of my boyhood. We stopped at a juice centre and drank some sugarcane juice. When I was paying for the juice, Digoo Mama looked at the notes in my wallet with a peculiar expression. As we climbed onto the bridge, we stopped for a while, pressed against the railings. I took out some notes and gave them to Digoo Mama. 'If I take them you'll feel a sort of release, won't you? All right then,' he said. 'The notes feel new. Did you get them from the bank?' he asked.

Beneath us on the rails, the trains were going up and down with their lights on. 'Sadoo, why do you think I'm agonising over that man Shirodkar?' said Digoo Mama. There was a long silence. Then he began to speak again. 'In 1960 I had come to Mumbai on work. Through a connection, I stayed in Shirodkar's house. And in those two days – you have to believe me when I say this – I experienced bliss with Shirodkar's wife. They had no children ... After that I went to Karwar. The memory of the pleasure remained, but I could not remember her. But now in my last days I can't help thinking,. what if Bhame – that was her name – had had a child because of our two days together? This strange desire is plaguing me. What if I had a child ....' He stopped talking. He stared at the rails below. This old body had carried its desire to continue living thus far – the thought gave me goosebumps. 'Did I frighten you, Sadoo? See how funny it is. At the time of dying one wants to live on in various ways.' He laughed like a child.

'Come, at the next corner one can get good apples. Let's have some.' He bought apples for us to eat. 'Eat fruits regularly. They're good for health,' he said. 'Sadoo, I'm going to remain here until I die. You must do me a favour.'

'What is it?' I asked.

'I want you to donate my body to the anatomy department of a medical college. Please,' he said. I couldn't eat the apple. He ate his with great relish. As I dropped him at his relative's place, he said again, 'Bring me any lawyer you know. Don't forget what I said. I want to make a will about this body business. And don't tell anybody else about it.' His relatives were all asleep by then. Someone opened the door in the dark and he entered. I returned home to Thane.

I felt as though I had left one dream and moved into another. I couldn't sleep. I moved from station to station on the radio and tired myself out. Not feeling like switching off the light, I kept sitting. Who but I could do justice to the life that was mine? Digoo Mama kept on living, with blood coursing through his veins, with his muscles and brain intact. He had his own expectations about how his body should be used after his death. And what were the interrelationships between those naked bathing women who had enthralled us at Mahim Station, and Shirodkar's wife who held Digoo Mama's attention as though like a glowing time capsule, and those crisp new notes I had given him? How was this time occupied by sixty-year-old Digoo Mama and twenty-eight-year-old me different? The time we were living in, this minute, in Mumbai, how were we experiencing it differently?

I stretched out my legs on the cot. If Digoo Mama had jumped to his death from the overbridge today, the notes in his pocket, the notes I gave him, would have no meaning. Why should I close my eyes if life in the shape of Anuradha had come looking for me? Why should I cheat myself of the boundless freedom and happiness of turning life into my own personal secret? My heart seemed to grow heavy, and then very light. I went to the bathing area, filled a bucket with soapy water, and soaked all my dirty clothes. I stood under the shower and had a cool bath. Then I fell onto my bed. As my hair dried under the fan I thought that I should take the lawyer to meet Digoo Mama tomorrow to prepare his will, and that I should take Anuradha with me. Decisions taken, I fell asleep.

Nimithha
1983

Threshold

At the turn of the last alley, as one goes towards the marketplace, was Muchhi Miyan's secondhand goods shop, a *modaka dukaan*. Both those terms need some explaining. Muchhi is moustache. And although his real name was Pratap Singh, because of the common perception that most people in the resale trade were Muslims, everyone called him Muchhi Miyan, Miyan meaning Sir in Urdu. But to be called thus in the unique commercial lingua franca of this city didn't offend him in the least. When someone addressed him as Muchhi Miyan, he would stroke his greying military moustache and twirl its edges upward.

His was a shop that sold what could be salvaged from ruined or demolished houses, from rusted pieces of tin to weathered window- and door-frames, a worn-out wooden threshold, a splintered mirror, hundreds of handle-less screwdrivers, a huge fridge like a blind ogre, old radios with their stomachs split wide open, old rexine sofas that looked like artefacts from an Indus Valley civilisation site. In the language of this city, a place like Miyan's was also called a *bhangaar*. In some ten square feet or so, all of these objects sat together, and in the midst of them sat Muchhi Miyan on a tattered throne from a wedding hall, with a cigarette between his fingers, looking like a king who had abandoned the field in mid-battle.

Each day he arranged the goods differently, as though they were props in a playhouse, making sure to dust them first with a yellow cloth. Like a mono-act performer, he would sit first on the throne and then on the sofa, and sometimes also on a three-legged cot that was propped up on stones. There was space to move around because the drain was covered with wooden boards. A nearby tree that looked like it was part of the shop offered some shade. Into this stage set of a 'social' play arrived one day a large, full-length mirror with worn wooden peacocks on both sides. This etched rosewood mirror took pride of place in Miyan's shop, where he placed it in such a way that it could be seen from the road too. When he stood scrubbing the mirror to make it shine, sometimes the huge vehicles on the road seemed to come straight at him through the mirror, making him tremble. When it appeared as if the vehicles were about to collide with their image, their muzzles turned away and they sped off. In this mirror which seemed to contain all the movement to and from the market in its eye, the sun too sometimes played around. Miyan lay on the three-legged cot, watching all this out of the corner of his eye.

One day, waking from his afternoon nap, Muchhi Miyan saw an astonishing spectacle. A beautiful woman was shaking out her thick hair as though fresh from a bath. She turned this way and that, admiring herself in the mirror. She floated through the old film songs coming out of the broken radio. Miyan sat still, like a statue, afraid that if he moved or closed his eyes the woman would run away and the scene would vanish. Her face was elusive, visible only in occasional glimpses. The scene was suffused with a light fragrance. Just then the teaboy Popat came up shouting in his shrill voice, 'Tea, tea, chai, chai' as he knocked his kettle with a coin. As Miyan wondered how he could stop him shouting, a double-decker bus came by and the woman disappeared in the cloud of dust it raised. Muchhi Miyan jerked to his feet and with a feeling of unease looked behind the cupboard next to the fridge. No one there. But the fragrance of her luxuriant hair was still in the air. Popat poured him a glass of tea and moved on, as usual. On the road, there were the usual people, the usual pushcarts, the usual vehicles. When he looked up, he could see the sulking trees that had stopped talking to the electric wires.

Although he finished his cup of tea, the festive feeling generated by the dream did not go away. Feeling it might be spoiled if he thought it real, Miyan tried not to think about it. That beauty, whose face did she have, whose gait? Was it the woman who scrubbed the dishes in the police chawl nearby? The sharp-nosed girl with the curly braid who went to the big school? The silly girl in the vegetable market who badgered customers to buy her shiny sour limes? Or was it the quick-tongued woman in the purple dress who had bargained with him the other day and bought two old iron chairs for a hundred rupees? Miyan was scared to put down the empty tea glass in front of the mirror. Popat came along collecting glasses and cash. 'Where are you, Muchhi Miyan?' he asked meaningfully. Miyan looked intently at the boy, who had become accustomed to spreading himself out regally on the chairs and sofas in his spare time. Then he leaned against the tree trunk, sitting with legs outstretched, looking at the world going by in the mirror, as though he were watching TV. In his nostrils he could still smell the fragrance of soap and a tiny bit of perspiration. A light young breeze wafted over him, and he sat inspired, not lighting his cigarette.

Every night, Miyan would tie all his goods to each other with string and then tie the end of the string to the tree, after which he would lie down on the three-legged cot. In the early morning, he would go to his hut near the railway tracks to have a bath. The women from the other huts nearby often came to his empty dwelling to pick stones from the rice before cooking or to put their little children to sleep. Whenever Miyan came in, they would vacate the hut. After a while, children who had nothing else to do came to play cards there, and Miyan could not stand this. He began to lock the door behind him. The people who lived in the neighbouring huts, on their way to the market, would come to the modaka dukaan and sit around as though it were a house to visit, looking at themselves in the mirror before leaving. The women liked to touch and feel the rusted gas stoves and the remains of the fridge. Popat came there to sleep at night. Sometimes thieves would come to steal nuts and bolts, wires and old LPs. So Miyan always slept in a state of half-alertness. To avoid the piercing headlights of passing vehicles, he covered the mirror with an old lungi.

But tonight, Miyan hesitated to cover the mirror. He could see the reflection of occasional lights. The skies seemed smoke-covered, the stars invisible. The dark shadows behind the cupboard seemed to twitch. As though foreseeing what was to come, Miyan sat without moving, propped against the tree. She came rushing out from behind the cupboard. Wearing a nightie like those of the chawl women. As though she was hard at work, she had hitched up the nightie a little. Anklets shone on her feet, although they did not make any sound. Adjusting some of the furniture, she sat down in a corner to sew something. She had tied her hair in such a way that the escaping curls fluttered pleasingly in the breeze. She hummed as she sewed. If the occasional vehicle went past, she would close her eyes against the headlights and place her hands on her ears. She wasn't just singing to herself. She seemed to be complaining softly about something.

On the rusted gas stove, dinner was bubbling. Before one could blink, she had placed a plate with appetising smells and a glass of water on the table. Miyan did not know what to do. It was clear that the plate was for him. But if he went up to it, what if she disappeared? Before he could fully articulate this doubt, he had already walked towards the table. In the yellow light of the streetlamps, the leaves had a golden hue as they fell from the tree. She carefully caught a leaf that was about to fall on the plate and flicked it aside. Until Miyan finished eating and let out a burp, she stood with a hand against the fridge, as still as a model on a wall calendar. She looked as though she had walked for several miles but still appeared fresh. As though she had put down a heavy load from her head and begun doing the housework. Roti flour clung to her curls. The sharp smell of chilli came from her fingers. Below her navel was a shiny drop of sweat that quivered with Miyan's breath. The lap he wanted to place his head on looked like it had the softness of an old cradle blanket. Miyan gulped down a large amount of water, saying that the chutney was too spicy. She came closer and filled his glass. Her eyes were not visible. The damp armpits of her blouse were distracting the breeze. Miyan's eyes misted over and he started gasping, too spicy, too spicy. As though she had committed a crime, she slipped behind the cupboard. Miyan got up, scared. Followed her, but she wasn't there. He ran into the street. The tender-coconut seller's discarded shells were gleaming in the yellow light. She seemed to appear for an instant at the cement rubbish bin outside the distant wedding hall and then disappeared behind it.

Miyan was trembling. The plate, the grains of food remaining on it, the water glass were all gleaming yellow. With shaking hands, Miyan washed these by the side of the road. The yellow water sloshed down. Even in this golden world, the streets were sleeping wearily. All the pieces in Miyan's scrapyard seemed to have come to life. In the yellow hour, a home seemed to have appeared there. Miyan couldn't tell when Popat had come and fallen asleep, but the boy's limbs were dangling from the sofa. Gently, Miyan rearranged his legs. Popat muttered in his sleep, opened his eyes suddenly, looked around, and then went back to sleep. His eyes, which had opened for a second, were blank. On his little hand the dark lines of hard work gleamed yellow, as though he had demanded to have mehendi applied the night before his sister's wedding.

Miyan looked around at all the objects in his shop. He felt like opening the door of the cupboard that didn't have a handle. Inside it were her saris and bangles and a small box of jewellery. And his clothes were there too, nicely washed and ironed. A blue shirt from thirty years ago was there too. Without opening the door fully, he came back to his cot and sat down.

When he woke up the next morning, Popat was already washing himself by the tap. His tea glasses, piled high like a small Qutub Minar, were shining in the dawn light. The municipality handcart had come to take away the roadside rubbish and the coconut shells. The dawn people were already rushing to their jobs. Having gone to his hut for a bath, and then to Shankarvilas Hotel for breakfast, Muchhi Miyan felt his body and mind glow. He felt a lightness even without speaking to anyone or sharing anything with anyone. As though he had sat under the waterfall from heaven, where ten roads meet, and bathed for hours. He lit agarbatthi in all corners of the shop. He turned the mirror away from the road, as though it might otherwise reveal something private. Now you could see only its back from the road. From this side, you could only see all the goods in the shop and, reflected together in the mirror, there seemed to be some connection between them.

As Popat set out to fill his kettle at Shankarvilas, he asked, 'Muchhi Miyan, you're particularly happy today?' 'Nothing at all, Popat,' was the smiling reply. 'Just happy.' 'Put up a board here saying that whoever buys this throne will get a boy for free.

If you get a good customer, give me to him. I'll arrange to supply you with tea all your life,' said Popat, running off. Appreciating Popat's ready wit, Muchhi Miyan stood looking after him. He was drawn by the soft chinking of bangles. Turning around, he was startled.

There she was, sitting in front of the mirror. With a hairpin clenched between her teeth, she was applying kajal to her eyes. She was redoing her hair into a bun. Without her knowledge, a small yellow leaf had fallen from the tree on top of her head. Miyan wanted to speak but the words did not come. She stood up with the leaf still in her hair. She picked up a shiny metal pot and went to the tap for water. Next to the dirty gutter, navigating the rickshaws and handcarts and bicycles, she crossed the street like the wind and came back with the golden pot full of water. She sat down by the gas stove as though to chop vegetables. Then she seemed to remember something and stood up suddenly. She took out some coins from below the mirror, picked up a bag and strode off to the market.

The water in the pot was cool. Miyan touched the face powder spilt by the mirror. He saw a few long hairs caught in the comb. He removed them and put them into his pocket. As she became real through such signs and traces, Miyan felt he was losing something. He could not understand what. The fragrance of her luxuriant hair was stronger than the agarbatthi. He looked at himself from top to bottom for the first time in the full-length mirror. The crowfeet around his eyes were not visible. His hair looked shiny. The sag in his neck wasn't to be seen. Even his sagging belly seemed to have flattened itself. The breeze blew the hair from his forehead. I'm looking like the hero on a film-release poster, he thought. But on the mirror, there was the shadow of a crack. He ran his finger over it dejectedly. The dust from the road had settled in the crack. The wind brought onion peels from the wedding hall's dustbin along with the smell of rotting food, and the peels were whirling around the worn-out wooden threshold.

In the last four decades, Miyan hadn't once dreamt of having his own family. So why had this domestic bliss come to him now? What could he give this beauty who was bringing both disturbance and distance into his life? The Junk King's throat swelled up. The connecting threads seemed sad and fragile. His heart felt heavy as he thought of her, who might be haggling in the market over five paise for a bunch of coriander.

He needed to do something. He was sitting with his arms folded. For how long would she come to this used-goods household? He began to wield the towel vigorously to take the dust off the objects lying around. He took the broom and swept up all the dust and the dry leaves. In that heap of rubbish, everything looked like a lie. He sat with his hand to his head, feeling stupid. Then he thought about the long hairs in his pocket, the fragrance around the mirror, and the pot of water – these brightened his dwelling. Such signs hinted at something blooming, but as he approached it, why was it that a peculiar distress came over him?

A man clad in just a lungi and a banian came shouting through the street, disturbing the crows in the tree above. 'Let me catch that slut, I'll take off her clothes and drag her through the street,' he was screaming. His voice, which sounded like a public announcement, slowly became less audible as he moved away. As though they hadn't heard anything, people continued to buy their vegetables in the market. The shout sounded like he was begging for his life. There was a lament behind all that noise. Taking it as a warning of some catastrophe to come, Muchhi Miyan crouched like a sparrow behind the mirror.

Pouring tea into a glass, Popat shook him. 'Miyan, drink this, Miyan, drink this.' He brought the news that the municipal truck had already come to the vegetable market and was confiscating all the roadside stalls, throwing the handcarts into the back of the truck. Normally, when Miyan heard this, he would hurry to put all his goods into the neighbouring compound, away from the street. But today, Miyan did not move. The tender-coconut seller was moving his coconuts into the compound in a complete frenzy. The man selling oranges on the road stuffed all the fruit into his sack and ran from his spot, panting. Popat felt scared. 'Miyan, Miyan ... hurry,' he said, trying to pick up some of the smaller items. Miyan looked confused. All he knew was that the woman would return from the market, and until then he didn't want to change anything here.

'Here it comes, here it comes ...' the crowd roared as the red-striped municipality truck, an old Ford that looked as though it had a grinning mouth, came into view and stopped suddenly in front of the threshold. In the back were a number of handcarts. 'Miyan, it's here!' Popat tried with all his strength to drag some of the furniture into the compound. Miyan stood speechless.

The grey-uniformed municipality workers were already moving around, picking up Miyan's goods. The vegetable vendors who had followed the truck tried to save Miyan's things. Big items like door frames and window frames were tied with a rope and hauled to the truck. The municipal workers made fun of Miyan's shop and kept laughing as they took away the goods. When the cot propped up by stones was lifted, it almost fell apart. The workers started to guffaw. 'What money can you make in a modaka dukaan? Let him be,' pleaded some people. 'Haha, the king of junk,' roared the workers. Popat was stuffing nuts and bolts and wires into his own pockets and Miyan's as though they were jewels.

For Miyan, who clung to the tree as he stood waiting, suddenly all the action seemed to be playing on mute. The fridge swayed like a swan with a broken wing. Miyan was praying that she would not appear in the midst of this mess, but she did. She came running from the market and joined the group of people who were desperately following the truck. As Miyan watched with his mouth open, she hitched up her sari, and along with the vegetable vendors, she began to pull out things from the truck, shouting. Her voice had joined that of the crowd. The sweat poured from her forehead. The municipality workers standing in the truck were pushing her away. She jumped ahead with renewed fervour and started yanking at a chair, a basket. To make her step back, they seemed to be tickling her under the armpits. She would retreat as though someone had poured water over her and then leap into the fray again. Sometimes she shrieked, sometimes she pleaded. Once she pretended to laugh as they tickled her. The water of anger and humiliation filled her reddened eyes. The truck began to increase its speed slowly. As though the dam had finally broken, Miyan shouted, 'Hey!' As if only she could hear the shout, she turned to look. As she turned, she stopped fighting and stood very still. The jostling crowd erased her altogether.

The lath that was covering the drain, the weathered threshold, the heavy three-legged cot and a completely rusted gas stove were all that remained. Miyan did not even feel like checking what was left. He sat clinging to the tree. The fact that he had shouted 'Hey' and that she had actually heard him was the unrivalled truth of his life. Nothing before and nothing after. Miyan sat like a cloud that had emptied out; in front of his eyes there were only her eyes. The distressed eyes of one who had experienced all that there was to experience in this world. Slowly, Miyan stood up and went to the tap. Bending down, he let the water run over his head and face.

'Muchhi Miyan, you have to shake my hand! The mirror is safe. My friends have taken it near the railway crossing and hidden it. Shake my hand!' Popat came up to him, whooping. Miyan silenced him with a sign and then signalled with both hands to indicate that he did not want the mirror. Then he held Popat close to him and walked heavily towards Shankarvilas.

Near the railway tracks a dozen children surrounded the long mirror, watching in astonishment an entire train go through it.

Hosthilu
1997

A Horizon for Each Eye

'Don't look for a reason for my suicide. If I knew the reason, perhaps I wouldn't have committed suicide.' These lines written by Sunil were like a slap in our collective faces. What was the connection between his words and the rain hurtling down to the ground right now? The rain was as true as the cool breeze that blew over us.

Perhaps anyone could have written those lines. But it was only through those lines that I sought to conquer my agitation, my sorrow, my fear, my depression after Sunil's death.

Sensing that the rain was wetting the curtains, I stood up to close the windows. Below in the street, someone holding an umbrella was paying a rickshaw driver before entering our building. Since Sunil died a month and a half ago, I assumed that anyone I saw was coming in search of me. And there were many such. Earlier, Kusuma would sit with me and the visitors, offering them coffee, describing all the dimensions of the incident in great detail. But nowadays, she had taken to being by herself. Sometimes I felt a strange confusion as to whether Sunil was my relative or Kusuma's. Whenever that happened, I tried to come out of the confusion as best as I could.

As I started moving slowly towards the door, the bell rang. Opening the door, I saw an old man whose clothes were dripping even more than his furled umbrella. Since he didn't carry any luggage, he was unlikely to have come straight from our native town, although he said, with great difficulty, 'I have come from Tadadi.' 'Please come in,' I said. Leaving his chappals by the door, he slithered with his wet feet into the living room and sat down on the divan before I asked him to. He seemed very tired. The raindrops that fell from him made my feet damp. It became apparent that although he had come from Tadadi, he had stopped at someone else's house first.

I had great trouble talking to strangers. This man must be a relative of Kusuma's, or Sunil's uncle, or something like that. 'Isn't Kusuma home?' he asked. 'No, she has gone to work. She'll return by evening,' I said. 'Hasn't she left her job yet?' When I heard that question, I began to think this man was closer to Kusuma than I had thought. 'No, no, she just keeps getting that urge sometimes. She hasn't left her job,' I said. 'I see,' said the man, laughing weakly. It was already nine a.m. In another forty-five minutes, I had to get ready to catch my train. There was no time to chat with him. 'Will you have some milk?' I asked. 'No, no, I don't drink milk,' he said awkwardly. And almost immediately, 'All right then. Give me some.' I went into the kitchen and brought him a glass of hot milk and got ready to eat. Kusuma had left all the dishes on the table. Somehow, I felt I was being indifferent to this man. 'How long is it since you came from Tadadi? Where are you staying?' I asked. 'I came this morning. Now that there's a direct Gokarna–Mumbai bus ... I came on that. It arrived promptly at dawn. I got down at Dadar and went to Kausalya's house. I put my luggage there, had a bath and something to eat, and then came here.' When I heard the name Kausalya, lights went on in my mind. 'I couldn't come when Sunil's thing happened,' he said. Must be one of Kausalya's numerous paternal uncles. Kausalya was Kusuma's relative.

'You must be in a rush to get to work. You carry on. I know that in Mumbai if you're a minute late, the train will leave you behind.' I began to eat hurriedly. He brought his glass of milk and sat near me. 'I hope Sunil's thing was not too much of a blow for Kusuma,' he said. 'She's recovered,' I said. 'Tasty milk. Must be from the dairy. It's not that I never drink milk. It's just that it's not easy to find good milk in our town, that is, good milk one can afford.' Laughing in an odd way, he drank up the milk and wiped his milk moustache with the edge of his dhoti. 'What time does Kusuma come?' he asked. 'About six, I said.' 'Mumbai life,' he said, shaking his head. When I got up to wash my hand, he looked all around the kitchen in an odd sort of way. When I opened the cupboard to take out a shirt, he came up to look curiously into it as though he wanted to wrench it open. When his eyes looked at me, his gaze seemed to change subtly. I couldn't understand why. 'Will you phone Kusuma and tell her I'm here?' he asked. In an irritated voice, I said, 'There's no phone here. Why don't you ask Kausalya to call? They have a phone.'

Although I felt that I was seeing him as a pest without any

reason, I had had enough of this. I began to fear that even when I went out to put on my shoes the man would stay behind. 'All right, shall we go now?' I asked. 'Yes, you're back in the evening, right?' he said, still sitting. 'I'll stay here. Why go back to Kausalya's house now? Don't worry, you go. I'll answer the doorbell if anyone comes.' I felt uncertain. Should I leave this man in the house? The stress was intolerable. 'Ok,' I said, 'be careful.' As I was leaving, the man asked, 'Is it true that Sunil's body was rotting when it was found? Just asking ... out of curiosity.' I don't know what I said in response. I went quickly down the stairs, got into a taxi and said, 'Station.' By the time I reached the office, the anger had built up inside me. I phoned Kusuma. 'Milady, some old man has come from Tadadi. The same enquiry about Sunil. He's in our house now. He went to Kausalya's first.' Kusuma cut in: 'Oho, that's Shankar Bappa.' 'Whoever it is, go home as soon as you can. He's new to the city.' 'I'll apply for half a day's leave and go immediately. Why didn't he come to stay with us? Why did he go to Kausalya's?' 'Ask him yourself,' I said, ending the conversation. I felt somewhat calmer, but my mind was still disturbed.

'Her feelings are even more true than she will acknowledge,' Sunil had said these strange words to me once about Kusuma. Although Sunil was not even twenty-five then, he seemed to be my contemporary. Carrying with him just a change of clothes, he had come to Mumbai, saying dramatically, 'Find me a job, brother-in-law.' In four years, he had become an integral part of our household. It took him a year to find a job. Until then, he said he had to earn his keep, and did all the housework after getting us to fire the maid. He made us get used to it. He fought with Kusuma. When she lied to him that I didn't like his being there, he fought with me. 'Don't be afraid, Akka,' he said to her. 'I won't spoil the image of your grand Mumbai life in front of our relatives back home.' With these words, he made Kusuma fearful and brought her to tears. At one time I became quite annoyed with him and found a place that he could rent. Four days in the week he would end up staying at our place. Then he moved back in so as to not waste rent. He gave away the indoor plants he had brought for us because we didn't like them. During that time, Kusuma had a miscarriage because of her anaemia, and Sunil berated me as though he were my father, sitting up all night spouting medical knowledge gleaned from his doctor friends.

Now Sunil had become a strand in my memories. Without my realising it, he had become an integral part of my ethical consciousness. Kusuma was thrilled by this at first. 'See, he's not discriminating against you although you're not directly related to him,' she used to say. Whenever she tried to browbeat him, he would shout at her. He would bewilder her by laying bare her mind, and that too in front of me. But she kept quiet when he brought her free vitamin tablets given to him by one of his doctor friends. Thus he slipped into her daily life too. This Shankar Bappa who had come today must be Sunil's uncle also. Perhaps I should have told him there was food in the fridge. Anyway, Kusuma is going home now, I thought to myself.

I phoned Sunil's office. There were some papers to be taken care of. In the lunch break, I went up to the third floor to see if

Shruti was there. She wasn't. I felt very bad about her. She was Sunil's friend. Or more than friend. She was his companion in his indeterminate frame of mind; she had shared his intimate moments with affection. She was the one who told me about what had happened. She took part with composure in his final rites. She was the one who took me by the hand to where his body lay.

Sunil had left home saying he was going on a picnic with some friends and not come back for a week. We searched for him. Me, and his friends and colleagues. We even went to Pune and Nagpur to see if he had gone there. When we gave up, Shruti was the one who went to the municipal morgue, searched for him there, and fainted when she found the body. When I sat down in the cafeteria to have my lunch, I thought of the old man's question about whether the body was decomposed. I couldn't eat anything. I went back to my cabin.

For a whole week, Shruti was like a silent statue, and her parents began to hate me. They blamed me for encouraging the emotional relationship between Shruti and Sunil. Once, when I was in their house and someone came to visit, they introduced me as a relative of theirs, wounding my self-esteem. They told me I could not come to their house anymore because they were looking for a bridegroom for Shruti. But she did not come out of the shadow of Sunil's death. She felt that he should now live on in her, she told me. 'Don't be afraid, I'm not going mad.' She felt pained that her family had offended me. Once, she came to my house when I wasn't there. I don't know what she and Kusuma spoke about, but when I came in, Shruti was looking very serious. Unable to stand the tension in the air, I escorted her back to her house, got blamed by her parents again for her leaving them, and ended up hurting her too. At home, Kusuma and I hurt each other with our words.

It was now over a month since Sunil had died. Shruti hadn't been coming to the office. She and I used to share so much of Sunil's troubles that there was a strange but reassuring bond between us. Once, Shruti had read in the newspaper that there was a particular tree in the forest near Jogeshwari that was one out of three such in the entire country. Insisting on seeing it, she took Sunil there. It warmed my heart to think of them going to see the tree. But as she told me later, it was the last time they went out together. Looking at the tree, Sunil had said, 'This tree is my friend. It's like I'm meeting him after many years.' His words uttered in the dusk made Shruti fearful. She had had a hard time getting him to leave the forest that day. When they left to see the tree, I had taken Kusuma to eat pav bhaji. There was a family sitting near us. Their little child came to where Kusuma was sitting, as though stepping straight off a baby calendar. She pinched his cheek and kissed him, taking in the baby fragrance he exuded. After that, she seemed listless and did not eat her pav bhaji. We returned home in an emotionally charged silence.

Around three, Kusuma called. 'When coming back from the office, please go to Kausalya's house and fetch Shankar Bappa's luggage,' she said. Thinking to get to Kausalya's before her husband came home, I left the office early. Her husband always wore a stiff smile on his face as though it was ironed on.

He talked about investments and the share market. According to him, money existed only to be invested. He made me tired. When I had insisted that Sunil's decomposed body should not be brought back to the house, this incomparable man had gone whispering gusugusu with his wife and managed to bring the body to his own house in Chembur and taken photos with it too. He got everyone to say that if Kausalya's husband hadn't taken responsibility, nothing would have been done about the body. When relatives came from Tadadi for the thirteenth-day ceremony, they all stayed in Kausalya's house and her husband took them sightseeing to the Gateway, Ranibag and Chowpatty, making himself popular in this way. 'Everyone in our town is saying we didn't look after Sunil properly,' said Kusuma. 'Yes, I bet when Kausalya's husband took his ramshackle car, which he keeps just to claim his travelling allowance from work, and drove down to Tadadi to eat fresh fish and ripe, seasonal mangoes, he would have definitely told them all so,' said I.

Kusuma appeared humiliated. 'No, no, my brother-in-law is not that kind of person. And what did he do wrong? You didn't agree to invite them home for even a cup of tea. What kind of person are you then?' she said angrily. Then, quickly realising that she was comparing me to him and that I might be offended by it, she said, 'They have money to spend on all that,' and turned the topic in another direction altogether.

Kusuma was of the firm but secret belief that I hated Kausalya's husband because he earned more than I did. Sunil was the one who brought this to my notice. Perhaps it was the first day we both had beer in the house that the topic had come up. Kusuma did not like the fact that we were drinking beer. Claiming that she had a headache, she prepared just rice with a basic dal for dinner and went straight to bed. Perhaps her mind was crowded with thoughts. One, that beer wasn't good for health. Two, that I was wasting money on Sunil, who was her blood relative but had gained entry into my innermost space. Sunil understood this. So did I. But we both said nothing. It was Sunil who started talking about 'the female mind' and ended the discourse with speaking about Kusuma. He was the one who came up with the idea that if we said beer was consumed in Kausalya's house, Kusuma would encourage us to do the same. One night Sunil woke me up, saying, 'I pity you for marrying my sister. She is a nut.' 'I've had a bit to drink,' he added. Another time he said, 'Shruti is saying that if I drink, she will drink too. What authority does she have to blackmail me like this?' Later, it seemed, they both calmed down.

As I approached Kausalya's house, her children who were playing outside shouted 'Uncle, uncle'. I suddenly realised I hadn't brought them chocolate. They said, 'Today our grandfather brought us sweets from the village.' Leaving them to their games, I pressed the bell. Kausalya opened the door. Her husband wasn't home yet. Without even sitting down, I said, 'Quick, give me Shankar Bappa's luggage. I'm in a hurry.' 'You're always like this. You never have a cup of tea in our house,' she said with dry coquetry. In the chaos around Sunil's death, she had dashed around in great excitement. She must be feeling a bit odd about that in front of me. That's why she sounded apologetic. 'Bappa could have stayed here,' she said.

'Yes, but Kusuma wanted him there. Let me see. I will bring him back after a while.' 'Perhaps on a day when my husband has a holiday,' she said. Before I flew into a rage, I grasped the bag she held out and left quickly. The children, saying 'Uncle uncle', came until the street and waved goodbye.

When I reached home, Shankar Bappa sat bare bodied on the sofa, his limbs spread out, as though he had somehow conquered that space. Kusuma took the bag from me and placed it in the bedroom. It appeared as though they had talked and shared their grief for a long time and were now spent. As though to draw me into that silence, Bappa said, 'Immature mind. What could we have done?' 'Yes, no one could have done anything,' I said. 'Maybe he couldn't do anything either.' I did wonder if I was talking too much. 'So ... so ... is the reason known now?' The old man sat as if on tiptoe. As though I didn't hear him, I went inside. Why did everyone have this strong desire to know the reason? Even strangers talked like this. 'Why did he die?' Did they want to look for these same reasons in their own lives and try to conquer them? Kusuma came up to me and hissed, 'Speak properly. Otherwise, he might go back home and spread all kinds of things about us.' While I sipped my tea, Kusuma and Bappa continued to talk outside.

I thought of the tree Sunil had gone so eagerly to see. What did it tell him? 'Bro-in-law, when the cyclone rages in Tadadi and the sea is foaming and turning red, and the boats don't come back, and in a hut somewhere a child is born into this world, wouldn't it be foolish to call that accidental?' How could I look for that Sunil in all the talk about him tonight?

Outside Kusuma was saying, 'Bappa, this time you should stay with us for at least a month. Every time you come, you stay at Kausalya's.' She came inside to give me more tea, saying, 'Look at that Kausalya, she's kept all the sweets from our village for herself. There should be a limit.' 'Don't fret,' I said. 'There, at least the children will eat it.' She turned and went out.

When we sat down to eat that night, Bappa said, 'We should have a puja for Sunil in the temple at Gokarna. But it will cost quite a bit.' 'Don't bother about the puja,' I said. 'Sunil never bothered with the gods.' 'Don't listen to him, Bappa,' said Kusuma passionately. 'Do whatever needs to be done. I'll give you the money. Don't tell Kausalya about this puja.' Bappa finished his food, saying 'Hanh' to everything. Later, as I sat outside in the balcony, I thought of Shruti.

The watchman of our building had come to tell me how much his little son had loved Sunil and what a fine person Sunil was, getting ten rupees out of this praise. Bappa came to sit near me in the balcony, burping. He sat fidgeting, as though he had something to say but couldn't find the courage to do so. I couldn't see his face clearly in the dark. I moved my hand over the plants that were sleeping in the corner. Bringing us a plate of fruit, Kusuma asked why we were sitting in the dark. As though struck by a wild thought, she said, 'I wonder what's happened to Shruti. I hope she isn't pregnant or something.'

I couldn't sleep for a long time. Mumbai could swallow anyone. It had swallowed me too. I was just a bunch of lies and explanations. Was Sunil my strength because he seemed to have swallowed Mumbai and not the other way around? Was it only someone like him who could choose their death? Did he have an abstract privilege that I didn't have? These strange thoughts went through my head. Downstairs, in the compound, someone was arguing in a loud voice. I went to the balcony to lean over and check. In the darkness, the voices were rising high. Why should they? What was the relationship between these voices and the voice of Sunil's inner world? Was his suicide a natural act? As natural as stepping out to water the balcony plants, as natural as inviting the watchman's son to stay for dinner? Who decided, in which world, whether suicide was natural or unnatural? In this world, Bappa, Kausalya, Kausalya's husband, Kusuma and myself – how did we make ourselves belong? And what was the meaning of belonging?

The dark became darker. Light played on the wet leaves. The chlorophyll was asleep. Perhaps I was building a tomb for Sunil with my own thoughts so that I could keep on believing in them. Feeling sleepy, I went to the bedroom. Kusuma was already asleep and dreaming. This woman, born as a free being, who could have become anyone anywhere, was now here. What kind of arrogance was this, that made me feel I could judge Kusuma or even the watchman? How could I disregard Kusuma's dreams? I lay down and closed my eyes.

In the morning, Bappa was awake before me and had already had his bath. He seemed to be in a hurry, having decided there was no use talking to me. 'I'm not going to work today,' Kusuma said. 'I have to take Bappa to a relative's house in Chunabhatti. The aunt who raised Bappa is now ninety-eight and lives there with her granddaughter. She wants to meet Bappa.' 'We'll eat lunch there. Come and fetch us in the evening,' she added, giving me the address and directions. I left for the office.

As soon as I reached my office, Kausalya's husband called. He wanted to know something about his life insurance policy. I gave him whatever information I could. Then I worked on clearing all the files to do with several years' worth of accidental deaths on our factory floor. A lot of details about the deaths, investigations, facts and figures. I signed off on everything and came out of the office to walk along Nariman Point in the rain. All the plants by the roadside were drenched and the scent was exhilarating. Or maybe it was the coolness that I translated into fragrance. It was on this same street that Shruti had told me, 'Sunil was a really genuine person. And he had his way.'

Wasn't that so? Why couldn't I just accept it? Why did I find it so difficult to accept that this person full of life had welcomed death by lying down in front of a train and that was 'his way' as Shruti said? Why couldn't I accept it as she did?

For some reason, at this juncture, I thought of Kusuma and Shankar Bappa, who seemed to be the happy ones. If Sunil had been walking with me now, he would have said, 'Hey, hey, you ball of arrogance. Who do you think you are to parade your pain at my death or anyone else's? You have no right to grieve anyone's death unless you know what it's like to die.' He would have dashed off to get a cigarette at that point. To calm myself, I lit a cigarette. As I puffed on it, I could see dark clouds massing near the ocean and coming closer. I ran back to the office. From the window, I could see the sky darken. On the road, countless feet submerged by rain could be glimpsed below the umbrellas.

In the distance, the red sea roared like a lion. For this sea, and for the sea at Tadadi where Sunil came from, there was only one horizon. And where my gaze ended was my horizon.

I left office early to go to Chunabhatti, to look for the house where Kusuma had taken Bappa, but it didn't take me long. The chawl was spread out on both sides of a narrow lane. Opposite the chawl flowed the kitchen water from each home where people had grown basale greens and tulasi. In bottles hanging from the eaves, money plants grew. All the people in the chawl came out to watch me as I approached. Kusuma came out and took me into the house with pride. In the cramped house I saw only beds and trunks everywhere. In a corner on the floor on some bedding lay a very old woman. Bappa was sitting next to her. It must have been the granddaughter who said Kusuma's husband is visiting us for the first time, and sent off the boy from the neighbour's house to buy some sweets. The granddaughter was supposed to have six or seven children. Her husband had been killed in a union fight several years back. They mentioned that one of her sons had come to me looking for a job a long time ago. Looking at how she had raised these seven or eight people, I felt shocked. On her lap was a baby. Someone said her daughter had delivered a child here the previous month. The daughter sat nearby, shyly.

Kusuma came up to me whispering and fished out my wallet. She took out twenty-five rupees and called out to a girl who was playing outside, 'Tulasi, come here.' She gestured for her to take the money. 'Why all this?' said the mother, at the same time indicating to the child to accept. At that point the sweets arrived. Tulasi looked unblinkingly at the packet that lay in the middle of the little gathering. The woman of the house said, 'Sunil liked coming here. He has eaten here at least a couple of times.'

I managed to get Kusuma and Shankar Bappa out of the house and onto the main road. When I turned back, I saw Tulasi of the sparkling eyes, in her dirty skirt at the edge of the street. She was looking at me against the strange backdrop of those teeming chawls, like we would never come to her house again. I waved goodbye to her. She waved back. What sort of language was this? Why did I wave my hand? Was it my hand that waved? In a disturbed state of mind, I reached home with the others. I wondered if I had imagined it, or if Shankar Bappa had actually fallen at the feet of the old woman before we left the chawl in Chunabhatti.

As we prepared to go to sleep, Kusuma said, 'This month, too, I'm bleeding very heavily. Let's go to Dr Rao tomorrow.' I sat stroking the curls on her forehead. 'If Sunil had been here, he would have taken me. I wouldn't have troubled you,' she said. 'May I say something?' I began. 'I respect the fact that Sunil chose to die. Please don't be sad about it and do him an injustice.' Her body seemed feverish. After a while, Kusuma whispered, 'I found out something. It was Kausalya's husband who called Shankar Bappa over. He wrote to him that there's a lot of money from office funds that the family would be eligible for, and that Bappa should come and sit on Kusuma's husband's head and get this job done. Shankar Bappa didn't know how to ask you, so he's making me do it.' I wasn't surprised. I sat in silence. Kusuma ran her hand through my hair and asked, 'Are you upset? I certainly was. What sort of people are these? They forget that Sunil lived with us for four years. Now they want to snatch money from us. And why is Kausalya's husband meddling in all this? How much money do they think they'll get?' I kept looking at her. 'I have a stomachache,' she said. I rubbed her belly for a while, and she went to sleep.

I came out onto the balcony. The rain was pouring down. In the living room, Shankar Bappa was tossing and turning on the divan. Why was I not able to understand why the old man couldn't sleep? Even if he got a few rupees, he would feel that he had accomplished something. What was the harm in that? The entire city was drenched in rain. In this same city, under different roofs, lay Shruti, the girl Tulasi, Shankar Bappa, Kusuma. The truth of the rain was like the truth of this moment's sleep. And could truths ever be wrong?

I left the balcony and went into the house. 'Shankar Bappa,' I called out gently. 'Hanh,' he said, sitting up bolt upright. 'Tomorrow you come with me. We'll go to Sunil's office and see if there's any paperwork to be done,' I said. 'No problem, sure, no problem,' he said. 'Sleep now,' I said, and went inside. I took out my wallet, looked at Sunil's photo, and then went to sleep.

Kannigondu Kshitija
1982

The Scent of Bakula

In the moment Shashank opened his eyes he couldn't immediately tell whether it was early morning or twilight outside. Slowly floating through the mix of voices, sights, exhaustion and drowsiness, he saw the light outside. The light too seemed indifferent – he could see a tree in it, its leaves trembling. The tree also held the whoops of children playing in a nearby field. If the voices had receded and the tree was drooping, it meant a day had helplessly faded away. However, if the voices increased in volume and mingled with the sound of traffic, making the tree stand there as though with ruffled hair and ready for a street fight, it meant a new day had dawned.

The same window. The same tree. But the tones were different. Folding his pale blue sheet embroidered with the name of the hospital, Shashank looked towards the next bed. It was empty. The Nepali youth had been taken early in the morning for his surgery. Erasing all traces of his having slept there, the morning nurses had changed the sheets and made the bed ready for the next occupant. The Nepali youth had been a bit down yesterday. He kept looking at Shashank with unblinking eyes. When Shashank raised his eyebrows at him, asking 'what', the youth closed his eyes like a thief.

'Don't be afraid. The operation will be a long and pleasant sleep. Skilful doctors, beautiful nurses – they'll all look after you while you sleep. When you wake up, it'll all be fine. Everything will seem like new.'

As though not having heard Shashank's words, the youth asked: 'Is it true that there's a backdoor to the operation theatre? If you get "out" they'll take you away through that door?'

'No, no ... you'll be the one to get discharged first and go home. Look at my state. The doctors still don't know what's wrong with me. They're conducting a test a day. Maybe all my blood will evaporate in tests,' Shashank laughed. But the youth looked at him without blinking.

Lucky fellow, he must be asleep in the operation theatre, thought Shashank, as he walked towards the washroom. Since it was already time for the morning doctors to come on their rounds, the toilets had been scrubbed clean with phenyle. 'Shashank, your scan is at eleven a.m. Don't eat anything. Drink a lot of water. Go to the T Ward and get a prescription,' said a nurse, hurrying him. Tying his pyjamas more tightly, Shashank walked towards the lift that was in a corner of the verandah.

The lift was descending from the seventh floor. At every floor more people got in. On one floor a wheelchair was suddenly brought in. The ayah pushing it held a saline bottle in one hand. The lift man stood up from his stool to allow the wheelchair to pass. Standing amongst all the people who were looking at the floor numbers as they clutched flasks of tea to their chests, Shashank bent to look at the wheelchair patient whose drowsy head was arched back on the chair. He thought he had seen her before. He peered closer. Was startled. Arre, Sarojini! Wasn't it her? He looked away and then looked back at her. The figure with eyes half shut was clad in the blue hospital gown. From the bottle held by the ayah, the saline was slowly dripping into the patient's veins. As she held up the bottle, the ayah began to chat with the lift man. 'Hey, are you continuing your shift or what?' Sarojini's slender and chiselled nose, the slight cleft in her chin – just like she used to look. He was seeing her after thirty years, in this big city hospital, in this lift, in a drowsy state in that wheelchair. Where had she come from? What was wrong with her?

After descending another floor, the lift halted. The ayah turned the wheelchair around and began to push it out. Sensing this strange moment slipping away, Shashank moved his legs that seemed to have turned to wood and went out of the lift to follow the wheelchair, holding back the doors that were closing. Since it was the Intensive Care Unit, he stopped at the reception desk. The ayah handed over the case papers to the duty nurse, wheeled the chair into a ward, settled Sarojini on her bed (yes, it was Sarojini), hooked the bottle onto a stand, adjusted the flow, and came out. To Shashank who stood there the ayah said, 'Someone you know? Come back later. Now it's time for the doctors' rounds.'

Shashank tried to stretch his neck and get a better look. His sense of time had changed drastically all of a sudden. In the midst of these white beds and blue hospital gowns, how could he reach this dear friend who lay still, like a doll? Where was her world? What kind of world was it? How could he touch it now? Shashank trembled, as though in despair. He sat down slowly on the bench nearby, thinking of how much he had been – he had been spellbound by that face whose radiance never let up. Just then he heard a voice on the speaker asking him to go for his scans. He stood up and made his way to the radiology department.

Slowly the scent of Sarojini's faded bakula flowers, worn in a string in her hair thirty years ago, pervaded his senses. When Shashank was made to lie down for the scanning, the scent became stronger. Sarojini was fonder of the smell of faded flowers than fresh ones. So her mother would wear them on the first day and Sarojini on the second. As the scanning machine sent forth its beams, in Shashank's heart there was the warmth of Sarojini's sighs. In that warmth was a bakula forest.

It was afternoon when Shashank finished his scans and was brought back to his bed. Because the nurse insisted, he ate two morsels of food, and then closed his eyes. Sarojini, who had appeared in the lift that morning. Sarojini, who was now lying alone on the third floor. She had come in the pouring rain, fully drenched. Without worrying about what people in that small town would say, she had climbed the big wooden ladder panting, come to his small rented room and stood in the doorway. Before he could sit up on his bed, she spoke from the door: 'You have to decide.' (The word 'decide' in English.)

'You have to decide. To hell with caste and other things. If you want us to be together, you have to decide. Come to my house. Tell them. Today. Now.'

The rain was washing the entire town clean. From Sarojini's broad forehead both raindrops and sweat were shining as they rolled down.

What was there to decide. I was lying on the mat. Although I'm now past forty-five, I still don't know the art of deciding. Not only that, no one is able to decide what disease it is that's devouring me.

With the background noise of the rain, the tendrils of hair that had escaped from her braids stuck to her wet cheeks. 'Come, sit down,' I said. She did not listen. 'No, there's no time. You must come now,' she said, and melted away into the rain. A long time after she left, I could hear the ladder creaking. The rope that was tied to it to help people climb still dangled. The town where I had come to study, that ladder, that room, that mat, that rope, that storm ... they receded far, far away. Wasn't it possible to live without making decisions all the time? I moved from town to town. The houses had steps but not the hills. There were steps in the parks, not in the forests. Clouds changed their shapes. What happened to the forest of bakula flowers? Merged with the dust. It became a tar road. It became the vehicles with winking lights that disappeared on the mysterious roads of the dark and distant hills. Where was all that now? Nowhere. Here. In this lift, in this wheelchair, and in the green shoots of the tree by my window.

Shashank woke up to the sound of the afternoon tea trolley. As though suddenly remembering that he had a train to catch, he drank his tea in a hurry and ran towards the lift. As he stepped out on the third floor, the ayah from that morning signed to him that he could go in and see the patient. Diffidently

Shashank approached the spotless silence of the room. Quietly he pulled out the stool that had been pushed under the bed, sat lightly on it, and looked at Sarojini as though gazing on a newborn infant.

It seemed to him as though sketches made of her at different stages of life had been laid one on top of the other. In this face that was now past forty, one could see the adolescent face too. There was also the face of the infant in the cradle. And the face that had told him in the pouring rain to 'decide'. He was seeing her today in the light of all those faces. Like the flower of eternity.

Just then a man came in with a plastic bag, put it down on another stool and looked at Shashank as though asking who he was. Shashank stood up, saying, 'Isn't this Sarojini? I knew her in college. She was in Arts, I was in Science.' This man could have been her husband, her brother, anyone at all. It seemed meaningless to ask who he was.

'All those medicines they give for those tests have made her really drowsy since yesterday. When she's awake she talks a lot. I'll call you when she wakes up. Give me your ward number,' the man said, and took down the details. A sort of white silence descended on them. There was something in the silence that erased the bonds to which society might have given a name.

'Let me know if you need anything,' Shashank said. As he left, he gently picked up Sarojini's dangling arm and placed it by her side. Feeling that she was watching him even in her sleep, he smiled. He felt as though he was standing in the sky inside her dream, without the earth beneath his feet. As he walked towards the lift, the blue sky dissolved under him.

The rays of light from the streetlamp attached themselves to the tree outside the window as the visiting hours ended and the watchman asked people to leave the hospital. On her rounds, a nurse came to take Shashank's temperature and check his pulse, looking like a bright new soap freshly taken out of its packaging. Seeing her slender fingers taking his pulse and observing her tiny wristwatch, Shashank began to blabber with the thermometer still in his mouth. 'Sarojini, if you had come with me your life would have been ruined. Everything I've touched has come to nothing, and when I go near something it disappears. Whatever I tried to make mine has become disfigured. You escaped all this.' The nurse said, 'Ah?' and laughed. 'What are you saying?' Before she left his bedside, the nurse did not forget to say, 'Has the friend who admitted you deposited any more money? Otherwise no tests from tomorrow, because the amount he deposited is finished.'

Sarojini brought fried fish secretly from her house in a steel dabba to supplement Shashank's meals in the cheap mess where he ate. He had put it into his cupboard in the chemistry lab where he kept his instruments and forgotten about it. Next day he lied to her that it had tasted wonderful. Then he dumped the stale fish in the pond near the college and returned the dabba to Sarojini after washing it. 'Dump the pond fish in the pond only. But first fry it and then dump it,' teased his friends mercilessly in front of Sarojini. Sarojini loved fish like her life. The tiny transparent belli fish – bellanji – was her favourite. She was proud of the fact that she could relish it bones and all. Shashank turned over on his side. It felt like the pond had come into his ward, as though the legs of the beds were submerged in water. In the pouring rain, a tiny boat carrying a fisherman with a dark blanket over his head was floating on the pond.

The ward boy was turning out the lights when, like a shadow, Sarojini's relative appeared and woke Shashank. 'Come, come, Sarojini is calling you. She seems very cheerful. The moment she heard your name she forgot this was a hospital and screamed "Arre!" In case you took fright and didn't want to come back to her ward ... she's insisting that I bring you now itself.' In a sort of stupor Shashank followed him.

They had to wait a while for the lift. 'There's something I need to tell you,' said the man. 'We're at a critical point in her treatment. As we proceed further, her memory, her personality traits, her consciousness – all of these might diminish, the doctors are saying. If we want her to be as she is, and stop the medicine, there's danger to her life. She's at that stage. We're unable to decide what to do.' As they got into the lift – with the man holding Shashank's hand – and it began to descend, he asked, 'And at what stage is yours?' 'I don't know,' said Shashank.

When the lift door opened, he could see Sarojini sitting on the bed with her knees drawn up, covered with a pale blue sheet, looking at him through the glass barrier of the ICU. As he walked up to her, it seemed as though she was the one coming towards him, not the other way around. Looking at her anxious face, her nose and the sparkle in her eyes, he did not know what to say, but just said, 'Sarojini'. As though saying 'Present, sir', when her name was called by the schoolteacher, she crinkled her eyes, shook her head and smiled faintly. Touching the arm that had the saline bottle attached to it, he said haltingly, 'Get well soon and go home.'

As though he had cracked a joke, she laughed in a peculiar sort of way. This laughter was unfamiliar to him; it was not part of the old portraits. Pointing a finger at Shashank's hospital dress, she gestured as if to ask, 'What's this avatar of yours?' 'Oh, just a routine check-up,' said Shashank, dragging the stool closer to the bed and sitting down. 'Don't bluff. No one comes to this big hospital for a routine check-up. But don't worry. Nothing's wrong with you. Nothing at all,' she said. Her relative, cheered by her forceful talk and the ease of their interaction, said, 'You keep talking. I'll just come back.'

'So then?' she asked, looking at him intensely. There was no answer. Shashank was looking for those eyes he had seen in the pouring rain, between the wet braids, but these seemed different. Here there was no room for questions, nor any meaning. The atmosphere was calm. Nothing could give the lie to this feeling – where were you, what happened to you, who's that man, who's this man, where is she, livelihood, rice, money, pregnancy, house, family welfare, victory, defeat, kitchen sink, illness, double bed, children, body – none of these false notes would reach here.

'Come, sit here,' she said as though to a small child, moving her feet further back so he would have enough space. He sat diffidently at the foot of her bed. She kept saying, 'There's nothing wrong with you, you're fine, really', but he looked odd to her with his wispy hair and pale lips. Like a cursed

Gandharva. He opened his mouth to say nothing had gone well for him, but he could not bring himself to say it. Neither his aspiration nor his realisation had taken shape, so what could he say? Noticing that it was time for the dinner trolley to arrive, Sarojini said, 'Go now, it's dinner time. In your bland hospital dinner I wish that a fried bellanji fish appears.' 'And in yours I hope you find basale greens, clams and ganji,' he said. They laughed uproariously.

'Go to sleep now,' said Shashank, rising and covering her with the sheet as she stretched her legs. 'In college throughout those two years you wore one pair of pants and two shirts, one with blue checks, one cream, striped,' she said, smiling as she closed her eyes. He tucked a pillow under her arm which had the saline tube and patted her gently. He felt like he was standing without being able to feel the ground. 'I'll come in the morning,' he breathed, and floated back to his ward, where he lay looking at the window.

Who was Sarojini if both memory and consciousness were erased? When we speak of love and relationships, do we think of our memories or of the breathing, living individual in front of us? This question stood between two mysteries – it wasn't merely a matter of medical choice. Shashank was perplexed. Even if Sarojini had experienced marriage and family in the past thirty years, all of it seemed a lie when he saw her today. Those years of not being present to each other meant nothing when they met today. What more could anyone want?

The dinner trolley came by, making a slight noise. The smell of food pervaded the ward. In the clink of plates, in the gentleness with which someone was feeding a patient, it felt like the aroma of the hurulikattu saaru that had been cooking on the hearth for a week as the coconut trees swayed in the rain. The other day, when he had come to be admitted here and felt dizzy, a stranger held him, helped him to a bench and then called for a wheelchair – the smell of that man's sweat was here too.

The tree by the window had already stopped talking to the breeze. So that the sulking breeze wouldn't come in, the ward maids were closing all the windows. Feeling someone touching him gently, Shashank saw that Sarojini's relative was sitting by his side and had taken hold of his hand. In a whisper he said, 'Look, we have to decide tomorrow. She has to survive. We are willing to do anything to help her survive. Please help us continue with her treatment.' He sighed as he spoke. The person in this half-light could be Sarojini's brother, husband, father, son, friend – none of them or any of the above.

Shashank was flustered. If I want the Sarojini of my memories, don't they want the Sarojini they remember? 'It's important that she remain calm. Please decide as she wants,' Shashank said. The man held Shashank's hand. 'After seeing you, she has become really stubborn. She says she doesn't want any treatment at all. She knows that with the treatment her memory, her energy, are growing dim. So far she hadn't refused the treatment. But today, after you came and went, she has been behaving like a madwoman. If we continue the treatment she says she will jump out of the hospital window. I don't know what to do.' He began to sob. Someone in the ward said 'Sshh'. He wiped his face on his sleeve. 'Please don't come to see her again,' he said, his head bent, and walked out of the ward.

Shashank sat up in bed for a long while, then got up and went towards the lift. It was midnight and the lift was empty. It looked quite large, devoid of the patients it carried up and down during the day. Hospital lifts don't have mirrors. Yes, that's appropriate, isn't it, Shashank thought. He pressed the buttons one by one. Where the door opened at each floor, there was a ward. The wards were asleep in a silent turmoil. Relatives of patients slept haphazardly. Wouldn't everything be different if I hadn't been in the lift this morning and encountered that wheelchair, thought Shashank.

Although what the two of them had experienced at the accidental encounter was real, it was already becoming a memory. We shouldn't touch it again. Shouldn't think of it again. It's a whole new forest of memories that has entered the mind. When we grasp at something, it wilts. Makes us stunted. That which comes by itself grows with us. Saves us. When we call it a memory, it appears like a new experience. It's the flower that has just bloomed on an old tree.

The lift stopped at the third floor. When the door opened and then shut again, Shashank prayed: 'God, please keep giving everyone new memories.' Then he closed his eyes as though playing a game and pressed a random button. When he opened his eyes, the lift was going up. He stood with curious eyes, wondering where it would stop.

Bakula Gandha
1999

The Right Side

Varsha, whose right side had been weak and deformed since birth, absolutely refused to go to the studio to take a full-length portrait photograph. In the one-room house in a chawl on the western side of Mulund suburb, her brothers stood like suitors in a court of law. Her mother as usual was brimming with unsaid words, and her father sat on the iron cot as serious as a judge. The gravity of this 'photo demand' situation was evident even to their neighbour, who was sitting across from their open door, washing vessels outside her house.

Since she was young she had been told, 'Don't walk around in front of strangers for no reason.' 'How many times to tell you that you should cover your right hand completely with your dupatta?' 'When you're pointing to something, why do you insist on using your crooked arm, you stupid girl?' Despite all this constant needling and correcting, Varsha had completed her tenth class from the municipal school about a dozen years ago. She, who was used to helping out all her family members with her left hand, including her father – when he set out for his factory shift, she would be ready to hand him his train season ticket, his comb and his handkerchief, and when he returned home she would take from him the bag he might be carrying and give him water to drink; this was her routine over many years, practised with great zeal. Today when all of them besieged her with the photo request she felt her arms and legs go cold.

All these years she had hidden the right part of her body to such an extent that she seemed to have no right side at all. More than her individual pain, she guarded her body for the sake of her family's social health. When she began to feel that the small mirror on the wall wasn't big enough for her face, around the same time her father decided to buy a metal cupboard on instalments. At that time, a similar conference had taken place. The discussion was about whether to have a cupboard with a full-length mirror or no mirror at all. The two brothers raised a hue and cry, saying they preferred to have a mirror. Varsha went pale and started trembling. She went out of the house and stood by the public tap in the dark. Finally, even though the father wanted the mirror cupboard too, the family decided to buy only the plain mirrorless one.

One brother had completed a diploma in radio and found a job in an industrial estate, while the other younger brother was growing up out of sight, like an actor who hadn't found a role. Her father wanted to continue working even though the factory was offering voluntary retirement packages. The little brother began to argue with his father that he should take the package so that they would get some money with which to do something. 'Look at the mug of the one who will "do something",' shouted the father.

Sometimes the father would proclaim that Varsha was his true son, his sanctuary when he became old. Although this proclamation made Varsha temporarily happy, she would begin to worry that it was the blueprint of her future. She would quickly say in a jokey voice, 'Don't worry so much, Appa. I will get married too, just wait and see.' None of them knew how to respond to her. Her mother, seeing it as impudence, would tell her to speak softly softly.

But Varsha's Appa kept up his futile efforts through his co-workers to find a match for her. At the same time, her mother began to persuade her to wear new clothes, to put on jewellery, to wear an anklet. But her new salwars all had long sleeves. She wasn't allowed to wear her brothers' half-sleeved t-shirts even at home. When they were about to go to sleep at night, the mother would say to Appa, 'You've explained everything clearly, I hope.' Varsha understood what this 'everything' was. Knowing the inevitable relationship between marriage prospects and her crooked limbs, she would feel a shudder run through her belly and sit up straight, shaking off the bedsheet that covered her. When her mother woke up at four in the morning and turned on a light to prepare her husband's lunchbox, she would see Varsha fast asleep with her limbs spread out. Seeing the girl's undeveloped right arm and leg, she would feel a pang. She would align her limbs properly, cover her with a sheet, and only then start rolling out the chapatis.

Varsha's old classmates would drop in once in a while and turn the talk to matters like 'There's someone in my husband's office ...' Varsha would immediately ask: 'And what deficiency does he have?' As though they were waiting for this question, they would quickly say, 'A bit of a lisp' or 'Misshapen ears' or 'Hard of hearing' or 'Can't see so well'. The details would come tumbling out as though they were adding to his credentials. When before she would seethe with anger, now Varsha just said, laughing, 'Chheh, don't you worry about me, I'll marry a handsome man with all his limbs intact. It's my birthright.'

In this way, a sort of theatrical distress around Varsha pervaded the household. This distress moved like a dark cloud over the brothers too. When colourful dupattas, high-heeled slippers, nail polish and hair remover entered the house with Varsha's flowering womanhood, her mother was mutely happy, but the brothers felt strangely aggravated. Why all this display for you, they seemed to convey, as they averted their eyes and made annoyed faces like brinjals. Neighbour Sonali in the furthermost house got married, and the night before, influenced by TV serials and movies, she had a 'mehendi' ceremony. Varsha took part in it with great delight and came home with mehendi-painted hands. 'You should have got married too while you were about it,' said her youngest brother harshly. Their mother turned on him and there was a ruckus. Another day, in the vegetable market, when she was bending down to pick up ladies' finger from the street vendor, this same brother said angrily, 'Wear your dupatta properly, cover yourself.' This boy, who she had seen from the time he was an infant, was displaying such absurd masculine grandeur. She felt simultaneously affectionate and sad. She tapped his cheek and smiled. 'Don't laugh on the road,' he said.

Varsha felt that her interaction with the people in the town, the market or the chawl – the milkman, the dhobi – with this whole wider universe, was marked by a certain freedom that her classmates did not have. She understood that her crooked limbs played a role here. Other people too used to behave with her in a free and unburdened way. In trains and buses, those men who would hesitate to sit beside a woman or hold themselves stiffly even if they did so, sat beside Varsha comfortably and sometimes even went to sleep. If she asked them questions like 'Which is the next stop?' or 'What's the time?' their voice did not begin to sweat. Varsha sometimes played a strange game with men. She would keep her crooked limbs hidden and then stretch out her hand suddenly and watch them squirm. Slowly she got tired of that game too. When her women friends went out with their boyfriends to the side of the cinema or to a park, they would take Varsha along as a chaperone. Varsha would be positioned like a chambermaid some way off, cleaning her comb with a hairpin, watching them stand like scarecrows at a safe distance from each other, engaging in babytalk. This kind of social service, too, she stopped doing after some time.

In that house were several photos of her taken over the years with different people. Whenever she stood to be photographed, she would press behind the person to her right so that her limbs were not clearly visible. Appa had shown only such photos to potential bridegrooms. Once, her youngest brother's friend had come over with a camera and made her stand half hidden by a curtain while he took her photograph. These photos too disappeared like worn-out currency notes. After all these failed games, when her family wanted her to go to Roopam Studio and take a photograph, she was infuriated. 'Absolutely not!' she cried out loud, and putting on her slippers she rushed outside. She did notice that her youngest brother was about to say something and was shushed by her mother.

Since she couldn't think of what to do, Varsha began to walk briskly and aimlessly towards the hill to the west. The thousands of huts covering the hill seemed to hold it down to the ground. On top of the hill was a ruined haveli. From there one could look down on the entire suburb. Today there seemed to be a large number of people on the path. They all seemed to be running towards the hilltop. 'There's a film shoot at the haveli, with the actress Rambha and a hero, also from the South,' said people in the crowd. Varsha's gait also quickened. She was panting as she ran.

Several feet from the haveli, the onlookers had been brought to a halt. There were large, shiny reflectors, wires, lights, operators speaking a strange language, and a peculiar sort of sunshine. If one looked back, one could see the suburb down below in a thick haze of dust and smoke, as if gasping for breath. Varsha wondered in which corner of that ocean her house was, and her parents, and her brothers. In front of her, sitting like dolls on two coloured chairs under two coloured umbrellas were the made-up lead players. Both held round mirrors with coloured frames and handles. Both were immersed in their own reflections. The hero in particular seemed to be ensouled in the mirror and was stroking his own hair gently. Two unit members were standing in front of him and behind, flapping plastic fans to keep him cool. From time to time, he put his tongue to his palm and patted down his hair with the damp hand. He did not look around him. Rambha, too, had established a soulful relationship with her mirror. A maid was fanning her with a plastic hand fan. Another maid was making sure the actress's curls stayed in place. Rambha acted as though she was speaking to the maids, but she was actually trying out various kinds of superficial laughter for the entertainment of the hundreds of people who had gathered there.

The entire hill was plastered with the small huts covered with tarpaulin and plastic sheets weighed down with old cycle tyres which seemed to be assaulted by the hot wind, while the coloured dolls under the coloured umbrellas looked distinctly absurd. The onlookers waited for the shooting to begin. Feeling nauseous and bored, Varsha made her way down, passing by the flour mill. The mill operator was sitting outside smoking a beedi, fully covered in flour. Only his eyes and beedi glimmered red. In his absolute self-effacement, the man looked quite beautiful.

When Varsha entered her house it was mid-afternoon. Appa had eaten and gone to sleep. The youngest brother was watching TV. Varsha felt sorry for him. 'Are you going to marry me off, little boy? Come, I'll give you whatever pose you want. I'm ready to get my photo taken. In the studio you name, in the pose that you want.' The startled boy began to weep noisily, as though helpless. Seeing him cry after so many years, Varsha thought he looked like a schoolboy. The arched brows, the dimple in the chin, the fold beneath the nose – all belonged to that boy from long ago. Feeling moved, Varsha bent down and stroked his back. 'I'm not lying. I'm ready, truly.' The boy appeared embarrassed at his outburst. He stopped crying and climbed onto the cot next to his father and lay down facing away from them.

When they were eating, the mother said softly, 'Not for a marriage proposal. Poor boy, some STD telephone booth idea has entered his head. If you're handicapped, you can get the booth allotted very quickly and at a discounted price. He's saying, if you get the booth in your name, he will run it himself. You don't have to do a thing. Just give a new photo.' Along with her meal that she swallowed without chewing, she absorbed her mother's words too. The brother was listening while pretending to be asleep. His body trembled with the effort.

After having a cup of tea, Varsha prepared to go out with her brother. Instead of her usual long-sleeved salwar kameez, she wore a short-sleeved shirt and a skirt that reached just below her knees. So far, she had not been allowed to wear such clothing outside the house. Her mother pretended to be engaged in frying something and did not look at her. From her silence, Varsha could make out that her throat was choked with tears. When Varsha and her brother alighted from their rickshaw at Roopam Studio, there was a crowd. A nearby school had had a fancy-dress competition and the mothers had brought their children there for photographs. Varsha got a kick out of watching the costumed children. A parrot, a monkey, a tube of toothpaste, a tree, a brinjal, a sunflower – all these children were waiting with tired eyes for their turn. A fairy with milk-coloured wings had gone to sleep on her mother's lap.

The photographer, who was fed up with the fussy mothers and their noisy children, had them make way for Varsha as though clearing the traffic for an ambulance. She and her brother went inside and looked up at the spotlights. There was a blue curtain. When her eyes adjusted to the light, Varsha saw that there, too, was a line of quietly sitting children: a squirrel, an Adivasi, a yellow butterfly, a tiny police inspector, a fisherman holding a fish as big as himself. When Varsha's brother mumbled, 'We want full-size,' the photographer – as though he knew exactly why they had come – placed a white curtain in front of the blue one and called Varsha to come and stand in the centre under the light. He told her to lean to the right. Varsha was about to say that she could stand straight, and then realised her slip and bit her tongue. The photographer tilted her to the right and pulled out her crooked right hand. 'The moment they see the photo they should give you your certificate. No need for an interview. That's the kind of pose you should give. Yes, like that.' He made her right leg come forward a little at an angle. 'Don't move,' he said in English. And went to get two shiny metal crutches. On seeing them, the brother blanched. 'One's enough,' said the photographer, and went to put away the other one. In the glaring light, except for this crutch Varsha could not see anything else.

Slowly she tried placing the crutch under her right armpit. Its cushioned part felt rough. This too was a set prop, like the plastic flowerpot, the coloured tablecloth, the necktie and the hat. In front of the gleaming eyes of the yellow sunflower, the joker, the bunch of grapes, the drip-nosed tree with 'Don't cut me down' written on its chest, the squirrel, the butterfly and the little fisherman, Varsha struck a pose as though in a dream. She transferred all her weight to her crutch, her limbs hanging. The photographer pushed them forward a little more and went to stand behind his metal eye. 'Ready?' he asked. She was expecting him to say 'Smile' and was gearing up for it when he said, 'No smile please ... Be serious.' Lightbulbs went off, the lights crackled like fireworks, the sound of the camera's click was heard. As though freed from a spell, Varsha smiled.

Just as the little parrot took off her cardboard wings, Varsha handed over the crutch and came out of the booth like a newly bathed infant. Outside, the mothers were still being noisy. Two of them were talking. 'I hear the photographer's wife is a real beauty. So beautiful that when he comes to the studio, he locks her up in the house.' The fairy woke up from her nap and demanded ice cream. Varsha grabbed the hand of her brother who had come out after paying the photographer. 'Buy me some ice cream!' she said.

Aparoopa
1999

The Master's Son

In ten minutes the bus would leave the Ankola terminus for Mumbai. It took Neelkanth five minutes just to find his seat and stow his luggage. As he was about to get off to talk to his father, the conductor started ringing the bell. Narayan Master gestured to his son to stay where he was, and went close to the window. That Neelkanth was entering an important stage in his life for which he was leaving town made Narayan Master feel choked with emotion. Neel too was trembling. Narayan Master was facing up to the idea that his son, off to his new job in Mumbai, would soon enter a world that wasn't controlled by his father.

Narayan Master was known in the whole town for his short temper, his discipline, a detached behaviour that made him seem eccentric and self-centred. His son Neel, who had grown up in the shadow of this detachment, was unemotional about this leave-taking. But at this moment both felt a strange bond surfacing of which they had not been conscious before. The bus started to move. Narayan Master waited until the bus had passed the second turn in the road and then made his way to his bicycle. He felt an overwhelming sadness. When the bus disappeared from view, he held the edge of his dhoti to his face, rested his hand on the bicycle seat, and sobbed bitterly. Without knowing whether he was crying for himself, or for his son, or for something beyond them, he wept. When the women with their baskets of abbalige flowers near the bus stand began to look strangely at him, Master wiped his face and began to push his bicycle. If anyone had seen Master and told Neel that his father was crying, he wouldn't have believed it.

In the bus Neel felt teary for the first half hour, but then, as they passed Masti Katte village, he sat up straight with a strange excitement. Hiregutthi, Ankola, exams, vacations, social gatherings, cricket tournaments, the Shivaratri 'company plays' in Gokarna, the one or two better-looking girls in the class whom he admired – all of these were part of a certain familiar routine for Neel. Now, on the one hand, there was the excitement of going beyond this established routine, and on the other hand was the feeling of a boulder-like responsibility sitting on his chest which made him feel fearful. In the last ten to fifteen years since he had come of age, he had felt he was being liberated from the peculiar pressure of his bond with his father. But in the haste to push away his past, Neel also felt agitated. At the Yellapur bus stand he ate a banana. At Haliyal he bought a copy of the latest *Filmfare*. In Belgaum he watched with interest the cowherds in their dusty turbans. After Nippani he observed on the left side of the highway the many colours of the sunset. As though not knowing that the same sun was setting in Hiregutthi, he stared at this one as he drowsed off.

At night when the bus stopped in Sangli, Karad and Pune, he went to relieve himself, and by dawn he got off at Dadar to be met by a t-shirted relative. As this relative threw his Hindi and Marathi-mixed Kannada at Neel, Mumbai started breathing within him.

In Hiregutthi, Narayan Master continued with his routine of going to the fish market, the bus stand, the platform around the peepul tree, sorting out the problems the locality's children faced in their lessons. Someone might say to him, 'Master, soon your son will settle down in Mumbai and ask you to come. You should definitely go. There's nothing here – just mud.' 'But mud is what I want,' Master would say straightaway. If he got invited to preside over a flag-hoisting or a debate competition, he would take part in the event as though he belonged to the school. From the right way to fold and tie a knot around the flag to how those on the stage should not stand with their buttocks towards the audience, Master displayed his 'discipline' to the new generation of masters with their budding moustaches, sometimes even arguing with them and making them feel they wanted to have nothing to do with him.

When Neel was about ten or eleven years old, Master lost his wife. Radhabai had kept on doing housework through her illness and passed away, neglected by her husband. No one knew whether Master's temper flared up more often at home than in the school. Neel had never looked his father in the eye. He registered Narayan Master's presence through sounds: the unlatching of the wooden gate, the cycle being raised onto the stand, the lid clanging on the water heater. All his students and their parents were scared of Master's temper.

When there was a year to go for Master's retirement, Neel entered high school. That is to say, Neel came under his father's rule for a year. It was the most difficult year for him. Master taught his class history. He shouted at Neel for no good reason, all his towering rage directed against the boy. Everyone knew that Narayan Master would not show any favouritism towards his son, yet he beat him mercilessly, as though beating everyone who doubted him. Although his classmates displayed a sort of pity mixed with fear towards him, Neel was left quite alone. Throughout his primary school days, his father had troubled him in peculiar ways. He once jumped on the science teacher and asked whether he did not know even simple science. After that the science teacher kept getting after Neel.

His friends appeared to see Narayan Master in Neel and kept a safe distance. But Neel always fell behind in his studies. His elder brother Madhukar, who had joined the army and was ten years older than him, had left home because of their father's temper, although Neel did not know this then. Madhukar always wrote in his letters, 'Study well.' He sent Neel shirts and pens and shoes from time to time. Never once mentioned their father. Except for his love of the perfumed eraser and the globe and the compass box sent by his brother, Neel hadn't the least interest in studying. The other teachers, expecting Neel to be more active in class and disappointed in their expectation, began to complain softly to Narayan Master. Master would get annoyed. 'Why should he be intelligent just because he is the Master's son' was his logic, as he brought this anger also to bear on the boy.

Fear became Neel's primary emotion. When there was a debating competition, he would shiver, because his father would make him stay up all night and memorise his speech. Next day, at the competition, Neel would say, 'Teachers and elders, my classmates ...' and sit down, stammering, having forgotten everything else. But he didn't feel humiliated. It was as though he was taking revenge on his father. At such times, as though carrying out his own revenge, Narayan Master would not eat dinner. Savitrakka, the woman from the neighbourhood who came in to prepare one meal every day, used to tell everyone at first that the Master abused his motherless child. Then she became frightened of the Master's temper and fell silent.

Neel used to delight in playing cricket in the unploughed fields. Whenever he got out, his playmates would taunt him, saying, 'Don't go and tell your father now', but Neel played on with great absorption. However, he never played cricket in school. Narayan Master would bring home his small misdeeds and beat him, saying, 'How will you become strong if you keep on doing these things?' It was as though he was preparing his son for the kind of future that was beyond his own imagination. His impatience was not just with his son but with everyone. He also felt that he would have treated Neel in the same way even if he were not his son. Finally, the year ended. Neel passed by a hair's breadth. Gaonkar Master whispered to Narayan Master that he had had to give Neel grace marks in mathematics. 'No need,' raged Narayan master. 'Fail him if you want.' Understanding that the rage was directed against him, Gaonkar Master grumbled. That year Narayan Master retired.

During his farewell ceremony, he sat down without being able to finish his speech. Even Neel felt bad for his father that day.

After retirement Master began to give free tuitions to the children in the neighbourhood. In his free time he would pick up a shovel and spade to clean the backyard, or repair the roof. Now that he was always at home, he asked Savitrakka to stop coming and took over the cooking himself. When Neel returned from school, he threw his bag in a corner and ran to play cricket in the fields.

Until the tenth grade, whenever Neel asked for help, his father would tutor him. But now, rather than shouting at him about his grades, Master paid more attention to keeping the house clean, scrubbing all the clothes with bar soap, putting the books into neat piles, sweeping the house two or three times a day. If Neel uttered a lie, the earth and the skies would join together. 'You have to hold up the world by yourself. Be strong, be strong!' Master screeched as he hit his son. Exceeding everyone's expectations, Neel got a first division in the school-leaving examination. In spite of knowing that this in itself didn't amount to much, Master made arrangements to send Neel to a college in Ankola. How he began to pay more attention to his studies after Appa retired was a mystery even to Neel. He wielded the cricket bat like a lone warrior and approached his exams in the same way. Maybe he had become a better student because his father had stopped hounding him. During the summer holidays, his father sent him to Dharwad to stay with his younger aunt. If the aunt had showed any interest, Master would have enrolled Neel in a Dharwad college. But she showed no interest at all. Narayan Master muttered that everyone had their reasons. 'We should not become another reason for them,' he said mysteriously to Neel.

As college began, Neel noticed that his father was becoming gentler. He set aside his peculiarly emotionless behaviour and talked openly to Neel. Whatever the boy said he would listen to very carefully without missing a word. For Neel this was not easy to digest. Even though he could have stayed in a hostel at Ankola, he began to travel up and down from Hiregutthi. It's not as though he took the decision thinking his father would be alone at home. But that's how Master saw it, and kept telling him, 'Stay in Ankola if that's easier for you.' But Neel kept commuting. Except during the exams, when he stayed with a friend in his kholi. As though having taken up a new vocation, Master began to do all he could in the service of Neel. If Neel and his friends came home during his tuitions, he would send the children away so they wouldn't disturb the bigger boys. He quelled his enthusiasm for giving lessons. He washed Neel's clothes regularly. When Neel's friends came over, so as to not trouble them, he would take his bicycle and go off. Neel felt this behaviour wasn't natural. But how could he bring it up?

Master had never been inside a college, although he had acquired strange-sounding certifications that were common in the Bombay Presidency region. After entering college, Neel had moved out of the range of his father's authority. Or was it Master's aging and his retirement that was making him loosen his hold? Sitting in his armchair, the old man began to think again about his desire to make his son an unbeatable warrior.

Although he couldn't give him anything of significance, he could at least behave in such a way as to not obstruct him. He wasn't yet certain about the source of his fierce anger, his obsession with discipline, and the concern with small and useless details. Were these intended to help him cope with a mundane routine? Whenever he sat in his armchair now, all the old issues would crowd around him like freshly scrubbed and sparkling brass vessels. They shone even more as the thoughts clashed in his head. *Wasn't it because of my anger that the older boy Madhukar ran off to the army? How did I have no feelings at all for him, my son, who has no space for me in his mind now? When Radha died after her illness, my uncaring nature reached a new height – why? What was it in my make-up that made me insensitive to my home, my children, my life as a householder? And it's not as if I pursued education and made the school central to my life. Wasn't this lack of caring related to my inner anger?*

Madhukar used to spit out in his letters, 'Our mother died because of your lack of responsibility. If you didn't want a family, why did you get married and why did you wash your hands of us? Please put Neelkanth into a hostel. Don't keep him with you and eat up his life.' Yes, his behaviour had the power to eat up someone's life. Perhaps Madhukar had strummed the right string. Marriage, relationships, the necessary interaction with other people, blood relationships, the family tree – his spirit felt hemmed in by all these and that's why marriage felt like a log tied around his neck. Is that what had bothered him all his life? With no friends and no connections with relatives, engaging only with lifeless ideals and lessons, had he done an injustice to his wife Radha? In the light of the evening sun, Master seemed to repent his past behaviour. When Madhukar left for the army he had thought it was a weapon launched at him to disturb his equanimity, and had turned furiously on Radha. When Radha had died on the way to hospital, it had not occurred to Master to call Neel, who was then in primary school. Madhukar, who came for the final rites, did not say a single word in the face of Master's helplessness. It was like pouring oil on fire. Little Neel faced his father's wrath alone. He began to run towards cricket and sport and away from himself, even as his father ran away from the world and retreated into himself.

Once, Neel went off to Karwar to a cricket tournament without telling his father. He couldn't return that night and only came back the next morning. A surprise awaited him. His father had not gone looking for him. He had calmly eaten and slept at the usual time and gone to the market in exactly the same way as always. Neel felt like he had lost a big battle.

Four years in college went past without any kind of obstruction from his father. When he was in his Intermediate year, a theatre company from Jamkhandi in northern Karnataka camped in Gokarna for the Shivaratri fair. In a pit dug in a field they had set out chairs and a tent. It was close to exam time. Neel started going there every night to see the play. It's not as though he had a troop of friends with him. He went alone, cycling. And came back at dawn. Through the jangling of the bell when the benediction was sung – '*vatapi gana*' – and the smoke of *lobhaan* Neel was transported to another world. Roadside scenes, trick scenery, scenes in which gods appeared on earth, peacock dances ... Basavayya, who played the foot organ, produced waves of music between the scenes when the stage went dark. Neel seemed to be under a magic spell. He took pride in exchanging a few words with the night-time actors when they sat eating fried bhajji at the teashop in the morning with sour faces. Instead of studying for his exams, Neel spent the entire fifteen days with the troupe. He even went around in the broken-down van to distribute handbills. And before Master got to know what he was doing, he had gone off to Sirsi behind the troupe.

Master's nervous system was being put to the test. Was it his youth that drew Neel to the theatre? Or was it that Master's control was slipping? Should he be worried about Neel going away? What if Neel's future was at stake? Should he go to Sirsi to fetch the boy? Or should he send someone? On the third day after Neel had left, Master went to Sirsi. He asked at the theatre company tent but got no information. He asked at the paan shop and the soda shop – no news. At this time Neel was travelling through the villages near Sirsi in the company van distributing handbills. Master wandered here and there too, all evening. Then he told the gatekeeper and the company owner, 'Neelkanth, my son, has come from Gokarna following your troupe. Tell him I was here.' Master didn't see any difference between Neel's escapade and the way in which, as a teenager, he himself had gone off with the Bharat Seva Dal. He had followed them up to Talaguppe without telling anyone he was going. Now he left the choice to Neel and returned home. This was enough to shake the boy. The next day he was back.

When Neel sat up studying at night, Master made tea for him. Morning and evening he checked the tyres of the bicycle and filled them with air. He brought from the market only the kind of fish that Neel liked. Neel could not understand Master's earnestness. He kept looking for reasons for his father's behaviour and his affectionate attentions which had now become a burden for him. He began to get angry. Master did not respond to these outbursts. He felt he had committed a grave injustice against his family and was now trying to make amends. If Neel asked angrily why he had stopped giving tuitions, he would start them again. If he asked him why he went to sleep so early, Master would try to stay awake longer. Master's unsolicited tenderness became a new chain for Neel. He tried his best to stay away from the house for as long as possible. One day Master called Neel to his side and explained, 'I'm not trying to do all this because I think it's my duty.' He couldn't understand why he said this, and Neel couldn't understand it either.

When Neel's BSc results were announced, Master was surprised at how happy he felt. But he was perturbed as to whether this happiness had something to do with the insecurity of old age. His disciplined self was shaken to the core by the thought that he was looking to Neel for security as his vision grew dim. He felt tired after drawing just four pails of water from the well, and found it hard to pedal the bicycle up even a slight slope. But if this were true, how could he fight against it? It was a blessing that Neel hadn't thought about it like that. Neel was pushing away the emotions that were coming at him as he saw his father melting like camphor in the fire of his repentance. But then there was the behaviour of Master when Neel went off with the theatre troupe or when he went to Karwar for the cricket tournament, a dispassionate attitude that went counter to Neel's calculations. Finally it boiled down to his own understanding of it, thought Neel. For all these comprehensions to become part of one's experience and then to result in action – if this were possible, humankind would have reached its highest point. Narayan Master's weeping while Neel's Mumbai bus rounded the corner was perhaps because of some guileless pain.

Setting foot on Planet Mumbai brought Neel into contact with its qualities, its smells, its responses, which turned him into a rolling stone. He became so smooth that the grammar of the city slid off him as soon as it touched his body. Between the day and night shifts at the factory and the business-like conduct with his colleagues and his relatives only in name, he did not have the time to fight against the routine He forgot dates. Once in fifteen or twenty days he remembered his father. Gokarna and Hiregutthi would come to him only in his dreams. Once a month, when he sat down to write a postcard, 'Dear Appa', just during those ten minutes he seemed to be in a vacuum, liberated from everything else around him. From North India would come Military Madhukar's letters: 'Mumbai, beware, don't trust anyone.' Once he suddenly visited Neel and on some pretext fought with the relatives with whom Neel lived. This put Neel in an awkward situation. But the relationship that he feared might deteriorate began to improve as soon as he started paying for his lodging.

Neel, who had begun to adopt the formless, featureless character of the city suddenly began to understand his father's lifelong and stubborn attempt to develop these same qualities. The morning alarm, the three-minute shower, the ten-minute bus ride, the one-hour train ride, the eight hours of 'duty' and then again the one-hour train ride and the ten-minute bus ride, and the TV demon that killed all conversation in the house, this is how the day went. But just before falling asleep Neel tried to crawl into his shell like a tortoise, a formless, featureless shell. Sometimes he thought that his mother Radha, who he could now barely remember, had also sought such a retreat. And of course his father had always been like that. *Here I have the demon-like train and there my father has his bicycle. Here the world around me is as though it exists but doesn't exist, and it's the same for my father.* Solitude helped him meditate on his existence just as his father's disciplined routine did for him. His father's dedication was self-chosen, whereas Neel's daily routine existed below the level of consciousness.

In the midst of Mumbai's featurelessness, Neel began to melt at the thought of how his father had behaved during his college days. As he began to grow harder living in the city he thought tenderly about his father. Master had receded to the background of his emotionless city life.

One day Neel received a letter from his father. He wrote that an old neighbour from the neighbouring gully, Mahadev Ajja or Madevajja, was seriously ill and had to be brought to the Tata cancer hospital. He was bringing the old man himself. If possible come to the hospital on such and such a day. Not a word about when they were arriving or where they were staying. Neel did not bring up the topic in his relatives' house where he was lodged. On the day his father had mentioned, he took a day's leave and went to the Tata Hospital in Parel.

Until the afternoon he could not find them. In the OPD, in the radiation department – wherever one looked there were cancer patients – on benches, on stretchers, on wheelchairs – patients looking vacantly into the distance. He came back during the visiting hours in the evening and went through each ward looking at the occupants of the cots. He saw Madevajja sitting on a white cot in the general ward, coughing. As soon as he saw Neel, the old man made as if to stand up, then sat down again. 'Come come, sit sit,' he said, as if he were welcoming Neel to his house. 'Narayan Master has gone to buy medicines and to fix the tests for tomorrow,' he told him. On seeing Neel in that place full of illness, the old man's eyes sparkled with happiness and a sort of peace. Master came in and handed over a bag of medicines and the prescription to Neel, asking him to check if everything was correct. Neel did so. He looked at his father. The same dhoti he wore while cycling. A snuff-coloured shirt with a big pocket. A two-day-old beard. That night Neel stayed in the hospital. He and his father sat on the wooden bench outside the ward.

All night long Narayan Master told him about Madevajja's illness, how it had reached the second stage, how they might have to come back here after two months. Neel couldn't ask questions like, 'Why didn't his children bring him?' In between Master asked, 'How are you? How is your job? Pay attention to your job. If you do your job well, it's like winning the world.' Neel wasn't surprised that he didn't ask questions like 'Where do you eat your dinner? Do the people you stay with look after you properly?' Neel took his father out to the Irani restaurant just outside the hospital and bought him bread and bhaji. 'Mustn't give Madevajja any sweet lime. He'll get phlegm. Bring some apples tomorrow if you can find them,' said Narayan Master. The restaurant looked like it too had been stricken with a whitish pallor. It was a white that confronted the darkness outside. A white that absorbed all colours into itself.

In the midst of all this whiteness, father and son sat on the bench through the night. Neel drowsed where he sat. When he woke up, his father was not by his side. He could see him sitting next to Madevajja. When he too went to sit there, his father sent him off, telling him to get some sleep. Even though his father had not asked him to, Neel applied for another day's leave. 'Your work mustn't suffer,' said Master. 'I can manage here, but when it comes to the local language it's better that you're around.' The next morning Madevajja was subjected to a dozen tests. In front of each examination room were patients waiting on rows of stretchers. Some had barely weeks left to live, others had months perhaps. Outside the hospital building was a rose garden. On the large verandah of the hospital, the patients who could walk or move around in wheelchairs sat and looked out onto the street. Madevajja was tired and fell asleep. Neel and his father sat in the verandah. As it grew dark, the patients returned one by one to their beds. The shift changed for the nurses, wardboys and doctors. As though looking at a hotel menu, the new nurses checked the case papers and popped pills into the patients' mouths. Master did not eat that night. Neel and he went out to sit on the bench again. At some point Neel went out to buy bus tickets for the following day.

The night looked even whiter than before. Narayan Master took out the *Prapancha* and *Kaanada Vrittha* newspapers from his bag which he had brought from Hiregutthi and began to read them. Neel wandered around the wards. How meaningless it was to feel a sense of duty only towards professional colleagues and kindred. People who were not related to the patients – nurses and doctors – were battling death for them, visibly and invisibly, in a deeply committed way. Madevajja was a name on a list. His, Neel's, was also a name on some other list. So was Narayan Master's.

The hospital at night. The doctors who kept changing. The relatives who sat close by to wipe away the patient's phlegm.

Neel came and sat by his father again. If he had gone with the theatre troupe or if Madhukar had not gone into the army, what might have changed? If he strung all the events thus far into a simple narrative or a circular one, what cause and effect could he find and how did everything relate to Narayan Master, who had been living such a clearly defined life? If he felt the tug of duty now, he should consider it strictly accidental, thought Neel.

Around sunrise, Neel's father fell asleep where he sat. Neel helped him lie back on the bench and covered him with a small towel from the bag.

The next evening Neel helped Madevajja and Narayan

Master get into the Karwar bus. He bought some fruits for them to eat on the way. 'Next time I'll come to fetch Madevajja myself. Just write a letter,' he said. He did not have the courage to give his father the envelope of cash he was carrying in his pocket. When the bus left, Madevajja waved goodbye with the same sparkle in his eyes. Narayan Master was busy wrapping a scarf around Madevajja's neck. As Neel came out of the bus station, the tears came boiling up. Not knowing whether to suppress them or not, he began to walk briskly. He could not hold back his tears now. Near the traffic signal, when he was in the middle of a large crowd of people, he moved to one side and wept bitterly. As though realising this was making him feel lighter, not weaker, Neel offered himself up completely to the sobs that engulfed him.

Kondi
1989

Lanterns in the Rain

Prakash of Chikalwadi Chawl, full name Prakash Ramdas Kulkarni, about twenty years old, had a few months ago obtained fifty per cent in the school-leaving examination, making his chawl proud. Every Divali, Prakash made sky lanterns for everyone in his chawl. For his grandfather Nana, who was past seventy, Prakash had fashioned a walking stick out of a branch he had found on his treks. The same Prakash had just been arrested, handcuffed and taken away in a blue police van. His father Ramdas hadn't returned from the night shift. His mother Tara had gone on her errand of taking the children from the neighbouring apartments to school. Only Nana was in the house. He was tying thread around the broken arm of his glasses when the police came. He sat up and asked weakly why they were arresting the boy, where was their warrant. Even as he objected, the van had driven off.

When Nana had left his small town and come to live in his son's kholi, Prakash had been eight or nine years old. His sister Shakoo was about five years older. Nana had never dreamt that he would sell his little house with its backyard and have to live under the roof of his only son. He used to draw water from the well to tend his vegetable garden. Nana, a freedom fighter, cooked for himself after his wife Kumuda died. He never showed his freedom fighter certificate to anyone. When the other freedom warriors rushed about to encash their patriotism, Nana continued to draw water from his well and tend his plants. Suddenly, one day, his son Ramdas arrived. 'The children are growing up. My job isn't stable. I need money urgently. What will you do here alone? Let's sell all this. You can come with me.' It was as though Ramdas had sat on his chest. Nana, who never spoke much, said it was all right with him. In just a week the entire transaction was completed. When Nana said he would stay on there in a rented house, Ramdas shouted: 'Will you throw our family's self-respect into the streets?' As though he realised that his son was only shouting at himself, Nana quietly left with him.

Tara and the children were not happy that Ramdas had dragged his father to the city to live in their one-room kholi. 'What's all this about self-respect? He could have lived happily in his town. Why did you bring an old man to this prison?' grumbled Tara. Shakoo, who had dropped out of school, had begun to talk exactly like her mother. She too expressed her irritation. There was only one iron cot in the room. Ramdas used to sleep on top, the children underneath, and Tara to the side. Now they had Nana on top, and husband and wife underneath. Since Ramdas used to work the night shift, he would often sleep on the cot in the daytime. With the money he got from selling Nana's house, the first thing Ramdas did was to buy an iron cupboard. It had been Tara's longstanding dream to have a cupboard. She now put all the contents of her many bags and pouches, and all the clothes from her trunk, into the cupboard. She would do this only when there was no one else in the room. She would never open the cupboard in front of anyone else, not even an inch. Because the water from the *mori* might spoil the cupboard, Ramdas moved it near the door. But when he realised it could be accessed by anyone from the chawl who was going past, he moved it further back into the room, this time covering it with a cloth. There had been a huge discussion about whether or not to buy a cupboard with a mirror. Ramdas argued that it would be a thousand rupees cheaper to get one without. 'This is a house with a daughter who's growing up. You want her to use only a hand mirror?' argued Tara. Finally they bought a cupboard with a mirror. Shakoo sat up day and night and stitched the curtain for the mirror. Learning how to embroider from her friend, she added an Air India maharaja on the curtain. Since it was her first effort, the maharaja looked as though he would tumble down any minute.

Tara took from her father-in-law the freedom fighter certificate he kept folded inside a bag and had it framed. She then put it inside the cupboard, saying, 'Never know when this might come in handy. Let's keep it where we can find it easily.' When Chauthi, Navaratri and Divali came around, the cupboard was opened for the children. From inside a small steel box, Tara would take out tiny rings and necklaces for them to wear. But they were allowed to wear them only inside the chawl. Now Shakoo's new hair clips and anklets went into the cupboard. Ramdas gave them his insurance policy to keep inside.

Except when they were eating or sleeping, if there were more than two people in the room, it felt very crowded. As for Nana, he felt stifled even when he was alone. Which is why he preferred to sit on the steps outside.

He would wake up and fetch milk in the morning, read the neighbour's newspaper, check Prakash's homework. Some evenings, when he went for a walk, he would stop at the Irani restaurant for a cup of tea. Nana was upset that Shakoo had been taken out of school. He would talk about it whenever he got a chance. When Nana saw Shakoo learning how to cook or mend clothes, or gossiping about others just like her mother or expressing astonishment in an exaggerated way like grown-ups, he would feel very bad. 'There's no wealth greater than education,' he would say, and Tara would raise her voice to say sarcastically, 'And I suppose you've set aside a big sum for their education!' Shakoo laughed at that, and Nana – feeling deeply hurt – left the kholi. Tara and Shakoo used words that pricked only when Ramdas was not around. But Prakash always hung around his grandfather, saying Nana, Nana. Sometimes the women would make bhajiyas and eat them in Nana's absence, having kept some aside for Prakash and Ramdas. When Ramdas came home after his shift and ate the snacks, he was too tired to ask whether they had given some to his father.

When Prakash came back from school, he loved to tell Nana all about his day. He was enthused by Nana's interest as he listened to the boy with his eyes and ears open. But Shakoo hated Nana like poison. Shakoo loved to tie her chunni in various styles and admire herself in the cupboard's mirror. She tied her hair in different ways and pouted as she figured out which one looked best. If she was satisfied, she would go out and walk up and down the chawl. Sometimes she would close the door and dance a little to the song coming from the radio. With Nana's arrival, all of these activities had been obstructed. So she flared up against him at the slightest provocation. If he asked her a question, she never gave him a straight answer. Once, when Nana was eating his dinner, Shakoo tossed a chapati at his plate from high above. Hurt, Nana got up to leave. 'No problem if you want to get up,' said Tara, 'but don't waste that chapati. Eat it before you leave.'

If Prakash had to do some craft work for his school, Nana always helped him. This Divali, Prakash was particularly excited because Nana had made a number of old-style lanterns with six corners. All the children of the chawl came to see these. Nana had used some wheat paste he had prepared at home. From that day onwards, Nana became the sky-lantern guru of the chawl. He made lanterns for every home. People brought him their paper, bamboo sticks and paste. The children stood at the ready, holding scissors and paper. Even the older children came to see this lantern workshop. Shakoo and Tara found the commotion unbearable. One day Shakoo began to bawl, claiming that the older boys were coming there just to look at her. So Nana went to sit in someone else's kholi to continue the lantern making. One evening, those people asked Nana to stay for dinner. 'Go, go tell the whole town that your daughter-in-law doesn't feed you,' screamed Tara. But Nana refused to get angry at her words. He always remembered Tara's enthusiastic attitude when she, as a small-town girl, had married Ramdas, dreaming of a happy and comfortable life. Poor thing, what a life she led now. Nana felt only pity when she flew into a rage. Even selling his home and yard had not brought them any comfort, he thought, feeling sad. Although he wanted to do something for the children, only Prakash would come near him.

Shakoo was growing up, ripening. Nana did not like the way the chawl boys tried to touch her or passed comments about her. The little children of the chawl would come over to get Shakoo's help for their homework. She called it 'tuition'. The money she got for it went into a peppermint candy box which she placed in the cupboard. Shakoo would deliberately choose to give tuitions when Nana was having his siesta. Just when he was drowsing off, she would shout: 'Nana, out!' Trembling, the old man would go and sit on the steps of the chawl in the hot sun, nodding off. Sometimes, even if the tuitions were done, Shakoo would not call him in, and would lie down on the cot herself. When Ramdas did not have a factory shift and was at home and awake, he would bang out applications for the neighbours for a few paise on his broken-down typewriter. Nana would say to him, 'You should get some rest, my boy.' And Ramdas would reply: 'Can't do that. This is a kholi with a girl child. We need every paisa I can earn.' Nana helped him with small tasks, arranging the blank sheets neatly, rolling up the typed applications and putting a rubber band around them, handing them to the customer if Ramdas was not around. Whenever Ramdas came home late, he would ask, 'Has Nana eaten?'

Prakash treated Nana with great care. He took him to see the science exhibition at his school. When Nana's glasses developed a crack on one side, Prakash brought it to his father's attention. When he went on a trek with his schoolmates, Prakash found a strong branch that he shaped into a walking stick for Nana, who then applied some varnish on it to make it shine. Shakoo would mock her brother: 'Pakya, has Nana set aside a special bundle for you?'

One day Prakash came home from school, saying, 'Tomorrow there's a celebration at the August Kranti Maidan. Our teacher told us. We're all going as volunteers. I heard they'll be honouring all the freedom fighters. You should come too, Nana, maybe they will honour you too.' Nana was flustered, but thought it would be a good idea to see such an important place from where Mahatma Gandhi had made his Quit India speech. The next day, both Prakash and Nana woke up at dawn and got ready to leave. Tara, who worked in the milk booth, was also up. When Nana went to the cupboard to retrieve his freedom fighter's certificate, thinking it might be a good idea to carry it, Tara flew into a rage. 'No one except me should touch this cupboard,' she shouted to Prakash. When the boy said that the cupboard had been bought with Nana's money, Tara hit him on his mouth. Then she pulled out the certificate and thrust it roughly into Nana's hands. 'If they give you anything there, don't refuse,' she said. Nana felt very tired. 'You go, my child,' he said, and sat down. Prakash did not know what to do. 'No, no, you should absolutely go!' said Tara, pushing them both out. Nana worried that his certificate, his walking stick and Prakash by his side were not enough to get him to the Maidan. He stopped at a nearby circle, saying, 'Prakash, I'll wait here for you. When you're coming back home, just fetch me from here. Don't tell anyone I didn't go with you.' He sat down on a small stone bench. Prakash was already late, so he rushed off in his uniform, weaving through the traffic. To Nana it felt as though all the vehicles on the street were heading to August Kranti Maidan. He sat with his plastic folder on his lap, like a patient holding an X-ray in a hospital, his eyes half-closed.

Prakash's only friend was Qureshi, whose father owned a shoe shop near Prarthana Samaj. Once in a while, Prakash would go to Qureshi's house to study. It made him happy, seeing the spacious rooms, the electric fans, the tea in a flask. One day, it got very late and so Qureshi's older brother Babloo dropped Prakash home on his scooter. Prakash felt he was in another world. Sitting on the pillion seat, he felt he had sprouted wings. That night he dreamt that he was riding on the scooter. Somehow he should earn enough money to buy a two-wheeler. But how? *Nana keeps badgering me about school. Appa is slaving away at some job and then types out applications for a few paise. Shakoo is busy shaping her eyebrows with a thread. My Aayi seems to think her life is inside that cupboard.*

Between sleeping and waking, the sound of the scooter's engine starting crept into Prakash's dreams. He didn't notice something else that came with the scooter. Babloo had filled his eyes with Shakoo's presence and took every opportunity to drop Prakash home. Shakoo, too, would dress up and wait for the scooter to arrive. Slowly Babloo began to come over when no one was home. Until noon, Tara would be busy ferrying children to school, and then at three p.m. she would bring them back. Babloo came to the kholi like a stealthy cat at that time. The two behaved as though Nana was not present. One day, Nana came and sat outside. He thought they might feel embarrassed and come out also. But they banged the door shut loud enough to break Nana's heart. Without realising what he was doing, Nana began to bang on the door, shouting, 'Shakoo, Shakoo!'

Nana could not help but tell Tara about what had happened. Tarabai felt as though the cupboard had fallen on her. She waited for Ramdas to come home, requesting Nana not to go anywhere. When Ramdas returned, Shakoo had gone to her friend Shubha's house. Tara blurted out the whole story, mocking Nana's inability to stop this unfortunate incident from happening. 'He was right here, but couldn't do anything,' she said.

'You are the one responsible,' said Ramdas. 'You're the one who took her out of school.'

'She would have done far worse things in the name of going to college,' said Tara.

All of them felt helpless, not knowing how to face the situation. Just then Shakoo came in, with a sort of adamant glow on her face. The elders fell silent – not knowing what to say, afraid that Shakoo would reveal far worse things if provoked. Watching this inquiry as it proceeded silently, Prakash burst out: 'All my fault! I should never have brought that *chutiya* Babloo here.'

Hearing this swear word from his son for the first time, Ramdas thought he would go mad. Dragging Shakoo by her arm and bringing her to the calendar gods, Ramdas thundered, 'Tell us! How much cow dung have you eaten?' Tara began to hit her head against the cupboard's mirror. 'Aayi, Aayi,' Shakoo wailed, trying to slip out.

'Where are you off to?' yelled Ramdas, pulling her back into the kholi. She fell on the bed and began to weep loudly. It was only when Ramdas shouted, 'Don't break the mirror, you donkey!' that Tara stopped banging her head on it.

As Prakash's school-leaving examination approached, the kholi took on a different demeanour. Nana and Tara sat up with Prakash in turn. Tara stopped going to her evening job. Nana gave Prakash warm water to drink, putting glucose into it from time to time, making sure the boy didn't drop off to sleep. 'You must bring fame to the chawl,' Nana would say. 'Who cares about fame? As long as he can stand on his own feet,' said Tara again and again.

Because Prakash wasn't brave enough to quarrel with Qureshi's brother, he had a small fight with Qureshi instead and so couldn't go there to study anymore. Prakash's studying affected Ramdas's and Shakoo's sleep. So Shakoo stitched a few eye bands from black cloth, and anyone who wanted to sleep wore one. By about three in the morning, everyone except Prakash would have fallen asleep. Looking at them with the black bands around their eyes, Prakash felt afraid. They resembled homeless people sleeping on the footpath. As he turned out the light, Prakash wondered whether all those people sleeping in buildings and flats looked the same at this time of the night.

Finally, Prakash's exams were done. On the day of the final paper, Nana took him to the nearby Irani café and bought a cake for him with his favourite Thums Up. Watching the cars and scooters go by, Prakash said to Nana, 'I won't look for a job. I'll set up a business. I won't touch the feet of any son of a widow. I won't bow to anyone.'

Later they went to the municipal park. There were some daily-wage labourers lying under the trees. Children played with their ayahs, looking like rosy apples. And at every foot or so was an embracing couple. Hundreds of them. Embarrassed, Prakash said, 'Let's go.' As they turned to leave, the blue dress of a girl who was rubbing her face against her partner's caught their attention. It was Shakoo. Nana was worried that Prakash would recognise her, and he in turn was afraid that Nana might. But the boy didn't seem to be Babloo, who would have been recognisable by his long Sanjay Dutt hairstyle.

As Prakash and Nana entered the chawl, Nana said, 'No need to say anything at home.'

'No need to roam around the town because your exams are over. Look for a job now. No more studying,' said Tara.

Just then Shakoo came in, in her blue dress. As soon as he saw her, Prakash uttered a strangled cry and made as if to hit her. 'Look at you! It's because of you that I'm not allowed to study further!' he said. Without mentioning the park, he kept saying, 'I know everything, I know everything!'

'What do you know, what do you know, are you the one who feeds me?' shouted Shakoo as she put away her bangles.

Prakash got busy with polytechnic admissions, enrolled in the employment exchange, tried to find a job in the cassette library. Next to their chawl the temporary workshop for making Ganesha idols for Chauthi was set up as usual by Harchande Master, who came from Ratnagiri every year and made hundreds of idols from May to August, returning to his hometown after the festival. Prakash began to assist the Master in kneading mud for the idols, pouring it into moulds and other such tasks. Nana went too, to help make cardboard flowers and swords, and to prepare *trishuls* from tinsel. Slowly Prakash became adept at touch-up work on the ears, eyebrows, legs and arms, fixing the trishul between the fingers and affixing the modaks. Prakash worked there day and night. Harchande Master began to give him tasks that were more demanding, such as fixing the garland around Ganesha without breaking the elephant trunk and painting the shades on the pleats of the idol's dhoti.

Around this time, Prakash got his exam results. He had passed with a Second Class. Nana was even happier than Prakash. He went from kholi to kholi with the news, carrying powdered sugar to distribute to the neighbours.

Prakash had a new idea. Just as Harchande Master did his Chauthi business, why shouldn't he set up a business for making sky lanterns for Divali and kites for Sankranthi? Perhaps he could take up the decoration of pandals for Navaratri too. Enthused by his idea, Prakash hoarded the money Harchande Master gave him instead of giving it to his mother. Not heeding Nana's advice, Prakash insisted that this money would be his first bit of capital. Let those who had money spend it on festivals. If he could feed himself because of other people's celebrations, why not? Why should he fall at anyone's feet?

He began to buy coloured paper, bamboo sticks and paste. As soon as work on the Ganesh idols was finished, Prakash got to work cutting paper for sky lanterns. 'Who gave you the money?' Tara kept asking, but Prakash never gave her an answer. Instead, he worked like one possessed. Nana devoted his entire day to him. They set up their workshop in the space behind the chawl. One day, Ramdas, perhaps spurred by Tara, came there after his second shift and roared: 'Is this why we made you study until the tenth grade? To sit beside the public toilet and lose your self-respect making lanterns?' When Nana tried to mollify him, Ramdas told him to be quiet. 'You are the one who's put ideas into his head.' Scolding him thus in front of their neighbours, Ramdas walked away.

Navaratri came closer. As the time for garba dancing approached, Shakoo's rushing around increased. This kind of festive dancing, with its opportunities for mingling with boys, for touching and looking, for losing oneself for nine whole nights, was for Shakoo like moving around in a dream. If the girls from the apartments wore two different sets of clothes each day for nine days, Shakoo wanted to wear at least three or four sets during the entire period. She began to get her clothes ready. She borrowed a dress from her friend Shubha. She stole the new pair of scissors Prakash had bought for his work and gave them to another friend in exchange for nail polish and lipstick. Prakash couldn't even complain about his missing scissors because Tara would then ask him where he had got the money to buy them.

Prakash now acquired a small diary and went around the lanes and bylanes collecting advance orders for Divali. Concessions for group orders, higher rate for plastic paper – Prakash had a range of options. He collected five rupees as advance for each lantern and wrote down the details neatly in his diary, on the first page of which he wrote: 'Prakash Kandeel Industries Limited. Office: Chikalwadi Kholi No. 12; Office: Chikalwadi Backyard'. Every now and then he checked the orders. Checked to see whether the balance he had was correct. He had orders for five hundred lanterns. As people began to wander around looking for garba dances, Prakash's single-minded focus was on making lanterns.

Ignoring her parents' opposition, Shakoo started going boldly to the garba events. She would put on her make-up and announce that she was going out with her friends. She said that the brother of one of her friends had a taxi. That they went in that taxi to the garbas in different suburbs of Mumbai. One night, when she had not returned till two a.m., Ramdas, who was still typing away, woke up Prakash. Although the boy said that the dancing would go on until dawn and that Shakoo would probably return in the morning, his father told him to go look for his sister. The streets were silent. From a couple of distant pandals they could hear music. Borrowing a bicycle from their neighbour, Prakash set out to check the venues where the dancing was still on. Tara, who didn't like to show her concern in front of others, was standing by the roadside waiting for her daughter. In the commotion, Nana woke up. 'She must have stayed back in a girlfriend's house.

Don't worry so much,' he said. Ramdas thought of going to their neighbours' houses and talking to Shakoo's friends, but Tara stopped him. The entire chawl was asleep. The time for the milk vans was coming close. 'Don't go to the milk booth today,' said Ramdas to his wife. 'Oh god, I hope Shakoo comes home before dawn, before people wake up. If anyone finds out she was away for a whole night, our self-respect will be in tatters.' Tara went out into the street again and stood clinging to the pole at the bus shelter, panting a little. As though remembering something, she came back into the kholi and said, 'No one should utter a word about any of this in front of others.' Once again she dashed out and clung to the pole at the shelter, still panting.

Prakash returned, having cycled all over their neighbourhood. He had even gone to Babloo's house, where Babloo's father had laughed and told him: 'Tell your father not to let your sister into the street.' 'Where will she go?' said Tara. 'She'll come to get her ring and her necklace and her tuition money.' Just then Shakoo's friend Shubha from the neighbouring chawl came over and handed a note to Tara. Tara opened the note and read it. 'I have married the man I wanted. I am fine. No need to worry about me,' Shakoo had written. 'She's dead! My daughter is dead!' Tara began to scream, beating her chest in anguish. 'All because of you!' she said to Nana and Ramdas, thrusting her clenched fists at them as though throwing a curse. Ramdas sank down, his blood running cold. Nana said to Prakash, 'Ask that friend of hers where your sister is. Let's go and see her.' Ramdas suddenly came to life. 'No, let her not step into this house again.

Don't you dare go near her, *khabardar*.' 'I won't let that creature spoil my chance of overtime,' he added, pulling on his shirt and dashing off to the factory.

They came to know that Shakoo was living in a hut near Kurla and that her husband had a taxi. They had met during the current garba season. In two days she had decided to marry him and had run away that very night. It was rumoured that her husband had links to the Dawood gang. If anyone comes to take Shakoo away I'll set him on fire, he was supposed to have threatened.

Bits and pieces of news floated in the air like scraps of paper. 'She is dead to us,' said Tara loudly as she went about her daily work. Prakash felt a sense of defeat. How helpless we've become, he thought. When Nana told him to go and do his work, he thundered: 'Yes, yes. Isn't it Shakoo's wedding? I'll light lanterns in all the lanes of the neighbourhood!' In a way, Prakash felt jealous of Shakoo's grand exit from her home to get married. How did she have so much courage?

Ramdas came back from work in the evening. 'Your daughter didn't even give us the good fortune of conducting her wedding properly,' he said, as he began to weep. As though embarrassed by her husband's weeping, Tara opened the cupboard and looked at the gold ornaments in the steel box. 'Why bother shedding tears for her?' she asked. 'This wasn't to be her lot, the whore.' She banged down the box on the shelf as she uttered the words. She picked up the pair of new bedsheets, pillow covers and bedspread that had been kept aside for Shakoo and threw them on the floor. 'Don't wrinkle them, you harlot,' shouted

Ramdas. Prakash picked them all up and folded them again. Nana seemed not to know who and where he was. In the midst of all this uproar, Shakoo appeared holding a plastic bag with half a kilo of apples, wearing a gold-bordered sari, flowers in her hair, and a *mangalsutra* around her neck.

Everyone was left open-mouthed. Ramdas made as if to hit Shakoo, but when Tara stopped him, he dropped down on the cot. Tara was undecided as to how she should treat her daughter, who had so shamelessly gone away and just as shamelessly come to the house the next day with her mangalsutra.

Meanwhile, the news that Shakoo had arrived spread like a bad smell and a small group of people gathered outside the house. Wisely, Tara shooed away everyone, saying, 'She'll come to your houses later.'

Eating one of the apples she had brought, Shakoo said curtly, 'I've come to take my things.'

Nana asked, 'Why did you come alone, my child? Why didn't you bring him too?'

'He doesn't have time to come just like that,' replied Shakoo. 'His taxi is in the airport line. If he gets the right customer, he could make thousands in just one trip.'

Shakoo moved to a corner of the house and started folding her clothes and thrusting them into a bag. A half-used bottle of nail polish, face powder, sticker bindi, she grabbed them all. Tara, who was looking at her carefully, shouted, 'You will get nothing from the cupboard.'

From where he was lying on the cot, Ramdas said, 'Give her her tuition money. We don't want even a paisa of her earnings.'

Tara examined Shakoo's gold-bordered sari as the girl bent over the mori to splash water on her face.

'I'll go and visit Shubha,' said Shakoo, stepping out.

'Not only is she eating cow dung, she's come to smear it all over our faces,' said Tara.

Nana said softly, 'Give her whatever is hers. Let her live happily with her husband.'

'Cheh cheh, you think I'm mad? We don't know anything about her husband. If he throws her out on the street tomorrow, who's to look after her? Let the money stay here. It can be her hard-times fund.'

In a tired voice, Ramdas said as he tried to sleep, 'I have a night shift. Don't make so much noise.'

A little later Shakoo came back with a group of women. Some of them made lip-smacking sounds. 'Tara, you must give us some sweets. What a wonderful son-in-law you got, without wearing out your slippers.' They surrounded Shakoo, who was sitting on the floor, touching her sari and caressing her chin as they talked to her. Tara watched closely as Shakoo's sari pallu shifted and various ornaments made themselves visible and the women pulled at each one to look at it more closely as though in admiration. Tara felt her blood boil. She began to sob as she washed the kitchen mori. When the women had melted away, Tara said, crying loudly, 'What I couldn't get from forty years of struggle you managed to get in a single night, and you've come here to show it off!' When Ramdas tried to shush her, she said, still weeping, 'Marrying you has spoiled my whole life.' She splashed mugfuls of water over her head and face.

'I'm off,' said Shakoo, standing up. Nana said, 'Have your dinner and go. Or go tomorrow.'

Ramdas said, 'Leave your address behind. When one of us dies we'll know how to inform you.'

Shakoo pulled out a piece of paper from her purse and left it by the side of the radio. As she began to put on her slippers, Tara said, 'Don't leave this house alone in the dark. Prakash will take you wherever you want to go. Don't walk alone in the dark.'

As though suddenly remembering something, Shakoo went to the cupboard and turned its handle. Tara tried to keep it shut by pressing her back against it and grabbed Shakoo in an embrace so as to push her away. Unable to stand it any longer, Ramdas started slapping them both. Nana ran out to the back of the chawl to call Prakash. By the time Prakash arrived, several people had gathered in front of the kholi. Shakoo was coming out, sobbing, clutching her bag. Although he was not wearing his sandals, Prakash went after her. Nana also went with them. When they had gone a short distance, Shakoo turned and spat in the direction of the chawl and ran across the road, jumped into a taxi that was waiting there, and vanished. Prakash stood looking in the direction she had gone. When Nana put his hand on the boy's shoulder, Prakash began to cry, 'Nana, this wretched whore has spoiled our name and destroyed my business!'

By the time they returned to the kholi, Ramdas had sat down to eat. 'Did you get to see his face?' asked Tara. 'What's he like? May he rot in hell for taking a chawl girl and putting her into a hut.'

Nana refused his supper and began to cut paper flowers for the lanterns. Prakash had dinner and went to his workplace. The sound of thunder could be heard faintly in the distance. Prakash's heart began to beat rapidly. He came running back. 'Nana, it looks like there might be rain. The lanterns will get wet. What should we do?'

'Let's put them in the common verandah,' said Nana. Panting, the two of them began to carry the half-finished lanterns into the chawl.

'Untimely Navaratri rain,' grumbled Ramdas, as he picked up an umbrella and went off to work.

The chawl was filled with Prakash's lanterns. To those who expressed their irritation, he begged, 'Please, please, just for this one night.'

Leaving only enough room for people to move around, Prakash filled every bit of the available space with his handiwork. The chawl began to look like a factory of colourful lanterns. The rain came down heavily. People went to sleep instead of going out to play garba. As midnight approached, the rain became even more heavy. Drops of water were falling on the lanterns and making them wet. Having cut out as many flowers as he could, Nana went inside to sleep. Prakash sat sticking the flowers onto the lanterns with paste. One by one, the chawl's lights went out. A tiny bulb glowed in the verandah. In its weak light, the raindrops glistened. The footpath dwellers had pressed themselves against the compound wall of the chawl, waiting for the rain to stop. Prakash stopped his flower pasting and looked disbelievingly at the rows and rows of lanterns crowding the sit-out. Had he really made them all? Without a lamp at their heart, the lanterns looked innocent and helpless against the rain.

Inside the kholi Nana slept on the cot without a sheet to cover himself, as though at a bus stand. Below the cot slept Prakash's mother. The cupboard seemed to tower above his mother, as though stepping on her. Prakash's head began to spin. Without understanding what was happening to him, he went into the kholi. He groped in the box that held the puja materials near the photo of the family god. Picking up the key he found there, he put it into the cupboard's lock and turned it. Moving soundlessly, he opened both the doors so that the cupboard stood with its arms open, revealing its inner world in that silent night. Almost without knowing what he was doing, Prakash put on the main light and began to shake the cupboard violently. Startled, Tara woke up and stared without uttering a word. She could not figure out what was happening. The cupboard's universe was crumbling. Steel tumblers, plates, old clothes, Ramdas's wedding cap, Tara's wedding sari, Prakash's and Shakoo's childhood blankets, wooden toys, all of them came cascading down. The embroidered clothes that had been part of Tara's trousseau fell in heaps on the floor. Nana's freedom fighter certificate was stuck in a corner of the cupboard.

Waking up in a rush, Nana grabbed hold of Prakash, calling his name. Tara, who had got her voice back, started bawling, 'Haiyyo, haiyyo, he's broken our cupboard ... broken our cupboard!' The footpath dwellers who were waiting near the wall came into the chawl and stood around the kholi. Searching through the things scattered across the house, Tara shouted,

'Where's the steel box, where have you thrown the steel box?' On trembling legs, Nana came out and waved at everyone to go away. People came out of other kholis irritably and shouted at the footpath dwellers, making them retreat back to the road. Nana closed the door. As Prakash sat looking at his childhood toys, Tara began to slap him across the head.

Next morning, someone from the chawl must have complained to the police about Prakash. 'Today he broke his family's belongings, tomorrow he'll do the same to us.' A blue van came and took him away.

Nana ran out, waving his hands in the air, stumbling all the way to the main road. His sweet boy who had just returned from putting all the lanterns back in the yard, was he hallucinating that his Prakash had been dragged away by the police? Tara had gone to drop the school children. Returning from his night shift and hearing the news, Ramdas rushed with the Shiv Sena pramukh, Gadkari, to the police station. Tara came to know about Prakash when she was on the way back from her school run and rushed into the house beating her chest. Shaking Nana by the shoulder as he sat lifelessly, she yelled, 'You were here, weren't you? Why didn't you stop them? Why did you let them take my child? Set all your lanterns on fire!' Tara hit herself on the mouth as she shouted. Some women from the chawl poured water on Tara's head and made her sniff a crushed onion to bring her to her senses. 'These children have really worn me out,' Tara sobbed into the lap of a neighbour. 'Has Shakoo been informed? Maybe her husband can do something,' said someone. Tara signed to them as if to say that was not necessary.

It was long after noon when Ramdas came home. Tara gestured to him from where she lay to find out what had happened. Nana, who had been sitting on the doorstep, stood up to see if Prakash was behind Ramdas.

'It took this long to get him released. If Gadkari hadn't been there, the fool would have ended up in jail. He didn't open his mouth at all. The son of a widow didn't have the guts to show up here, so he ran away the moment we came out of the police station. He hasn't eaten anything since morning. How far can he run? He'll come home when he's hungry, to eat cow dung,' Ramdas said in a rush, breathing heavily.

As though he wasn't present to himself, Nana was shouting: 'No, no, why would he come? Why did you let the child go?' Before Ramdas could turn to him, the old man, with his dhoti coming loose, stumbling like someone who had just regained the use of his feet, ran into the street and towards the crowded market shouting, 'Prakash, Prakash.'

Prakasha Varsha
1992

News for Sumitra

It was already three months since Sumitra had come to live in the flat where she would finish cooking in a trice and then station herself by the window that looked out onto the street. In this Mumbai flat were her younger brother's son and two bachelor friends who shared the rent. It was not more than a small room, actually. Adjoining it was a kitchen and a tiny alcove for washing dishes.

Sumitra's nephew Sudhakar was around twenty-five. Working in an office somewhere. Of his two friends, one was Jose from Kerala, who worked the night shift in a factory, rising when everyone was going to bed and dropping into exhausted sleep while they were making merry. The other one's name she did not know. He worked in the sales and service section of an agency, and for weeks and months he would vanish. All of them used to eat out. They shared equally the rent, the newspaper bill, the electricity bill, and the contributions for the Ganesh festival and Navaratri. Sudhakar, who had a delicate constitution, got jaundice after eating out all the time. He didn't inform his family in Honnavar. Once he was well, he wrote to his father. As soon as his father heard about the illness, he panicked. Eating all that rubbish in hotels, he thought, and rushed off to Mundgod where his elder sister Sumitra lived, separated from her husband. After searching everywhere for her, he finally found her in a government-run home. With tears in his voice, he begged her to go to Mumbai and cook for his son. Arranging for her to travel with someone he knew, he sent her off to this *akhaada* full of bachelors.

Having separated from her husband a while ago, Sumitra had stayed on in Manchikeri. She moved to Sirsi and then to Siddapur for some time, and for the last five or six years she had been in Mundgod in a Janata home. This delicate woman of sixty could not remember how many of her years had passed in helping others, in raising their children, caring for mothers after childbirth, packing tiffin boxes for those going to work. Here, in Mundgod, in the police chawl near the public home, she told stories to the children, put to sleep those whose mothers had to go to work, read every word without fail of the *Vanitha* and *Ragasangama* women's magazines. She put her old-age pension of fifty rupees every month in a corner of her trunk, and spent it as and when she liked. It was not very difficult for her to respond to her younger brother's plea. In a cloth she tied up her two saris, her spectacles, a few issues of *Vanitha*, put the remaining toor dal, sugar and salt in small packets, put everything into the bag, pressed a lime to her nose to ward off motion sickness, and got on the bus to Mumbai.

She had no special bond with her brother's family. In fact, she didn't have any connection with any relatives of hers. Why would she have bonds with those who were too frightened to ask how she was or what she was eating after she separated from her husband? But she did have bonds with different families that were not related to her. In Siddapur, she looked after the eight-month-old infant of a teacher couple until he started going to school. Lawyer Kalghatgi, who lay in hospital after a stroke, didn't he recover after eating the food that Sumitra sent every day?

When her brother came pleading to her, Sumitra hadn't realised how old her nephew Sudhakar was. When the boy had been a child, he used to come to her house in Manchikeri to stay during the school holidays. Her husband, Ramakant, who worked in the Forest Department, used to come home a couple of times every month. Sumitra remembered that once Sudhakar had tied a strip of banana leaf around his head, adorned his face with a moustache made of mud, and danced around shouting alalala keeha as he performed Yakshagana for them both. For the little boy, her husband had spent a whole day making a crown from cardboard and adorning it with tinfoil and sequins, she remembered that too. His drinking and beating had not yet reached their limits then. Even though he was gone for months, when he did come home, he filled the place with enough rice and dal and dried fish to last for a while. That she did not bear children or that those she conceived left her body before the ninth month seemed to be of no consequence to him, as though her psychic wounds did not matter to him at all. By the time she figured out why he was even bothering to visit her, he would have put on a pair of ironed pyjamas, oiled his hair and combed it, and be gone, back into the forest.

Sumitra began to grow dahlias in the front yard, which she would give with a big smile to the girls who passed by on their way to tailoring classes. She would give jaggery and water to the schoolchildren who milled around during their interval, and read every word of all the newspapers and magazines that came to her neighbours' houses. Sometimes she wondered who was undergoing *vanavas*. Was it she or was it her Forest Department husband? All the children from above and below the ghats, from the families of all her brothers, loved to come to her house for the holidays. Calling her 'Kakoo Kakoo', they would play freely in her yard. Sudhakar used to beg his parents to let him go to Sumitra's house and would not leave until there were just two days left for the reopening of his school in Honnavar.

This same Sudhakar was now a neat young man earning a salary and shaving his beard. Sumitra felt affection for him. Seeing him clearly through her cataract-less eyes, she laughed within herself to think that he had his mother's face and only the beard from his father. He didn't yet show his father's bad temper but maybe that would emerge only after he was married; maybe it was lying in wait. He was a respectful boy. He always laid out the mattresses of his roommates and rolled out Sumitra's bedding in the kitchen after sweeping the floor. He had given her his bedsheet. But when she said she was used to sleeping with an old sari over her, he did not insist. 'Kakoo, should I bring that, should I bring this?' he kept asking. Sumitra began to cook with a feeling of fondness towards this boy.

With the arrival of Sumitra, there were some necessary changes in the grammar of the boys' routine. Throwing their briefs here and there, the posters of Dimple and Sridevi with suggestive areas pencilled in, the weekly drinking sessions, turning off the lights and seeing if they could spot anything special in the bedrooms of the building next door, the self-stimulation in solitude, all of these came to a halt. The room began to look like a man who's just left the hairdressing saloon, everything shiny but also a bit too clean.

Having reached the point where he could tell which hotel it was by tasting a morsel from his plate, Sudhakar's eyes misted over with pleasure as he sampled the food with the aromas of childhood cooked by his Kakoo on the little broken gas stove in that rented room. Although Jose could not feel the same excitement, he kept saying 'Simpal homemade food' with great enthusiasm. What the food did for Sudhakar was recall his childhood, the memory of which he thought he had lost in this big city. With the help of a woman who was his office colleague, he bought two flowery saris for his Kakoo. Touching a new sari after many years, Sumitra clutched them to her chest and sniffed them. 'Chheh chheh,' she said, 'You should just have got ordinary ones. How much did it cost you? And why two? Save one for your mother.' Afraid that she couldn't hold in her gladness, she quickly went into the kitchen.

Within a week, Sumitra got used to the ways of this place. Earlier, Sudhakar used to go sleepily at dawn to buy milk from the booth. Now Sumitra began to fetch it, leaving him to enjoy the dawn's sweet sleep for a while longer. In her spare time, Sumitra would wipe the fan's blades, or the dust from the windowsill. The maid was given only clothes to wash, and Sumitra took over the dishwashing and sweeping. When Sudhakar told her, 'Don't do that, Kakoo, it's quite a burden for you as it is, to cook for us', she replied, 'This is hardly housework. And I love to do it. When we were little, we used to do much more when playing house house.' 'And don't think I'm doing it because you brought me those saris,' she added, laughing. Sudhakar was pacified. Kakoo kept the saris very carefully. Said she would wear them only on special occasions.

Now she started going to the fish and vegetable market by herself. Where to cross the road, which fisherwoman had the freshest fish, which vegetable vendor engaged in shortchanging, which little shop one should buy bread from, Sumitra figured out all of this and walked boldly on the road amidst all the other women going here and there. From the man beside the garage who repaired plastic buckets with a heated iron rod to the cobbler who fixed the broken toe band of her chappal for just twenty-five paise, Sumitra felt full of pride and happiness at having grasped the secrets of this strange city. The waste bin of the house, which used to be filled with banana skin, empty incense-stick packets and cigarette butts, was now bulging with vegetable and onion peels and fishbones.

Once a month, the wife of the flat's owner, Jacob-bai, used to come by. There were two iron cupboards of the owner in the flat. She would open the locked cupboards that belonged to her, put things in and take some out. Her husband, Jacob, had been working in Dubai for the past fifteen years. He came to visit once in three years, put more money in the bank, and bought some more apartments. It was strange for Sumitra to see the wife going around collecting rent, wearing lipstick, bringing up her children by herself. She didn't feel there was much difference between them in terms of marital status. The only difference was that Sumitra, who had walked out of her formal marriage, was outside of any monetary arrangements. She felt sorry for Jacob-bai. The woman would say, 'The house has become clean after you arrived' and leave with the rent. She would not forget to check whether she had locked the cupboards properly. She was sure these cupboards did not contain children's old clothes or tiny socks. She suspected that they were packed with silverware and perfume bottles instead.

Now Sumitra began to run the household with great ease. She went now and then to matinee shows in the nearby cinema. On her way back, she would sit for a while in the Maruti temple near the municipal market. Several neighbourhood women used to frequent the temple, women who were living, often without choice in the matter, with their children to look after the grandchildren. Using her broken Marathi, Sumitra became friendly with some of them. Following their suggestion, she began to use Jose's little transistor radio to listen to the early morning abhangs from the Pune and Sangli stations. So as to not disturb the sleeping men, she sat with the transistor glued to her ear like someone listening to a cricket commentary. In that dawn, even before the birds began chirping, pressure-cooker whistles could be heard from several apartments. Hurrying to finish cooking, spreading their washed saris on the line in the balcony, packing the children's lunchboxes, powdering their faces, turning back as they ran to the main gate to shout, 'Put a lid on the milk that's on the gas stove', winding and fastening their watches as they hurried towards the station ... Sumitra felt a strange sort of excitement when she saw these young women. The sight of these spirited girls winding their watches as they rushed past energised her. There was no space in their lives for grievances. They spent two hours in the kitchen, at the most, to make food for everyone, and then tied their hair with a rubber band as they went on their way to work. Seeing these women, Sumitra felt that her generation had wasted their entire lives just being in the kitchen. But then she would be reminded of Sudhakar who drooled over her cooking.

When she first arrived in Mumbai, Sumitra could close her eyes and feel herself surrounded by the government home in Mundgod, the smell of the dahlias in Manchikeri, the forests in Siddapur. But now they had begun to grow indistinct. The old issues of *Vanitha* she had brought lay face down in a corner of the kitchen. Sumitra hesitated to touch them, fearing that she would be immersed in her Mundgod life again. When the next-door neighbour Gupte Aunty called her over to come and watch TV, she hesitated at first, but then began to go. Gupte Aunty was the same age as her. She had a sewing machine at home and took in saree fall stitching as well as beading work. Sumitra had her do the falls for the saris Sudhakar had brought. She insisted on paying Gupte Aunty, even when she refused to take the money.

One day Sudhakar received a letter from Honnavar. Written by his father. After asking about everyone's health, he related a piece of news from above the ghats. Sumitra's husband

Ramakant had passed away. 'Ramakant died somewhere near Dandeli. Excessive drinking had ruined his liver. We did not know anything about his death. The news came via someone else and not from our relatives. Maybe that's why it took so long to reach us. Do give this news to Sumitra.' This last sentence shook Sudhakar. Not having the courage to read it again, he thrust the letter into his pocket. He said he had some work and went outside. Although he tried his best to return late at night, Sumitra was waiting up for him without eating dinner. Seeing that he seemed depressed, she served him only what he asked for and did not force him to eat. Then she told him to go to bed, because she was going next door to listen to Gupte Aunty relating the story of one of the old TV serials.

Sudhakar could not sleep. What would this news mean to the woman who had left her husband fifteen or twenty years ago to eke out a living cooking in other people's homes, caring for babies and finally ending up in a government home? For someone who never uttered the man's name, and seemed to appear humiliated only when she had to sign the monthly pension form with her married name, what would this news mean to her? Bolting the door from inside, Sudhakar switched on the light and read the letter again. Deciding that his Kakoo did not need to hear this news, he put the letter into his pyjama pocket and went to sleep. When Sumitra came back after midnight, to prepare for the next morning she soaked avare beans and urad dal in two pots without making a sound, and then lay down.

Next day, when Sudhakar returned from work, Jose said

to him, 'Arre bhai, what a mess. Today Kakoo took out all the old newspapers from the attic and sold it for *raddi*. She must have also taken all the old beer bottles we had piled up behind the newspapers. The attic is empty now.' 'Don't worry,' said Sudhakar. 'Let her know what we do.' Just then Sumitra came in, saying, 'How much rubbish you boys had piled up! I got seventy rupees for it. More than my pension.' She took the money out of her purse and gave it to Sudhakar. 'These fellows who come to the doorstep to collect raddi always cheat with the weights. So I got the raddi-shop boy to come and take it from here, and sold it directly to the shop,' she said. There was no mention of the bottles. 'If your flat owner Jacob had come and checked the attic he would have been furious,' she laughed. Jose and Sudhakar left the house, saying they would get some fresh air.

Handling all those bottles in the attic started affecting Sumitra a little. For a second, she felt Ramakant himself had been in the house. She sat looking through the Marathi magazines Gupte Aunty had given her. She searched for those cartoons that did not have any words. Sudhakar came in and rolled out the bedding. Jose must have stayed down in the street to finish his cigarette. He would not listen to Sumitra when she urged him to smoke inside the house.

At night, as the two young men slept, Sumitra stood at the window as usual. She watched the men as they lay huddled under the sheets. Suddenly, the thought came to her that if she had borne children, she would have been a prisoner of Ramakant's forever. Even after the vehicles on the road had lessened, and even after the watch-winding women had turned out the lights, Sumitra kept standing at the window. It made her happy that the watch-winding women, in spite of being married and having children, kept their interest in what they wore, pleated their saris in different ways, tied their hair in different kinds of styles. A neighbouring woman, who was quite plump, got her husband to plait her hair tightly in an attractive new style, the Sagar Choti named after the Hindi film. Sumitra did not see any relationship between this enthusiasm and the daily grind of the household. Gupte Aunty's interest in reading also captivated Sumitra. The woman loved to read autobiographies and had read nearly five hundred of them. She told Sumitra that in Marathi, the autobiography was even more popular than the novel. Gupte Aunty believed that one could find something special in personal stories that weren't to be found in other types of writing.

When she was younger, said Gupte Aunty, her husband used to run after other young women. After each affair failed, he would come crying to her like a child with a broken toy and sink into her embrace. I had to look after this man as though he was recovering from typhoid, said Gupte Aunty, laughing heartily. Her company began to give Sumitra more solace than going to the Maruti temple. Perhaps if Ramakant had given her the opportunity, she would have put up with his drinking and beating and with his forest disappearances. He had never let out his secrets. When she tried to ask him where he went, he retreated as though she was attacking him. An animal fit for the Forest Department indeed. Counting trees in unnamed forests, writing numbers on those trees. One day, Sumitra declared: 'If all you want to do is give me a few paise as though you're paying taxes and write your name on the ration card, then don't bother coming. I'll look out for myself.' As though he was waiting for that moment, Ramakant went away and never came back. Who knew in what gypsy camp he was spending his days? After becoming friends with Gupte Aunty, Sumitra felt satisfied that she had given Ramakant his freedom and perhaps lessened his burden too.

Sudhakar kept the letter close to his chest in his shirt pocket, feeling shaky about the whole thing. He could not for the life of him remember what Ramakant Kaka looked like. He thought of the time when he was little and Kaka had made him a cardboard crown. He remembered going with Kaka to look for jackfruit to make chips, and Kaka climbing trees in the Hasanagi forest to pluck the fruit, tapping it to see if it was a good one, and then cutting it down carefully so that the sap didn't fall on the body, and carrying it down the tree on his shoulder. He also remembered that many years ago, they had gone to see the Honnavar chariot and Kaka had taken all the children of the family in a launch to see the Idagunji temple. He remembered the tender bamboo shoots he used to bring from the forest. If so many shards of memory were in him, how many more did Kakoo carry? Would this news trouble her or give her some relief? Sudhakar began to feel that not telling Kakoo wasn't right.

Perhaps it was thinking of Manchikeri that made him ask Sumitra to bring bamboo shoots from the market that day.

'Jose doesn't even know that bamboo shoots can be eaten. He's never tasted them,' said Sudhakar as he set out for his office. 'No problem. It's been years since I had bamboo shoots. And Gupte Aunty has never tasted them either.' He stepped out of the house but came back in again, and in full view of Sumitra, pulled out the letter from his pocket and left it on the table. He wanted Kakoo to read this letter that had been bothering him for these past two or three days.

Around noon, Sumitra went to the market and bought bamboo shoots. She thought them too expensive, but she bought them all the same. Jose had gone to sleep after his night shift. She peeled the shoots and soaked them in brine. She woke up Jose, gave him lunch, and then had her meal too. The afternoon sun was beating down on them. Jose turned on the fan and went to sleep again. Noticing the letter on the table, Sumitra wondered with concern what it might contain that had bothered Sudhakar so much. She picked it up and read it.

That evening, when Sudhakar returned home, Kakoo looked as though she had just had a bath. 'Jose just left,' she said. 'I've brought the bamboo shoots and soaked them. Can make the dish only day after tomorrow. Today I thought I would make tambuli but there's no grinding stone here.' She went across to Gupte Aunty's house to grind the coconut.

'Buy a grinding stone, boy,' she said to Sudhakar. 'This is a rented house, Kakoo. I'd have to carry it wherever I go.' 'Get married first,' said Sumitra. 'Then we'll see how you'll carry your bride from one house to the next,' she laughed. 'There's a lot of soap in the bucket still. Do you want to give me your pants and shirt for washing?' She soaked the clothes and went over to Gupte Aunty's for a while, closing the door behind her.

Sudhakar looked at the table. The letter was still there. Believing that it had played its role, he tore it and flung it into the rubbish bin. He had a long bath. That night, as usual, after Sudhakar went to sleep, Sumitra went and stood at the window. Sudhakar rolled over in his bed. 'What's there in that bottle? Just bring it over here, just once. Don't be afraid. I want to taste it once. I want to know what it's like,' she said. Sudhakar heard her but pretended to be asleep. As the noise outside receded, Sumitra lay down on her bed and covered herself with her old sari. She told herself that she should call Gupte Aunty over the next morning to watch her make the bamboo shoot curry. She got up, took the pencil hanging from the calendar with which she used to do her accounts and wrote on a small piece of paper, 'Bamboo shoots – Gupte Aunty', placed it on the lid of the pot where the shoots were soaking and weighted it down with a spoon. She turned out the light, covered herself with the old sari, placed her head on her arm, brought her knees up to her stomach, and slept like a baby.

Sumitregondu Suddi
1991

Forest of Disappearance

Hopping off hurriedly when the bus stopped at the signal and getting shouted at by the driver, buying a packet of biscuits from the tiny shop nearby and wending her way to her parents' place through the alley next to the garage, Kusuma felt incapable of grasping anything new. Under normal circumstances, she would have noticed all the changes in this factory workers' locality where she had grown up, and later she would talk to her mother Yamuna and her sister Poorvi about it: 'Arre, how did that Xerox shop get replaced by a hotel? Where did that Solapur woman go, the one who had a sugarcane-juice stand next to the factory? How come there's still a lock on Dilawarbhai's door?' In this way, she renewed her acquaintance with the neighbourhood, in a sort of artificial way. But today was different. Her little brother Chhotu, who had left home twelve years ago, whose name was actually Makarand although everyone called him Chhotu, 'little one', because he was born after Kusuma and Poorvi, Kusuma had received the news that very day that the boy had been seen somewhere close by. She had immediately applied for half day's leave and made her way to her family with this news that might stir the pot again. But as she approached the house her mind was blank.

Her father Parulekar had been a senior worker in the factory and thus obtained a one-room 'quarters' a long time ago. Poorvi and Chhotu had been born here. Kusuma still remembered the day when as a young child she came with the family in a tempo with all their belongings from Dombivli in the suburbs to this place near the factory. She remembered that the tempo driver wanted five rupees more and fought with her father, abusing him in a disrespectful way.

By the time they could figure out how to bring up the three children in this one-room house, Kusuma had been married off. Poorvi had a love match with a factory worker, Suhas Bhalekar, who eventually came to stay with them. Chhotu disappeared a few days before this wedding.

Twelve years ago was when it happened. Chhotu, who had just failed his pre-university exams, lurked in the house, shamefaced. If someone told him, 'Hey, Chhotu, why don't you go out?', he would rage: 'Don't call me Chhotu, call me Makarand. Just because I failed my exams doesn't mean you can boss over me.' Poorvi's wedding plans had just then been made. Kusuma, who had come home to help with the engagement ceremony, said to Chhotu, 'Why don't you find a temporary job somewhere? If you keep sitting in the house, you'll fall behind.' The mother took Chhotu's side. 'Just because you girls are clever doesn't mean you should be so scornful. You don't understand his problems. He's staying in his own house, na? What's your problem?' In this way Yamuna made her daughters shut up.

One afternoon, a group of five youths came in, dragged Makarand out, beat him with a stick, and hit him in the face in front of everyone until his jaw began to bleed. 'You cheat! Until you return the money you've taken, we'll come and beat you every week like this, in front of your neighbours, just wait and see!' The youths left, staring at Poorvi, Kusuma and their mother strangely.

Makarand had listened to someone's advice and taken a sum of about twenty thousand rupees from several people to start a business. He had invested it somewhere and now it was all gone. When the beating happened, Parulekar was away on the second shift. But when he came home and heard the details, he stood speechless, trembling from head to toe. He had come from the Goa border to Mumbai to earn a living. From selling combs in the local trains to assisting in a radio repair shop, then doing double duty in the factory so that he could bring up his three children. For the first time, he talked about all this in front of the children, sighing deeply, almost as if telling his story to strangers. To Poorvi, who had gone to the neighbour's to get some ice from their fridge for Chhotu's swollen jaw, he said, raising his voice, 'Who asked you to go? Aren't you ashamed to ask for ice for someone who's cheated so many people and destroyed the self-respect of this family?' Parulekar refused to take Chhotu to the factory's health centre. After dark, Kusuma and her mother put Chhotu into a rickshaw and took him to a doctor in Bhandup.

Whenever Parulekar spoke loudly about his family, about respect, integrity, money, he turned his face towards the open door so that everyone in the row of houses could hear him. The neighbours stayed behind that carefully drawn line, that *Lakshman rekha*, commiserating with him. As though everything else was fine, they began to invite Yamuna to watch the *Chhayageet* programme on TV. They peeped into the small home, looking seriously at the young man who sat crumpled in a corner. Now that Poorvi's wedding day was close, Parulekar began to tremble again. 'Poorvi's marriage shouldn't be stopped because of your escapade. I've used up all the money earned during my service for this wedding. If it doesn't take place, I'll be destroyed. You're not likely to do anything for us. Go away, get lost!' He threw Chhotu out at midnight. Helplessly, like a wounded animal looking for protection, Chhotu turned his face towards his sisters. Slowly, he stood up, took the t-shirt drying on the thick string near the door, pulled it over his dirty, faded jeans, and limped into the darkness. Feeling she was losing control over what was happening, Yamuna sank to the ground, sobbing, beset by unknown fears about her daughter's wedding. Only Kusuma stood at the door, watching her limping brother until he passed the last streetlight. Even in that light she could see that the un-ironed pale yellow t-shirt he had pulled on bore the mark of the string on its back.

That string mark on the yellow t-shirt never faded from Kusuma's memory. She came to her parents' house more often than she visited her husband's family. Near the factory gate, or near the ration shop, strangers would accost her parents. 'Where is your son? Where have you hidden him? We won't let you get away,' they threatened. A fear that ruined their sleep haunted the one-room house. At those times, Parulekar would shout: 'He is dead to us!' His voice was deliberately loud for his fellow workers to hear him. The wrath seemed to safeguard his status at the factory and Poorvi's wedding at the same time.

Chhotu is in Baroda. Someone met him in Kolhapur. When such rumours flew past like pieces of paper in the breeze, the four people in the small house sat up sleepless, without talking, under the dim zero-watt bulb. The little boy who was afraid to light firecrackers has now outgrown this house, thought Kusuma, yearning to see him. She was the one who had cuddled him and played with him the most when he was growing up.

Poorvi's future husband Suhas Bhalekar used this opportunity to put his weight behind the family's decisions. He passed an injunction: 'In this house there shouldn't be any sign of Chhotu. Not a single picture of him.' Photographs were removed from their frames. It was decided that the wedding would be solemnised through a simple Arya Samaj ceremony. The money saved through this simplicity, Suhas wanted to receive as a cash gift. On the day of the wedding, Suhas said theatrically that if Chhotu appeared, he would abandon the wedding mandap and go away. Poorvi made all her girlfriends stand outside the Arya Samaj venue to prevent Chhotu from coming inside if he did indeed show up. 'My marriage ceremony will be stopped if he comes. My life will be destroyed!' she said. After the wedding, Parulekar and Yamuna went away to Kusuma's house for two days to give the newlyweds some privacy. By the time they returned, Suhas was in the process of throwing out Chhotu's old canvas shoes, sweaters, books. 'I'm a working man and even I don't have such fancy stuff. Big hero, your pre-university-fail brother,' he taunted Poorvi.

'Then why do you use his aftershave lotion?' asked Poorvi. 'Hey, I'm your husband now. Use the plural when you talk to me,' screamed Suhas. In front of the Parulekars, he started throwing Chhotu's things out onto the street, shouting, 'Is that *gandu* smarter than me? Just because he studied in English medium, he was full of himself!' Yamuna picked up all the things, her lips pressed tight. That same day, Parulekar rented a room in distant Kalyan. So as not to upset Poorvi, they stayed for a couple of days more and then moved to their new home.

After moving to Kalyan, the incident with Chhotu began to look quite different to Parulekar. Issues such as his status and his name, which mattered so much in the factory quarters, did not seem as important in this new environment where he did not know anyone. He began to feel that his son-in-law's behaviour in Chhotu's absence had been rather harsh. Of course, Suhas was now struggling for his own status and position in the factory quarters. In the new environment of Kalyan, Parulekar began to think frequently about Chhotu. Was his twenty-thousand-rupee incident such a big crime? Parulekar's colleague Nair had said to him: 'What's the value of money in these times, Parulekar? What can you buy for twenty thousand rupees? Forget a house or a rickshaw, you can't even buy a motorbike for that much money. His plan went wrong. Poor boy. Forgive him.' Parulekar remembered this and told Yamuna what his friend had said to him. Yamunabai stayed silent. When she heard rumours like 'Chhotu is in Nasik' or 'He is in Daman', what gave her solace was the knowledge that he was somewhere. She would close her eyes and think of their family deity. She would also call Kusuma often and ask her to tell Poorvi to give their Kalyan address to Chhotu if he came.

One day, someone told Parulekar that he thought he had seen Chhotu in the canteen at Vasai railway station. Parulekar immediately got onto the local train, changed at Dadar, and went straight to Vasai. It was eleven at night when he alighted. There were at least four canteens across four platforms. He climbed up and down the stairs and peered into each one. There was not a single familiar face. Maybe he had grown a beard? Parulekar began to look for a bearded young person. As the night wore on, people closed their businesses and rolled out dhurries on the platform to sleep on. After midnight, there was very little traffic on the rails. Parulekar took out his small battery torch and began to shine it on the sleepers' faces as he walked up and down the platform. As he approached someone covered with a green blanket, his hand shook. Someone behind him shouted. The person under the blanket sat up. 'You *chuthia*, are you a homo or what?' he said, kicking Parulekar hard. A few days after this, Parulekar died.

Yamuna stayed on in Kalyan alone, although both Poorvi and Kusuma asked her to stay with them. Finally, one day, Poorvi pleaded with her: 'My husband has started drinking heavily. They've announced VRS in the factory. What if he takes this voluntary retirement and drinks away all the money? If you stay with us, maybe he'll be a bit more under control.' So Yamuna locked up her house and came back to the old quarters.

When told to give up the place in Kalyan, she said, 'What if Chhotu comes?'

Her drunken son-in-law began to say: 'No one needs to give me a lecture on how to behave. They should control their own son first.' 'Let that fraudster come here, I'll show him who I am,' he yelled, facing the door. One day Yamuna stood in front of him, shouting, 'Look at your own face in the mirror first, and then speak about my son. Learn how to earn properly and look after your wife, you useless man. How can you send your pregnant wife to work in a book bindery? What happens to your status then?' Yet another day she said to him: 'My son has become a big man, you know. He has a flat on the Western Line. He has people who work for him. He is not so hard up that he must come to your door. Don't you dare mention his name.' As she spoke these words loudly, what she said appeared to become real, to become true in front of her eyes. 'Hanh!' she said, almost like an incitement. Unseen, out of sight, perhaps Chhotu had indeed grown into the man she described.

Next morning, when Yamuna went to the milk booth, she saw that Tailor Gopichand's house was locked. Oh no, I had bought that *dhoop-chhaon* sari from his wife on instalments, and if they're now gone, how will I ever pay back the fifty rupees I owe her? What will she think of me? When Poorvi woke up, Yamuna confided in her. 'Don't worry, Aayi,' said Poorvi. 'Haven't Gopichand's children eaten at our place many times? Didn't the couple leave their kids here all the time when they were away? In any case, don't break your head over an amount like fifty rupees.' 'No, no, we must not keep track of how many meals a visitor has eaten,' said Yamuna, but somewhere within her, she felt her burden lessen. Like yesterday, when she said Chhotu was now a big man, what was wrong in believing that? Yes, he was rich now, he was living in comfort, he was generous. Yamuna felt her world transforming.

Kusuma's husband found a job in a catering company in Dubai and moved there. She herself got transferred to the Cash Section of her office. She was the only one in her family who read the day's newspapers. But one thing she didn't want to read was the obituaries. After she joined the Cash Section, she learnt to count notes swiftly, to twist a bundle of notes back and forth to get the staples out, and other such deft mannerisms associated with a bank teller. However, the bundles of notes made her weary and afraid. The gap seemed vast between the modest amount she received as salary, the four rupees she gave to the bus conductor for her ticket, and this abundance of bank notes. They were not the same substance at all. While she was looking through account books mentioning crores of rupees, she suddenly thought of Chhotu's twenty-thousand-rupee incident. How pathetic and guileless it seemed!

Kusuma and her husband didn't have children. When she went with him for check-ups to a gynaecologist, she would sit in the reception area reading the old issues of *Stardust*, waiting for her name to be called out in the usual distorted fashion. Looking around at the posters of cute babies on the wall, she always thought of Chhotu when he was an infant. He loved batata vada and kept lisping 'Batade, batade' as he stretched out a hand for the snack. If he hadn't failed the pre-university exam, would the twenty-thousand-rupee incident loom as large as it did now? Had their small family thrown out this boy who was indifferent to school, unwilling to carry his burden? pondered Kusuma. She had tried to look for him on her own. She always carried extra cash in her purse to give her brother just in case she ran into him. Now that Aayi kept saying that Chhotu was happy, that her inner being knew it, Kusuma felt a great relief. Once she realised that she could not have children, Kusuma thought about her little brother whom she had looked after and felt even more sad. She kept thinking of the yellow t-shirt with the mark of the string.

Yamuna kept scolding her son-in-law, and suddenly one day Poorvi turned on her, her pride awakened. 'Aayi, don't go on like that. Did your great son come even once to see you?' 'Shut your mouth,' Yamuna replied. 'That boy went away quietly even though he was wounded because of your wedding.' Poorvi could not stand it. 'No one has made any great sacrifice for me and needn't do so in future. I was the one who decided to marry Suhas. I went around with him even though he had the bad smell of whisky on his breath. I married him to show you that I could do it. You kept saying to me, "Look at Kusuma. Learn from her. At your age she used to be like this and like that." You would keep praising her and mocking me for being useless. To get her a husband, you wandered all through Parel and Lalbagh holding her horoscope. And when she got married and stopped giving her salary to you, you'd wear a torn sari each time she came to visit and make a long face. I know all that. That's why I decided to get married on our doorstep, without making you run around and wear out your slippers. I married a worker from the same factory so that we would have the quarters even after Father's retirement. Isn't that why you all stealthily supported my "love affair"? Whenever I returned home late after being with Suhas and all the chawl folks looked askance at me, you felt the ground beneath your feet was giving way. But you didn't say a word, did you? It was eating you up from inside to support this love affair. But to cover that up, Chhotu's twenty-thousand-rupee incident came in handy. How Father grasped at it! You were silent. And me? I gave up Chhotu without saying a word. Why? Because his friend Nandu Jagtap saw me and Suhas coming out of a lodge near Mulund Paanchrasta one day. Although I walked straight ahead, as though I didn't recognise him, he's sure to have told Chhotu. And I began to feel that Chhotu was flaring up at me because he couldn't really tell you what was happening. Even his ordinary conversations felt like they contained barbed criticisms. When he hummed '*Dilwale dulhaniya le jaayenge*' or '*Hum tum ek kamre mein bandh ho*' I felt he was mocking me. I felt my crime was getting magnified by his behaviour, so when those men came and broke his jaw, I wasn't in the least bit upset. To conceal my offence, I began to scream that Chhotu's issue would stop my wedding. And you wanted that too. You just pushed him out!' Poorvi began to weep, her lips blanched. Distraught, Yamuna saw that the little girl Poorvi had grown up to become a tired woman who seemed to be weeping inside her own world. Things such as status, *izzat* and society were like flotsam thrown up on the shore of that world.

One day, Suhas began to shout, 'I see that you two sisters have got money from your brother and are enjoying yourselves. How could you have bought that VCD system otherwise?' As he spoke, he looked meaningfully at Yamuna, as though to suggest it was all her fault. She sat watching the TV screen as though none of this mattered to her. The images on the screen played across her face. 'If your son was so rich,' Suhas continued, 'why would you be stuck in this place? Why don't you go live with him in Malabar Hills? Or buy us a flat in a nice colony?' He began to laugh aloud. Poorvi, who was patting the baby to sleep, screamed wordlessly through her eyes. Shhh, shhh, shhh.

When Kusuma arrived with the definite information that Chhotu was actually in their suburb, and that he was barely two streets away, Poorvi's daughter Soni had gone to school. On the doorstep that had worn smooth with sitting over the years, Poorvi was perched with a steel plate heaped high with raw rice, picking out the stones with one hand. Her left hand was adorned with mehendi that had been freshly applied, and she held up that hand as though blessing the world. When Poorvi's eyes widened on seeing her sister, Kusuma signalled to her to be silent, and sat down with her on the doorstep. Yamuna was sleeping on the cot inside. Suhas had gone to the factory. Kusuma said, 'Chhotu is supposed to be right here on Kamani Street', Poorvi expressed her shock through her widened eyes and open mouth.

What did it mean that the unseen Chhotu, who had become part of their private struggles in so many different ways, was actually twenty or thirty minutes' walk away? In the stillness of the afternoon, there was a sort of helpless excitement. When Kusuma said, 'Come, let's go and see', Poorvi stood up as though in a stupor. When she leaned forward to stand up, Kusuma saw the tarnished safety pins suspended from her sister's mangalsutra and felt weary.

The women walked through the street that was lined with godowns of wholesale metal sheets. Once upon a time there were pharmaceutical production units here, but now those had been abandoned. Many of the plots had been bought by builders to erect skyscrapers, and the old compounds and empty buildings had boards on them with the builders' names. Security guards sat around guarding the corpse-like buildings. These were factories that had nurtured thousands of families like theirs. Kusuma and Poorvi walked along, wondering where those families had gone to in this big city.

Since marriage, the sisters had never come out together. Kusuma was following a mental map. Her chest was quivering. As they approached their destination, their pace slowed. When Poorvi stopped near a muskmelon-sharbat vendor and raised her eyebrows, Kusuma did not refuse. Stirring the ice inside the steel vessel, the vendor poured out two glasses of juice for them. When Kusuma made as if to pay, Poorvi put down her glass and held back her sister and, still not using the mehendi hand, pulled money out of her purse. 'I too am working. I bring book binding home. You're not the only one earning. Don't get uppity with me.' As they walked on, she said, 'How come you didn't bring Aayi a sari this time for Sankranthi? She said you must have forgotten. But don't tell her I told you this.' As though to use this afternoon's opportunity to talk about everything, Poorvi continued: 'So we heard that you've booked a flat in Kandivili? Two-room-kitchen? Is that true? You never said anything to me. You're only the two of you, no kids. Why do you need two rooms? You could have bought a one BHK! But it's your money and your house. None of my business, is it?'

'Don't say anything in front of Chhotu,' said Kusuma. 'We don't know what's in his mind now about us. Don't blurt out things that might spoil the situation.' 'You're talking as though we're definitely going to meet him. Don't worry, your highness. I won't ask him to buy me a colour TV, or to give me a gold ring because he didn't come for my wedding. I'll keep my mouth shut. If he does buy me all those things, where would that leave you? No, I certainly won't ask him. I'll just be happy with the black-and-white, all right?' She breathed rapidly, walking faster.

They stopped when they reached Kamani Street. On the other side from where they stood, they could see Shefali Scrap Centre. *See that paan shop nearby, that's Chhotu's shop. You can't see him, he is sitting inside. Wait, there's someone buying cigarettes, let them leave. How does it matter, let's go. Kusuma, you go. From that glass shop you can see better. Take a look. Having come this far, don't do drama now, Poorvi. Come. All right, you stay here. I'll go myself. If it's him, then I'll call you.* Poorvi stood holding on to the wire cage of a wilted municipality plant. Kusuma walked slowly up to the glass shop and looked at the paan shop, feeling some qualms as she did so.

One couldn't immediately tell whether it was him. With the cigarette and gutka packets, the jars of chocolate, chikki and peppermint, the shallow containers for paan ingredients, the shopfront looked like a TV screen. In that square frame, he was wrapping a paan, head bent. Above him was a god photo, a small one, with a red zero-watt bulb. The child who used to lisp as he asked for batata vada, how did this sweet little boy learn to wrap paan in a shop, how did he decide which god was his? thought Kusuma. His square box-like shop stood in isolated splendour. There seemed to be a strange boundary line between his world and theirs. Though invisible, Chhotu held them all together and had brought them to where they were. Between that Chhotu and this person here who existed on his own planet, one he had built with his own loves and hates, his business, his beliefs and fears, his t-shirt, his credit slips, his cash on hand, his sins and good deeds, there was no connection whatsoever. How had he carried the burden of those twenty thousand rupees? He was here, close by, only two and a half kilometres from the house, but was he related to them? Should we bring him back into our world of indebtedness and destroy him? Oh, little god, protect his little shop, his heaven and hell. Please iron his t-shirts for him.

'Chhotu ...,' a peculiar sound coupled with a sigh came from Kusuma. Lightly it touched the metal, glass and scrap material and flew away without touching him. Still clinging to the plant's cage, Poorvi signalled to ask what, what. With a crestfallen face, Kusuma shook her head as though to say it wasn't him. Slowly she crossed the road and came back to where Poorvi waited. 'I knew it, I knew it wasn't possible that he could be here,' cackled Poorvi as she walked ahead, as though emerging from an eclipse. From behind, Kusuma said, 'Slowly, slowly ...' as she leaned against the shutter of a closed shop. She covered her face with her hands, feeling besieged by the dense silence, feeling distraught like when she had her miscarriages. Thinking Kusuma was beside her, Poorvi kept walking, yammering under the hot sun, holding up her mehendi hand in benediction.

Kanmareya Kaadu
2002

Mithun Number Two

When Chandu begged a ride at the Karad check post in a sugarcane truck headed to Mumbai on the national highway, the skies were full of stars. After he had lied at home that he was going to the cinema, it had taken him half the night to find a ride. If the sugarcane truck driver had not agreed to take him, perhaps he would have had to make his way home. Since there was no room in the cabin, Chandu had to stand in the truck bed clutching the cabin's roof edge, with the passing vehicles flashing their headlights into his eyes. In the distance, the moon floated in the sky. And countless stars, many more than he had ever seen before.

Once, Chandu had banged his head on a door and tied a bandage around the wound. The neighbours in the chawl began to say, 'Arre Mithun Chakraborty', and that was the beginning of everything. At the time, a poster from one of Mithun's 'South' films was plastered all over town. Mithun stood in it with a band around his head and his hip slightly stuck out. Standing in front of the mirror, Chandu combed his hair so as to make it fall over the bandage, and said 'Arre, arre, it's true', and stuck out his hip at an angle. From that day on, his appearance and attitude changed. He washed his clothes vigorously at night. When they dried, he 'ironed' them by putting them under his mattress. Before his facial hair had a chance to grow, he would go to the salon and get a shave. Collecting all the money he had, he bought a pair of boots that looked like pigeons. Near Karad's sugarcane mills and past the State Transport bus stand, Chandu would stroll around stylishly with his hands in his pockets. Every day he went to the theatre and walked around until the show began. He began to believe strongly that the entire world was seeing him not as tobacco shop Pandhari's son Chandu but as Mithun Chakraborty himself.

This did not fail to come to the notice of his father Pandhari or his elder sister Baby. Although Pandhari dismissed Chandu's behaviour as the ways of an adolescent, Baby, who had brought up her brother when their mother died, felt he was overdoing it. Once or twice she tried to talk to him. When Chandu began to spend all his time hanging around in hair salons in order to read film magazines like *Ruperi*, *Mayapuri* and *Screen*, Baby confronted him one evening with a slap. Usually when he was slapped Chandu would weep like a child, even though he was as big as a man. But that day he didn't cry. Instead, he passed his hand over his face like a hero in a film and walked away. Baby was perplexed.

Chandu began to sit at the petrol pump near the highway. The trucks that went towards Mumbai offered him both comfort and pain. The goods piled on the back of the trucks reflected the desires of a magical city. He began to feel pity for himself

– for being the son of a man who packed tobacco in the Seth's shop. Looking as he did, exactly like Mithun Chakraborty, how could he be known only as a good kerosene-stove repairer or as a fast swimmer in the village lake, or as the winner of the running race at the Lakshmi temple festival? No. The real Mithun Chakraborty could balance a city on his eyelids. He could melt into the soft embrace of fair-skinned heroines. He could beat the life out of any number of villains. Chandu began to spit at the future that awaited him and his friends in the sugar factories and the juice centres and garages. He fretted. Even Dhonduba's daughter Manda now appeared to him like a mote of dust. He did not want to live his life in the mean streets of Karad, eating his sister's potato bhajiyas and hanging around with his friends. He stopped seeing his friends. Began to stay at home. One day, when his father asked him to work in the tobacco shop, Chandu flew into a rage. Putting into a small bag some money, some clothes, a comb, booklets of film lyrics, and his pigeon boots, Chandu came to the highway check post to beg a ride from a truck driver.

Standing at the back, behind the driver's cabin, Chandu felt a strange rush of passion as the truck gathered speed. Everywhere the darkness. The truck pierced through the night like a bull with its powerful headlights. A number of men were lying on the piles of sugarcane, fast asleep. The highway vehicles were rushing into Chandu's eyes. He began to drowse while standing, holding on to the cabin roof.

Having stopped briefly at Pune and Lonavala, the truck began to descend the Khandala ghat in the early morning. As the new day filled the valley with mist and clouds, Chandu opened his eyes, startled at the sight. He looked nervously at the challenging dawn. In Karad, Baby was running down the streets of Karad in her smudged white sari calling Chandu's name; in the truck Chandu made a great effort to suppress his sobs. The first rays of the sun caressed his cheeks. The breeze ruffled his curls. Ahead lay the highway stretching far away, green trees to either side. The truck had now descended the ghat and was moving swiftly. Near the Khopoli signal, Chandu saw a large poster. Mithun Chakraborty. Both hands outstretched, calling to Chandu. Chandu felt that a lost link had been established again.

Along with the sugarcane, Chandu was set down in Crawford Market in Mumbai on that hot afternoon, amidst trucks unloading grain, vegetables and wood. A thousand boxes, drivers, coolies with towels tied around their heads, hand-drawn carts, cages full of birds piled up for sale, a roaring sea of people shoulder to shoulder. Chandu began to wriggle his way out. Only the posters by the roadside seemed familiar to him. How many of them! Big and small, of cloth and paper and cardboard. Chandu walked slowly, looking at them. He sat leaning against the wall of the Metro Theatre. He bought a plate of cut fruit for a rupee and ate it. It had small pieces of papaya, apple, orange, grape and melon. Chandu fell asleep leaning against the wall. When he woke, the cinema crowd was coming out. A strange light – neither dawn nor twilight. Chandu felt a moment of fear – a moment which made him forget his name or which day it was. Even the bit of sky that could be seen was like smoke. When a lathi poked him in the ribs and someone shouted, '*Naam kya hai*, what's your name?' he began to sob, 'Mithun, Mithun.'

Chandu spent that night in the Dhobitalao police station. At midnight, two constables were trying unsuccessfully to light a kerosene stove. Chandu said he could do it, and got it up and running in a couple of seconds. The constables were impressed. They were addicted to tea. In the morning, they got him to light the stove again, made tea and gave him some too, before they released him into the streets of the city. One of the constables directed him to an old man in the Dadar area who repaired stoves. Like a straw coming to shore on a wave, Chandu arrived at the small shop on the Dadar footpath. With soot on his hands and face, he became part of this tiny shop.

The old man did not speak much. Didn't even ask where Chandu was from. He would tell him what work needed to be done, and made suggestions about how to do it. He gave him one meal a day and two rupees. In the evening, Chandu roamed around on the streets of Dadar. Marking off Chandu's space on the footpath, the old man would go to sleep. Chandu would wander through the crowds, as though looking for something. People looked scared. They seemed to be running, as though chased by someone. No one looked another in the eye.

Seeing the dozens of salons on the roadside, Chandu chose one, entered it and sat on a chair like a king. As though to belie the fear that everyone would see him as a country bumpkin from Karad, one of the hairdressers approached him. 'Mithun Chakraborty cut,' announced Chandu clearly. No one laughed.

Instead, his hair was cut with all due reverence. Three-fourths of an hour of tweaking and smoothening and the Mithun cut was ready. In the row of mirrors opposite, Chandu could see the green valleys of Kashmir. Sridevi, Madhuri, Kimi Katkar came running towards him, arms outstretched. Sitting up suddenly, Mithun paid eight rupees and descended into the street as though alighting from a plane. Graciously acknowledging the salaam thrown by the hairdresser, Mithun walked slowly along the footpath, looking for his spot.

When he put down his sheet and lay down, the person next to him asked, 'New here?' He said, 'Yes.' Before he could introduce himself, the other man had gone to sleep. In another corner someone was rubbing oil on his head. He asked Mithun/ Chandu, 'What work do you do?' 'I've come to work in films,' he said, without hesitation. His new friend said, 'Is that so? Near the postbox on that next footpath is Pakya, who's acted in many films. He knows a lot of studio contractors.'

Mithun now slept among the thousand bodies on the footpath. If he opened his eyes, he could see the stars. If he closed them, he heard the clacking of wheels as the trains went past. He felt a strange floating sensation as though unmoored from everything he once knew. Around him, workers kept going and coming to and from their shifts. The utensils on the food carts of the night kept rattling. Here was an opportunity for a new life to emerge amidst all these connected lives. Mithun slept more deeply than he had ever slept before.

At dawn the milk truck appeared in front of the milk booth and all the sleepers woke up and disappeared. When Mithun woke, the old man was pumping the stove to light it. It came to life with a 'phos' sound, and in its blue flame the new day drew its first breath. That day Mithun tried to meet Pakya from the opposite footpath. But Pakya would not even look at him. The old repairer mended each stove with great care. Had he been born old, wondered Mithun. 'Where do you eat? Can I come with you?' the boy asked. 'You look out for yourself,' said the old man.

In Dadar Market there was a great hustle and bustle because of the Gokulashtami festival the next day. Chandu waited eagerly to see how they celebrated the festival here. At home in Karad he would have played with coloured water and then gone swimming in the pond with his friends. He pushed aside the fear that between the bustle of Dadar Market and the magic world of Mithun Chakraborty there might lie a long and arduous journey. That night on the footpath there were no sleeping youngsters. They were all awake, discussing the 'Govinda' competitions for Ashtami. Before he knew it, Mithun/Chandu was part of a team. They went to the nearby Shivaji Park and practised climbing on top of one another to form a human pyramid. He listened eagerly as they spoke of pots of money and dahi tied on high, and how the group that formed the tallest pyramid and broke the pot would get to keep the money. Full of the competitive spirit of his Karad days, Mithun did not sleep all night.

At dawn the next morning began the game of breaking the pot. In a flash, the Govindas of each group had made a pyramid and broken many a pot full of money and flowers. Everyone's eyes were on a pot placed at a great height near Plaza Cinema. The Dongri group and the Mahim Koliwada group failed to break it. Even the legendary Lalbagh group could not succeed. Then the Dadar Footpath group tried its hand. In a lightning moment Chandu was on top of the pyramid. He grabbed the pot and hung triumphantly to the rope which held it in place. With elated cries, he was lowered down to the ground. They carried him high in a victorious dance. Afterwards the boys started dancing madly, throwing coloured gulal on each other. 'Cinema *mein kaam karta hai*.' It seemed as though everyone was saying this about Chandu, making him dance in a frenzy. 'He works in films.'

At night the footpath cassette vendor kept playing the Mithun Chakraborty song, '*Dance dance*'. He turned up the volume full blast, and Chandu danced as if possessed by his hero. Pakya came up to him drunkenly, saying, 'Tomorrow I'll take you to Film City, brother.' Mithun slept late that night. That moment when he was on top of the pyramid, with thousands of eyes watching him, all those people like ants, and he with his hand on the pot – the memory of that moment kept waking him up. He sat sleepless among the bodies lying on the footpath like corpses. Such happiness – he had never known the extent of his prowess before. Even the film posters looked pale in comparison. He slept on his back with his chest opening out to the skies as though to share his happiness.

Mithun now acquired several friends. Sometimes they would go to the seaside at Shivaji Park to swim. Mithun was always the one to swim furthest, making everyone anxious. Little boys who worked as hotel waiters pestered him to teach them to swim. He did that enthusiastically. One day Pakya took him to the office of the Film Extras Union. They took fifty rupees to enrol him as a member. It was a union that helped members find small film appearances in a group, in dance numbers or in a festive or funeral procession. Mithun just wanted to get some kind of entry into the industry – he thought he could fend for himself afterwards. Outside Film City sat rows and rows of people. Everyone waiting for their turn. Aging men and women, plump women in lipstick and slit blouses, well-muscled men. When a contractor came out of the gate and called a number, people ran towards him. Some had been waiting for months without being called. A few of them began berating Mithun: 'Who are you to come here like a big shot when we haven't had a chance at all?' Some others had surrounded the contractor and were shouting at him. The gurkha at the gate swung his stick and drove everyone back to the queue as though he was herding cattle.

A car approached in a cloud of dust. Arre, it was Meenakshi Sheshadri. Mithun ran towards the car. The actor was looking at herself in a hand mirror. The same woman who had kissed Jackie Shroff in *Hero*. As Mithun stared at her, the guard came up and shooed him away. The gate opened and the car drove inside, spreading more dust in its wake. First shift cancelled, someone began to say. A few people went to the gate to negotiate. What sort of magic factory lay beyond the weathered gate? Mithun wondered fearfully. Just then Pakya came out of nowhere and marched Mithun into Film City. Three or four men looked him up and down. One said, 'Go tomorrow to Filmistan studio.

There's a sequence of Mithun-ji being shot there. Let's try this fellow.' As he returned to Dadar on the local train, Chandu thought how strange it was that he would be playing Mithun Chakraborty's duplicate. He comforted himself that even a duplicate came in front of the camera. Pakya said, 'If you pass tomorrow, *teri toh zindagi ban gayi yaar*! You'll have made it. Mithun-ji is such a busy star. To be his duplicate is to hit the jackpot.'

At mid-morning the next day, Chandu was made to stand on the sandy meadow of Filmistan Studio. Wearing a thick wig, oil on his face, a red t-shirt, a light blue jacket, he was filmed from different angles. Run, they said. Fall down, they said. Jump, they said. Then they brought lights and reflectors, made him stand with his back to the camera, and said, 'Chalo, run!' Chandu ran. 'Cut,' they said. One of them called Chandu and said, 'You're not the hero, kid, to show your face. Try to hide your face as much as possible. The less you show of your face the greater the chances of your getting the job.' Again it was start, camera, action. Chandu hid his face as he ran, jumped, rolled around in drums, was chased by dogs, swung from a rope. His main aim was to keep moving without showing his face. He took note of where the camera was, and learnt how to turn his face away and run the moment 'Action' was shouted. '*Muh math dikhaana*, don't show your face,' they kept shouting, the people behind the camera. They told him to come early the next morning. That night on the Dadar footpath, Chandu kept running away from the camera in his sleep.

Chandu's 'action' began the next morning. Appearing as

Mithun's backside, as his right side or left side, he fell from a horse at a distance from the camera. Pulled himself out of a pond. Wrestled in slime with a bunch of men. He swallowed the pain from the blows and danced around in the mud. The wrestlers went off at lunchtime to eat biryani. Not having the courage to ask them for some, Chandu went to the gate and bought bread omelette from a cart. He was sweating profusely. It all felt like a dream. In his sweat flowed those small thrills at jumping higher than another 'extra' or actually being able to slip out of a wrestler's grasp. He drank some water. Then the action began again. Now there was the scene of Mithun Chakraborty being slapped. Chandu stood with his back to the camera. The man opposite slapped him hard. 'Excellent,' everyone shouted. By this time, Mithun-ji arrived, and was seated under an umbrella. All eyes, Chandu stared at his hero. He looked rather swollen. But Chandu gasped at Mithun-ji's costume. It was the same as his! The same red t-shirt, the light blue jacket, the light blue trousers. Chandu felt like it was he who was sitting under that umbrella. '*Aapka naya* double,' said the contractor, pushing Chandu forward. Mithun-ji cracked a joke, looking at Chandu. Everyone laughed. Chandu was peculiarly thrilled at the thought of them wearing the same clothes.

Once again, the shooting of the climactic scene began. Chandu's hands were fastened and he was tied behind a van. So that his stomach didn't rub against the earth, they tied to his front a small cart like those used by crippled beggars. 'Careful,' they yelled, as the van started moving, dragging Chandu along.

His knees got scratched. The pebbles in the field leaped up and hit his face. A bottle got stuck in the wheels and Chandu thought he was going to slip and fall but he managed to pull himself upright in time. When the van turned sharply, he somersaulted twice. He thought he might fall on his back but managed to fall on his hands and knees instead and saved himself. He was possessed in his daredevilry – did not even wonder when all this would end. The moment the shot was over, everyone broke into loud applause. Chandu was thrilled.

Mithun-ji was smoothing his eyebrows in front of a mirror as though all this had nothing to do with him. Chandu squatted on the floor. Now they tied the same beggar cart to Mithun-ji's stomach and started taking close-ups of his grimacing face. The actor was working hard at squeezing his facial muscles. The same red t-shirt, the same boots, the same silver bracelet, the same necklace. Mithun Chakraborty is imitating me, thought Chandu. He's lifelessly imitating the adventurous actions I performed in real life.

Chandu began to feel restless. He went towards the gate and bought two bottles of Gold Spot which he guzzled sitting there. He did not even have the energy to meet the contractor after pack up was announced. He went back to Dadar and helped the old man repair four or five stoves. Then he took his flower-seller friend and went off to the sea near Shivaji Park. In the dark, the sea, sparkling with phosphorus, beckoned guilelessly.

He swam quite far from the shore. The further he went, the more his exhaustion receded. Once he was far out at sea, Chandu floated on the water and looked at the sky. The stars were shining brightly. The entire city seemed to float on the water in the form of clusters of lights. In this floating city, where was Mithun Chakraborty with the cart tied to his stomach? How helpless he was that he couldn't even imagine encountering death, thought Chandu. Does he know how to repair stoves? Does he know how to climb a five-storeyed pyramid and capture the Ashtami pot? Does he know how to turn away from death by regaining his balance behind the van?

Chandu felt he was floating above the city. What could give him more happiness than these adventures. I shall swim, I shall run, I shall win competitions. He turned towards the shore, convinced that one day he would outswim the world's greatest swimmer. The flower-seller boy had gone. Since it was near midnight, there weren't too many people on the beach. As though he had been reborn, Chandu ran swiftly on the beach, like a bird skimming along.

Mithun Number Two
1989

Translator's Afterword

In my afterword to *No Presents Please* (2017), a collection of Jayant Kaikini's stories in English, translated by me, I reflect on the 'ruse of the ordinary' that for me is a characteristic Kaikini narrative strategy. The stories usually begin with a commonplace or 'ordinary' situation, but as you go deeper into the narrative the ordinary has been rendered surreal, or tragi-comic, or filled with profound melodrama. The sixteen stories in this new collection are further evidence of how this strategy works. Layer upon layer, fold upon fold, the stories open out into new developments, turn and twist in unexpected directions, often concluding in ways that are deeply unsettling.

There is never any happy ending. Varsha the disabled girl in 'The Right Side' agrees to go to the photo studio so that her brother can apply for a phone booth under a quota. The studio experience is rendered surreal by the little children in their fancy dress costumes. After the photoshoot, Varsha asks her brother gaily for an ice cream, but can she look forward to more than a life of dependence and the pity of strangers? The two sisters in 'Forest of Disappearance' go looking for their missing younger brother, but can they ever find out what happened to him? The trapeze artist gives birth to a child, but is it the kind she imagined it would be?

No happy endings, but sometimes there are resolutions. Chandu resolves to stop being film star Mithun's body double; Neel has a cathartic weeping fit about his father as he stands near the traffic signal; after the raid on his shop, Muchhi Miyan's magic mirror is saved by some children but he refuses to take it back; Sadanand decides to take his estranged girlfriend to meet his dying uncle Digoo Mama and help him prepare his will.

So many of the stories focus on children or young people in Mumbai, and the spaces they occupy, on streets, in slums, in chawls, or in apartments: the slum kids waiting outside the hospital for their artist mentor; the children in the remand home lined up like silent little owls; the eleven-year-old servant boy Punda; his tiny eight-year-old sister who has been hired to look after a baby; Chandu/Mithun who runs away from home to join the film industry; the missing boy Chhotu of the yellow t-shirt; Varsha the disabled girl; Prakash, trying to make a living through his new lantern business; Sunil the small-town suicide; Neel, the master's son who moves to Mumbai and gets sucked into its frenzied pace; Sadanand in Thane who agonises over his relationships with women; office clerk Sudhakar with his roommates in the kholi.

Except for the kids seen as a group, the other young people have their own interiority and modes of expression, and modes of dealing with their precarious existence in Mumbai. Punda the servant boy, for example, tells stories to his charge, little Pinky, that involve characters from the Mahabharatha like Bhima interacting with the paan shop near the apartment, or elephants and kings wearing mehendi when Pinky did. Remembering his previous life in a flower garden, Punda grows bulbs in a discarded vanaspati tin. He buys a paan from the mobile paan-wallah to take to his little sister whom he has not seen in a few years. Living in precarity, like the elderly Sumitra sleeping under her old sari in the kitchen of her nephew's kholi, but seeking out multiple ways of negotiating that precarity, like going to matinee shows in the nearby cinema, is what Sumitra and other migrants do.

The representation of the precarity of city life is heightened by the fact that several stories are partially or wholly set in Mumbai hospitals: 'The Recluse'; 'The Master's Son'; 'The Scent of Bakula'; and 'Spotless', with the protagonists often in the final phase of their lives. In that liminal phase and space, interactions in the hospital between people who are not kindred but are invested in saving lives reveal another aspect of Mumbai's impersonality.

For those coming from small towns where everyone knows you, impersonality is both desirable and terrifying at the same time, as is the need to do things just for oneself. After months of sneaking away to drink lassi by himself, Kekoo the Xerox shop owner in 'Kekoo and Pyarelal' grows so close to the migrant fruit-seller outside his shop that he invites him to his middle-class home for a meal. Pyarelal turns down the offer gently, just as he negates his friend's suggestion that he rent a kholi of his own instead of sleeping under a staircase in a dilapidated building.

Twelve out of the sixteen stories in this volume are actually about those who have migrated to Mumbai in their own lifetime. The arcs of migration in these stories include town and village names that people reading about Mumbai do not usually hear: Hiregutthi to Mumbai, Gokarna to Mumbai, Honnavar to Mumbai, Bhatkal to Mumbai, Mundgod to Mumbai, Tadadi to Mumbai. All these are coastal towns or villages with a long history of mobility connected to Mumbai city. When Neel in 'The Master's Son' comes to Mumbai for the first time, he is met by a distant relative at the bus stand, a young man wearing a t-shirt and speaking in Hindi- and Marathi-inflected Kannada. At that moment, Mumbai started 'breathing within him'. Soon, Neel (like Sadanand in 'The Recluse' or Sunil in 'A Horizon for Each Eye') is drawn into the 'formless, featureless' city life. The qualities, smells and responses of Mumbai rendered Neel 'so smooth that the grammar of the city slid off him as soon as it touched his body'. But for all of them, Mumbai is a destination, a place from which they will never return to that remembered village or town. This is true both of the young and the old, Punda or Digoo Mama, Neel or Sumitra, or Nana, the distraught grandfather from the Marathi-speaking hinterland. None of these characters will ever attain fabulous wealth in the city or achieve social mobility undreamed of, but the metronome of Mumbai has marked them forever.

The characters in Kaikini's stories are often caught up in unexpected situations even as they are living their daily lives.

Two unlikely friends, in 'Kekoo and Pyarelal', find themselves helping a teenaged pregnant girl to hospital on a bandh day when there is no transport; the owner of a used goods shop glimpses a beautiful woman appearing and disappearing amidst the clutter of old furniture; the nameless narrator of 'The Scent of Bakula' discovers his old lover from college in a ward of the same hospital he is in. Certain everyday objects function like doorways to other worlds: the wooden peacock mirror in 'Threshold'; the piano in 'Hello, Mike Testing'; Prakash's family cupboard in 'Lanterns in the Rain'; the blank sheets of paper distributed by the artist KK in 'Spotless'; the paan in 'Milk Moustache'; or the 'dark, silent tomb' of the remand home in 'Kekoo and Pyarelal'.

Jayant Kaikini and I selected these stories together. We trawled through his oeuvre, looking for stories set in Mumbai. However, unlike in *No Presents Please*, we have assembled in this collection not just stories about people living in Mumbai and speaking Marathi or Gujarati or Hindi but a substantial number of stories about people who have recently migrated into the city from the northern coast of Karnataka or North Kanara as it's called. The Kannada of these characters appears in the original story as Kannada, although sometimes with a North Kanara inflection. The others who don't speak Kannada in real life are speaking that language in the stories. When they do so, Jayant doesn't mark their usage as belonging to any particular dialect but presents it in a spare prose, peppered with Bambaiya Hindi. My strategy of dealing with this multiple-language register of the stories is to use a kind of English that does not draw too much attention to itself, in keeping with the tenor of the original text. I have thought at length about how to create an English that's appropriate for Jayant's stories. I've concluded that lean prose that hints at what I have elsewhere called the 'cultural vernacular' of Mumbai – that is, Hindi–Urdu–Dakhni – mixed with Marathi, works best. Since the narratives themselves are filled with intricate symbolic patterning (the trapeze, the piano, the paan, the cupboard, the mirror) that shines through the pared-down prose, they don't require further accentuation.

This translation has been enhanced by hours of animated discussion with the author, by our meticulous and perceptive editor Karthika V.K., and by the enthusiasm of our Mumbaikar first reader Ashish Rajadhyaksha.

Ahmedabad
November 2023